Diseased

Disclaimer: The themes surrounding this novel adhere to the idea that a person is shaped strictly by the traits related to their zodiac sign. Under no circumstances does portrayal of the zodiac signs in *Diseased* mean any derogatory connotation.

ISBN Number: 979-8-9906448-4-7

First paperback edition: October 2025

Edited by Adrienne Kisner
Proofread by Carol Trow
Cover art by Shirley Tran
Layout by Ava Frechette and Shirley Tran
Printed by Kindle Direct Publishing in the U.S.A

Dedicated to Mom, Dad, and Izzy
(Boden already got one.)

Author's Note

"I bet you thought you'd seen the last of me!"

-Emma Roberts

Wait, I'm only kidding.

Welcome back to the third iteration of the *Divided* series, *Diseased*! I promise, I didn't realize how similar those two adjectives looked until it was too late.

Diseased is a special book for me. You'll notice that for the first time in the series, we've shifted focus more intently to a singular character- Peter.

Of course, don't be alarmed. The other four in all their chaotic glory are still prominent, very much so. However, Peter holds a special place in my heart (as I'm sure he does in others' too) and I wanted to give him his own moment to be in the spotlight, even though if he were here, he'd tell us just how much he dislikes that.

Peter is a good human being, a great one, even. But in this book, you'll get the sense that bad things happen to good people all the time. You'll get the sense that even though Peter goes through a lot- too much- he has people by his side who dull the pain just a little bit. I took that from my own life, actually. Even though sometimes things suck (to be frank), having the right people around you make things infinitesimally better.

I also love *Diseased* because we meet three very exciting new characters. If you know me, you know that I'm a sucker for an ensemble.

Doctor Charles, Nurse Ruth, and Doctor Inesh Mahra have become a wonderfully fun team and a truly perfect trio that, in my humble opinion, are up there with the Stooges, the Golden Trio, and Charlie's Angels.

In reality, they're more like those three little guys from *Ducktales*, but let me have this one.

To start putting this author's note out of its misery, let me get into my thank-yous. Adrienne, Shirley, and Carol remain the most incredible team a girl could ask for, and the three of them somehow manage to bring out the best writing I have to offer, and for that I will always be grateful.

Like Peter, I come from a small town in Northern New Hampshire. While Conway has its flaws (welcome to the U.S of A), I could not do this without the lovely, kindhearted community that has supported me every step of the way.

And, in the spirit of family, found and otherwise, my village of friends and relatives who make me the best version of myself every single day. It would take me forever to list you all by name but know that I love you just as much as you love me, even on the days I don't show it as much.

Dearest gentle readers (not copyright, I Googled it), please continue being your shining, lovely selves. Especially my women, teenagers, LGBTQIA+ family, and Americans who sometimes feel like the world we live in now is eerily similar to our favorite dystopian books.

And now- third time's the charm- thank you for reading, and please enjoy *Diseased*.

Part One: The Taurus

Diana

As Cameron's voice echoes across the Plaza, everything that seems to happen after does so in a blur.

A staff member Diana doesn't think she's seen before grabs her arm and tugs her back inside, away from the incoherent shouting of the crowd. She watches as Barbara Oswald steps up to the microphone, gently pushing Cameron out of the way. She starts to speak but Diana can't hear her over the buzzing in her ears.

Stop, stop, stop, Diana- think, Diana. She begs herself. *You can fix this. You* have *to fix this.*

They're ushered down the hall, pausing in front of the spiral staircase as the group is finally released from the strong hold of their guards. Kiara leans against the rail, her chest rising and falling heavily, as Cameron and Lucas collapse onto the bottom step. Diana feels sick to her stomach.

She looks around as the buzzing in her head subsides. It seems as though the people who had brought them inside were Doctor Charles and his two bodyguards, a taller woman and a short, stockier boy.

"Charles," Diana whispers, eyes swimming with tears, his name a plea on her lips, "what do we do?"

The man meets her eyes and Diana's heart sinks before he even says a word. He shakes his head as he speaks. "I normally wouldn't dream of sugarcoating things when it comes to the truth-"

"So don't," Lucas says, cutting him off. Diana is almost certain that he doesn't mean to sound as rude as he does, doesn't mean to sound like the old Lucas.

Charles clears his throat. "-so I *won't*. Your people were not enthralled with the news of Peter's infection. He needs to be isolated as soon as possible, and he'll go downhill fast."

"Are we in any danger?" Kiara asks. Diana can barely stand to hear her speak, and her stomach roils with nausea.

"No," Charles states. "Well, not unless we get you separated from any and all contact with this disease."

"What do you mean, isolated?" Diana practically wails. "We didn't know about this!"

"No," Charles begins, "but the people don't know that. What they *do* know is that a member of the American government traveled to a diseased sector despite the risk and then came back with the infection, which is highly contagious and has no cure."

No one attempts to refute that.

After a silent moment, Barbara enters, flanked by her guards. She gazes down at the group, her eyes filled with sympathy and a tinge of disappointment. "Well, we sure made a mess of things."

"Yeah," they all chorus.

"What do we do, Barbara?" Diana asks.

"Lockdown," she states plainly. She turns to her guards and begins to bark out orders. "Joshua, go find Miriam and Reginald and get them to help turn their offices into temporary bedrooms. Wren, find Lucas a place to stay."

"Barbara, what's going on?" Lucas interjects, rising from his seated position. Cameron follows suit.

"You have seen what that disease is doing to Sector Five. I'm not losing another one of you. Effective immediately, you're all entering a lockdown here in the

Capitol," she replies. "As will us four adults. Safety precautions must be put in place."

"What?" Kiara asks, bewildered. "How the hell are we supposed to *work?*"

Barbara shoots her a look. "Any way you want to, my dear. As long as it gets done."

With that, they're quickly ushered up the stairs and into their offices, where staff members are already installing rollaway beds, minifridges, and other quarantine necessities that have appeared quick as a flash. Diana has no clue how they even got word of the quarantine so fast, and she has no idea how everyone else's brains aren't going as slowly as hers.

"What about the bathroom?" Diana asks.

"Down the hall, in the normal bathrooms. They'll be sanitized after every use and they're single-stall anyways," an employee replies.

"And meals?"

"In here," another worker says as she pulls a fitted sheet over a cot in the corner of Diana's once-tidy office. Diana barely recognizes her, and she can't figure out where from.

She turns to Barbara. "How do we communicate?"

"The phones," she responds. "No paper trail, to avoid the press."

Diana looks at Barbara, emotions swarming over her as she studies the old woman's too-neutral expression. "Barbara, I'm scared." She can't pinpoint exactly what is scaring her, but she knows for certain that it's more than one thing. It's *everything*, really.

Oswald shakes her head, features softening a little. "Darling, there's no time to be scared. You have to be strong, for the sake of the country. We start with a week-long quarantine, and if no one shows symptoms, we all will be out."

"And Peter?" Diana asks.

Barbara pauses, then sighs. "I don't know what will happen to Peter."

With that, she turns and leaves, heading further down the hall.

Part Two: The Scorpio

Cameron

"What do you mean, Charles?" Cameron asks, sitting down on his new rollaway bed as the doctor paces the floor of his office. The mattress beneath him is lumpy and not yet broken in, and Cameron fidgets both nervously and uncomfortably.

"What I *mean*, is that I cannot allow you to see him. The disease is too dangerous, and Peter is too sick."

"What if it was a short visit? No touching, only a few minutes? I'll wear a mask, or something. Can I?" Cameron pleads.

"I'm sorry, son," Charles says, crossing to Cameron and clapping a hand on his shoulder. Much to Cameron's dismay, the doctor sounds very resolute and very genuine. "I know how much he means to you, but I can't take unnecessary risks."

"How long until I can see him?" Cameron asks, ignoring the thump in his chest at the implication of the latter part of Charles' sentence.

"Until he gets better," Charles replies.

"And if he doesn't?" Cameron whispers, looking up at the man's kind eyes. "You said it takes a downturn fast. What if... will he get better?"

The doctor glances down at him, expression entirely unreadable. "He will if I have anything to say about it."

Cameron, to his own surprise, smiles at the man, giving his hand a firm shake as some of his worries melt away. "Fine. Help him, please."

The doctor crosses to the door, shooting Cameron a wink. "I will."

Part Three: The Aries

Kiara

"Hi," Diana begins as she enters Kiara's office quickly, to avoid the dozen staff members in the hall. Kiara has made up one of the two beds in her room- she assumes Diana is her new roommate.

"We're supposed to be quarantined," Kiara says teasingly. "Are you my new roommate?"

Before Kiara can continue speaking, Diana blurts out: "I need to tell you something."

Kiara quirks an eyebrow nonchalantly, but her heart gives one big resounding *thud* against her ribcage. "Okay." She motions to the chair across from her desk, but Diana doesn't sit.

Her breathing is erratic, and her eyes are red, like she's been crying. Something was scaring her, and Kiara needed to know what.

"Diana, you're making me nervous-"

"Henderson had a wife."

Kiara pauses. Something flushes through her body, a lukewarm neutrality, although she feels a cold tingle at the nape of her neck. "I know."

"What?"

Kiara speaks without thinking, like her body flipped a switch onto autopilot. "I know. He had a wedding band on the day of the revolt. I saw it when I stabbed him," she shivers. "You should've seen the blood running down his arm; it all pooled at the ring."

Diana stares at her, *really* stares, her eyes flicking over each of Kiara's features as if memorizing them. Kiara rises then, hoping Diana can't see her shaking fingers. "There must be more to that story than that, Di."

Diana blinks, and one tear slips down her pale cheek. "Yeah."

"Tell me."

Diana moves to Kiara then, her hands finding Kiara's shoulders, traveling restlessly and finally stilling only when Kiara takes Diana's hands in her own.

The two girls look at one another, and Kiara feels suddenly nauseous, like there was something coming which she was not and could not ever be prepared for.

"There was a daughter, Ki," Diana whispers. "Henderson and his wife had a daughter, and Cornelius said she was our age. And her name started with a 'C,' or a 'K'..."

Kiara feels that same feeling again, that flush of multiple emotions coming too quickly to process. She doesn't say anything, doesn't move, and she's distinctly aware of the fist-like clench in her stomach squeezing just as hard as Diana's hands.

Diana doesn't need to elaborate. Kiara is no fool, and she's able to connect the dots to get to the tragic conclusion that Diana was implying. A wife and a daughter, who was just about Lucas' age. A daughter who was hidden, a daughter who had a matching name.

"That can't be true," Kiara whispers, voice breaking. "My father wrote me letters in school. He- he's a Pisces, that's why I-"

Diana gives her hands a hard squeeze, as if reminding her to come out of her brain and back into her body. "Did he ever meet you?" she continues before Kiara can give the answer she already knows. "Wasn't it convenient that he said he was a Pisces?"

Kiara feels like she's burning, and some twisted part of her revels in the fact that she felt this way. "No, if Henderson was married just once, this daughter would be-"

"Almost eighteen."

Kiara half-coughs, half-retches, and Diana rushes to her side, only stopping when Kiara holds up a panicked hand. "Stop!" she demands. "Please don't touch me."

"Kiara, this doesn't change-"

"But it *does,*" Kiara cries. "It changes everything. I... I don't want it to be true, Di, but I *know* that it is. It even makes *more* sense now. Remember what Barbara said the day of the revolt about your mother and her power?"

Diana nods solemnly. "Why would my mother abandon me unless I'd done something to deserve it?"

Kiara inhales a shaky breath through dry lips. "That day on the steps, I asked Henderson why he hated me. But... but if his own *daughter* betrayed the sign she was supposed to lead? If I was supposed to take over, and instead I teamed up with the very people who destroyed everything. It... it makes perfect sense."

"God," Diana whispers. "Oh, Ki. I'm so sorry."

"Don't be," Kiara says, swallowing her tears and shaking her head. "I used to think it wasn't over until I killed him. That it eventually had to be him or me. But... now it'll have to be both, I guess."

She wasn't sure it was possible for Diana's cheeks to drain of color any further, and yet, her skin pales. "Kiara, please don't say that-"

"No, it's okay, Di," she says, finally looking Diana in the eyes. "That's how it should be."

Diana's shoulders convulse in a sob, and Kiara hangs onto her, the girls wrapping each other in a hug.

"This is personal, Diana. It always has been. But now... now I can't in good conscience let his family live, right? And that includes me."

"What about Lucas? Or Cornelius? They're his – *your* – family too."

Kiara sighs, pulling away and rubbing her eyes until they burn. "They don't know him."

"Neither do you."

Kiara nods slowly, wishing the truth of her words weren't deflecting off her skin. "Diana, could you please go? I just... I really need to be alone."

Diana nods and leaves without a word, and Kiara turns, taking in her desk, with all its papers and clutter and books that she used every day to help her country. Did Henderson – did her *father* – know that things would end up like this? Did he think when he abused her that she'd never find out? Or worse, did he know that she'd end up taking over Sector One – taking over the *nation* – and ruling with just as iron a fist as he did?

Part of it made complete sense. Why else would he try to kill her? Why else would his hatred run so deep?

His daughter, the Aries Heir, turned revolutionary under his rule.

Kiara sinks to the floor and begins to cry.

Part Four: The Libra

Lucas

This is *not* what Lucas had in mind when he pictured an American tour.

He was immediately swabbed and poked and prodded with every device imaginable to take all kinds of vitals, and while those were being tested (for what, he didn't know), he got to watch with anxiety as staff members haphazardly threw his things into a bag.

When he returns to the Capitol, though, he isn't marched towards his regular borrowed office, he's brought to one that's a little more familiar and a lot more intimidating.

"Kiara?" Lucas says with surprise as Hayley – one of the bodyguards he actually *knows* – shows him into the office, which has two matching cots on either wall.

Kiara jumps in fear and spins around, and Lucas can tell that he wasn't who she was expecting to see, based on the way her eyebrows shoot up and then immediately soften with something close to relief. "Hi," she mumbles, quickly turning back to a red, leather-backed journal on her desk.

"Am I... staying in here, too?" Lucas asks Hayley.

Hayley nods, seeming to hesitate, casting a glance at Kiara that's so brief Lucas almost misses it. "Same, um... you've got the same blood type. O-negative!" she adds cheerfully.

"Hayley, you can go," Kiara says flatly, and the guard hurries out as if she'd been waiting for the dismissal.

"You alright?" Lucas asks, sitting on the non-occupied bed.

"Just journaling."

Lucas nods, leg bouncing, and he focuses on studying the room rather than looking at Kiara.

He barely knew her. Well, he barely knew any of them, but Kiara least of all. Something about her was so similar to Lucas but also so entirely different, and that in itself made her... off-putting, to say the least.

"Cut that out," Kiara mumbles.

Lucas forces his legs to stop moving as he shoots an apologetic smile at the top of her head.

It's going to be a long week.

Part Five: The Aries

Kiara

"This is the worst," Kiara mumbles towards the ceiling as the stress ball she tossed falls back into her open palm. "What the hell am I supposed to do for a week besides stew in my own thoughts?"

"Well, you'll still have work," Lucas says from his spot on his bed, looking concerned. If only he knew the extent of Kiara's turbulent whirlwind of emotions.

Kiara groans from where she's lying on her back on the ground, burying her face in her hands. "I *know.* That's almost the worst part."

Lucas is quiet, engrossed in some book, and Kiara lays there still for a minute. *Breathe in, breathe out. Count to three,* Peter's phantom voice says in her mind.

But she can't really think. She can't get past one huge, life-ending roadblock that is threatening her very being. She blinks rapidly to clear her stinging eyes. She forces herself to speak even though her voice cracks. "This is gonna be a long week."

"At least we're almost an hour down," Lucas replies.

"Have you spoken to Di?"

"Not yet," he says, his voice dropping into a sadder tone. Kiara watches his face fall, too. Despite that, she's relieved, incredibly so. Maybe she had some control over this whole thing after all.

"Did they get you all your stuff?"

"Yup." He holds up the big book he's reading. "Brought lots of books too, if you want to borrow one."

They settle into silence as Kiara shakes her head, and after a moment, Kiara hucks the stress ball towards him and he yelps as it bounces off his shoulder.

"Kiara! That scared me!"

"Gotta keep you on your toes, Trust Fund," Kiara says with a chuckle. "We've only got each other for the next seven days."

"I guess you're right," he replies. "Seven days and counting."

"Seven days and counting," Kiara repeats.

A confession would have to wait.

Part Six: The Taurus

Diana

Diana opens the door to a staff member holding a tray. Well, she doesn't exactly know who the person is, since they're head-to-toe in a literal hazmat suit, with their face covered. "Dinner?" she asks tentatively.

Diana's stomach grumbles in response, and the staff member passes her the tray. "Thank you *so* much," Diana says with a polite smile.

"Goodnight," they say plainly, beginning to shut the door.

"Wait!" Diana says, desperately sticking her foot in the door to stop them from leaving. "Have you spoken to the others?"

They shake their head, and the noise of rubber suit material chafing makes Diana cringe. "No. I'm the only staff member assigned to you, so I don't cross-contaminate with the others."

Diana nods slowly. "I see. Well, thank you."

They leave without another word, so Diana sits down and eats, alone again.

Part Seven: The Scorpio

Cameron

Dinner got dropped off at almost six o'clock.

And yet it sits untouched on a tray on the desk because Cameron has been messing with the thermostat for an hour.

"Shit," he says as the dumb thing blinks red *again*. It's freezing in here, and the last time he had to fix it, at least he had help.

Peter's face flashes through Cameron's brain and he pauses, trembling fingers resting on the thermostat's button.

"Cam, you'll want it to be cold when you get back," Peter argues with a laugh as Cameron grabs his elbows and tugs him away from the wall.

"No, I like it warm. It was always freezing in Sector Three, especially in winter. I'm surprised your southern bones can even take this chill."

Cameron pulls him too far and accidentally backs into the desk, his legs hitting the large wooden structure. They both laugh as Peter stumbles into Cameron's chest, grabbing his arms to brace himself. His chest and thighs press against Cameron's, and Cameron looks into his amber eyes as Peter leans his forehead against his.

Cameron grins at him. "I love you."

"I love you," Peter replies.

"I'm excited to see your home," Cameron whispers.

Peter chuckles quietly. "You've already been to Sector Five before."

"Not with you," Cameron says. "Not as your..." he trails off.

Peter leans even closer. "As my what?" he whispers.

Cameron's lips brush his ever so gently. "As your boyfriend. I've never been to Sector Five as your boyfriend."

Peter finally presses his lips against Cameron's, and his hands travel down Cameron's arms to rest at his hips, moving him further back so he has no choice but to sit on the top of the desk. Peter fits himself between Cameron's legs and kisses him harder before finally resting his forehead against Cameron's as his hands stop on his thighs. Cameron kisses him on the forehead and pulls away. "But you're not touching the thermostat."

"Yes, I am," Peter contradicts sassily, "you'll want it to be cold in here, I swear."

Cameron groans. "Fine. But you absolutely have to put it back as soon as we get home."

Peter turns away from Cameron and starts rapidly pressing buttons on the thermostat. "You've got a deal, O'Connor."

He never did get the chance to reset it.

Part Eight: The Aries

Kiara

"Have you spoken to your dad?" Kiara asks. She and Lucas were running dangerously low on conversation topics, and to her horror, the broaching of the paternal curses that had befallen them both slipped out of her mouth before she could stop it.

"Nope," Lucas responds flatly.

Silence. Now was her chance.

"Do you think we all get the same thing for dinner?" she asks instead. In her head, she kicks herself. Hard.

"Yes, ma'am," he responds. "That's at least one good thing about this quarantine. The food is good."

"Very true," Kiara replies. "Have you gotten a call from Di?"

Lucas groans. "No. I'm gonna go crazy."

"Down, boy," she laughs. "She's the president. She's gonna be swamped with work for the rest of eternity, so you better get used to it."

Lucas chuckles and adjusts his supposed sleeping position. He could've been asleep hours ago, had his cot been at least a little softer than a block of cement. Kiara knew because hers was just as uncomfortable. "I miss her."

"I bet," Kiara replies. "Have you figured out anything concerning what you're gonna tell people?"

"What do you mean?" Lucas asks.

"A public announcement," she responds, as if it couldn't be more obvious.

"About... me and Diana?"

"About you and Diana," she replies plainly. "You guys haven't made an official announcement to the public since we got locked up within a *month* of being home."

Realization dawns on him. "You're right. But we can't do it from *lockdown*, can we?"

Kiara shrugs nonchalantly. "Why not? Arrange a conference the day you get out. You can play the whole 'I realize that she's my whole world now that I've been separated from her' angle."

"She *is* my whole world," he responds.

Kiara gags jokingly, and Lucas chuckles. "What?"

"That's the stupidest thing I've ever heard," she responds.

Lucas can't help but laugh a little more at her over-exaggerated expression of disgust. "It's true."

"I *know*, and that's the worst part."

"A press conference is... not a bad idea, though," Lucas responds after a moment. He considers her words, running a hand through his dark, unruly hair and studying Kiara's face closely. "Kiara, have you ever considered working in public relations?"

"I already sort of do," she replies, picking at a chipped portion of paint on the wall.

"No, I mean working strictly with speeches, and press conferences, and cutting out the whole traveling around thing."

She's quiet for a second. "No. I didn't think of that."

"Well, you should," Lucas says. "Hey, you know what's always been weird to me?"

"What?"

"You never had a last name, did you? I mean, if you're gonna be in history books, you'll need one."

Kiara feels suddenly nauseous, and she turns away from Lucas' gaze and focuses on the dusty bookshelf ahead of her. She doesn't want to lie, but she really, *really* does. "You're right," she croaks.

"You may as well just make one up," he says plainly.

Kiara suddenly feels that wash of neutrality again, and she can't help the small smile that creeps onto her face. "Yeah, I may as well, huh? It's not like it means anything anyways."

"Exactly. Well, unless you're royalty. Then it's everything."

Kiara laughs, somewhat mirthlessly. "You'd know better than me."

Part Nine: The Cancer

Peter

"How are we feeling today, Peter?" Charles asks as he enters the boy's room.

Peter does nothing but groan in response. He's shirtless in his rollaway hospital bed, feeling awful despite the doctor's cheery tone. Peter guarantees he doesn't look much better: his dark circles are apparent, his hair is tousled, and his head is pounding as if someone were slamming their fists against the walls of his skull. Besides, he is absolutely drowning in sweat.

"Not good, I assume?" Charles asks as he begins to unpack his bag. Charles usually stays with Peter for the morning, and then his nurse takes over for the afternoon.

"My head is *pounding*."

"The fever, probably. Perhaps just a bad headache."

Peter watches Charles flit about the room, wanting – wishing – he could just talk to him. However, his incessant coughing makes that just about impossible.

Instead, he sits in silence and looks around. Papers – no, old charts – are tacked to the wall, his desk, now shoved to the side, is covered in random junk: more charts, test medicines, and more importantly, his things: pictures, clothes, letter writing stuff, which he was somehow too weak to use already.

"Is this the first time you've had such a terrible cough?" the doctor asks, pulling Peter's chin with his thumb and index finger and then sticking a thermometer in his mouth.

"Mm-hmm," Peter mumbles.

Charles removes the thermometer and jots something down. "Any blood?"

"No," Peter rasps. He looks up at Charles. "Charles, am I going to-"

"Goodness, no. Don't ask that, already."

Peter nods as he mumbles, "I'll wait, then."

"May I ask if Cameron has ever shown symptoms of this disease?" he speaks without looking at Peter, instead studying the labels on the vials that rest on the desk and letting the conversation shift.

"I don't think so."

Charles sits at the foot of Peter's bed, and Peter just stares at him. After a moment, the doctor speaks. "Let me explain this to you, okay, Peter? This disease is almost a mimicry of tuberculosis, which was a bad infection that was common in Old America."

"Okay."

"Luckily, for the people in Sector Five who have it, there are some older treatments available that they may respond to better than simply isolating them. However, you have two things working against you. Your power, for one thing, makes you incredibly susceptible to worse illnesses because it physically saps strength and energy from your body, both of which are necessary to fight diseases. The second thing we found due to your biopsy and blood tests is Wilson's Disease. It's a liver complication that was biologically passed down to you."

So the parents he never knew cursed him with a shit body. *Perfect,* Peter thinks.

Charles pauses to readjust on the slim bed and then continues. "Luckily, now that we know you have Wilson's, we can begin treating it. However, this means you are at a higher risk of needing a liver transplant because of this new disease from Sector Five."

Peter takes a deep breath as best he can and nods. It wasn't that he wasn't listening to Charles, it's just that the kind man's words were deflecting off his sallow skin. He swallows as he looks down at his hands, wishing he could say anything at all that would summarize his feelings. After a second, he looks back up at the doctor, who is staring at him intently.

"I promise you, Peter, that I won't let you suffer like this for long."

"Thank you," Peter whispers, for lack of a better response. He can't help but worry that the end of his suffering might not be the same thing that Charles has planned.

Part Ten: The Scorpio

Cameron

Dear Peter,

Hi, loverboy. I'm sorry your headache is so bad, but I'm glad that even if things have gotten worse, you're still with us.

We're all separated, except for Lucas and Kiara. I'm not sure why they got quarantined together, but I guess the doctors have their reasons.

I miss you. A lot. And I love you, Peter Simon. I can't wait to hold you again. I get out in... I think three days? Maybe four, I don't know. But I've been trying to talk Charles into letting me visit you. It's not working so far, but I'm gonna keep trying.

What have you been doing to occupy yourself? You're lucky you get to talk to Charles and your nurse, at least. Even our dinner people don't stick around to chat. I've found that I'm really good at drawing (not really) and I did a killer still-life of the plant in my room. I still suck at reading. I think I can only read when I'm with you.

Oh, I had another question. Are you still eating normal food? Like, do you get sick-person food? We've come to the conclusion that our meals change every day but all four of us get the same thing, but none of us actually know what you eat.

I miss you so bad.

Can you please leave instructions on how to fix the thermostat? I can't figure it out and it's literally negative a million degrees in here.

I love you. And I miss you.

Love, Cam

Part Eleven: The Cancer

Peter

Peter couldn't hold a pen. So when Ruth read Cameron's letters aloud, he couldn't do anything besides listen to her voice and his heart breaking, and when she left, he'd let his fever-induced stupor take over.

If he couldn't talk to Cameron in real life, he could at least do it in his head.

Dear Cam,

Hi. I miss you, too. I think I'll mention that upfront, just so it's out of the way.

I've been doing nothing. I sleep a lot. And think, and mostly just sit and breathe and try not to panic.

I eat normal food, for the most part. I think it's the same meals as you guys. If I'm testing a new medicine, they usually keep me on liquids until it's out of my system, which sucks because the only thing worse than being sick is being hungry.

I miss you.

I think you're a psychopath for wanting that room any hotter than it is, but since I'm not there to be dramatic about it, here are the thermostat instructions:

1. Hit the 'on' button.
2. When the screen blinks green, turn the dial to 75. (I know that's where you want it because that's where it was when I reset it the first time.)
3. Hit the center button on the dial.
4. If it blinks twice, it's working the way it should and the temperature should be up within the hour.
    I love you. Write to me again soon.

Yours, Peter

Part Twelve: The Aries

Kiara

Today Kiara actually has *work* to do, which is good for her dwindling sanity.

From her office, Barbara has signed off on the press conference for Lucas and Diana, so Kiara has been meticulously drafting a speech for this Sunday afternoon, mere hours after they get off their lockdown. If Lucas and Diana stay in good health, they'll quickly be moved back into their apartment, then shoved in front of cameras and microphones to deliver their speech, one Kiara must have perfectly crafted by then.

While Lucas read and sketched and, well, lazed about, Kiara sat at her big desk and buckled down.

It felt good to do something again, not just sit and wait and feel uncomfortable in her own body. She also had less time to talk to Lucas, which was a good thing, because Kiara was slowly feeling more affection for the prince with the newfound knowledge of their familial relation, and she didn't exactly like it.

Kiara sighs and pushes the sixth draft of their speech up to the corner of her desk, swinging her legs up and leaning back in her chair.

"Lunch, Miss Kiara and Prince Lucas?" her designated staff person asks as she nudges the door open. She's clad in a hazmat suit, and the strange sight has become eerily and quickly familiar.

"Sure. Thank you, Hayley," Kiara replies, tapping the desk with her pencil, "you can leave it right here."

Hayley puts the tray down and quickly backs up, out of range from whatever invisible germs they may be spewing. "And your symptoms?"

Every time they get lunch, their waiter-slash-butler-slash-nurse-slash-astronaut takes their symptoms. Then they return them to Charles, who compares them with Peter's symptoms and decides whether or not they're getting sick too.

"Same as yesterday. Nothing," Kiara responds. Lucas nods too, a silent echo of Kiara's statement. Kiara watches as Hayley writes something down and then something nags in the back of her brain. "Have the other two shown symptoms at all?"

"I'm not sure," she replies. "I don't get that information, only yours and His Highness'."

Kiara nods, disappointed and nervous for some reason. "Well, thanks anyways."

She smiles politely and heads for the door. "Of course."

As soon as the door is shut, Kiara turns to Lucas. "Hey."

"Uh-huh?" he responds, nose stuck back in his big book once more.

"Can you read this speech? Try to imagine it as it will be read for real, on Sunday."

Lucas crosses to the desk, hovering over Kiara's shoulder as he reads. After a long, quiet moment, he nods, pulling away just a hair. "It's good. Really good, actually." He smiles down at Kiara, and she frantically searches for any signs of her own smile in his. "You're really good at this, Ki."

Kiara can't help but smile back at him, although her anxiety quickly pushes it away. Clearing her throat, she turns away from Lucas. "Thank you."

Part Thirteen: The Taurus

Diana

Okay. Diana hates to say it. But working during lockdown is kind of... not that awful.

She's at least gotten stuff done. That doesn't usually happen when you've got one of the boys barging in asking about lunch, or when Kiara is needing your opinion on a speech draft, or when Lucas comes in just because he misses you.

Sure, Diana loves those things, but it feels good to just... get something done. She also guarantees the other three are bored out of their skulls, so now is the best time to work before they fall back into their jam-packed routines. Plus, a respite for the sake of her sanity before Kiara's bomb of an announcement dropped would not hurt.

She's been catching up on bills that were passed through from the adults, and she was in the groove of editing, revising, and re-reading. According to Barbara, she was supposed to have gotten seven, but she only had six on her desk. Either way, fewer bills meant more time to focus on each one.

"Diana!" someone from across the hall shouts.

Diana groans and gets up, crossing to the door. "What?!"

"Did the staff give you my sweatpants instead of yours?"

Kiara.

Diana looks down at her sweatpants. The girls have the same ones, but Diana is just a little bigger than

Kiara is. Diana twists around to check the tag, and sure enough, a 'K' is written on it in black marker.

"Uh, yes," she yells back. "They must've grabbed them out of the laundry."

"Damn," Kiara replies, "I knew they were missing."

Diana pauses, realizing that each of their offices were almost like separate worlds now. She's suddenly envious of Kiara and Lucas, and the feeling makes her stomach feel sick. "I can have someone bring them to you?" she yells.

"No, it's fine!" Kiara shouts back. "Four days! Four days. "Yes, ma'am."

Diana sits back down, grabbing her papers and flipping aimlessly through them. Suddenly, the phone rings.

"Yes?" she says, this time speaking at a normal tone and not the one she adopted for shouting through the walls.

"Hello, Diana dear," Barbara says, voice slightly tinny. "Just checking in."

"I'm fine," Diana replies. "Four days, according to Ki?"

"Yes, four days. Oh, by the way, Reginald wants you to annotate that bill he gave you, when you get the chance. Don't sign anything yet."

"Sounds good to me," Diana mumbles, slumping back in her chair.

Part Fourteen: The Libra

Lucas

Lucas stands back and admires his and Kiara's shared office.

After *three whole days,* he can absolutely promise that this place is well ordered. When he'd arrived, the room had been a disorganized mess, perfectly chaotic in Kiara's regular fashion. But now, Lucas' hard work has changed the place for the better. There are no stray papers, the books are shelved, both of their clothes are folded away, the tables are dusted, and his bed is made. He didn't dare touch Kiara's overturned pillows and crumpled sheets.

Lucas can also promise that he's going completely insane, but it's fine.

He notices something on Kiara's desk which he'd obviously missed during his cleaning. It's a journal, carefully bound in red leather. A strap ties around the front, sealing it closed. He'd seen Kiara write in it every day, sometimes more than once.

Lucas knows he shouldn't touch it. It wouldn't be very prince-like to root through his friends' things, especially while she was in the bathroom of all places.

But he isn't in Alynthia anymore, is he?

He picks up the smooth journal, which is bent and warped from constant use. Pulling the strap gently, he flips to the most recently written page.

It's dated from the previous night, and Lucas tries his best to keep his eyes from wandering to the neatly-written words. Naturally, he doesn't succeed.

I find myself looking for similarities between Lucas and me. I haven't noticed many, but it's the sort of little things that we share. He snores, and the others always say that I do, too. His forehead wrinkles when he thinks just like mine does, and we have the exact same eye color.

It makes me think of mom, sort of. If I can even call her that. Henderson and Cornelius have green eyes that match, but Lucas and I must share the same eye colors as our moms. I've only ever seen photos of Anastasia, and I guess in the tomb I saw her, too. She's beautiful, and I find some peace in knowing that Lucas looks more like her than Cornelius. I only assume that I look more like mom than Henderson, but I wish there was something more I could do to know her.

When I think about all this, it makes me feel sick. I want to curl up and hide away, but that isn't really possible with Lucas of all people quarantining with me.

I'm scared about what he'll say when he finds out. He'll hate me, probably, and do I deserve that? If you ask me, I think I do.

Lucas wants to continue – he has questions, lots of them – but then the office door opens.

"Lucas?" Kiara asks, her voice confused and her face tight with worry as she enters.

Lucas jumps with fright and quickly spins around, attempting to hide the journal behind his back, but Kiara is too quick, and Lucas' hands are shaking.

"Is that my journal?" she asks, her voice now less confused and more outright angry. "Lucas, why do you have that?"

No, not anger. Fear.

Kiara yanks it from his hands as Lucas splutters for words, clutching it close to her chest like it's armor. "You can't just rifle through my stuff, Lucas!" she yells. "I... just because we share a room for a week doesn't give you the right!"

"I know," Lucas tries, "but Kiara, you wrote-"

"It doesn't matter what I wrote," she shouts, although her voice cracks. "It's private."

"Why am I in your journal, Kiara?" Lucas asks, unable to help the way his voice rises to match hers. "Me, your mom, my *father-*"

"Because in our country, they refuse to tell you about your family and I never got to know mine, so yes, Lucas, I do have some questions about my mother. I'm sorry if that makes you angry."

"Why me, though? Why am I in there, too, and none of the others?"

Kiara hesitates, and Lucas takes a moment to stare at her. What she had written was right – he did see his irises mirrored in hers. And if he could look in a mirror, he'd bet that his forehead was creased in exactly the same crinkled manner.

But this Kiara isn't the same girl he always saw. This wasn't the Kiara that he thought he knew. This Kiara's eyes were swimming in tears, her shoulders were tense, and her chewed-down nails and cuticles clutched that red journal tight, like it could buffer her from him getting too close.

And then he puts the pieces together in one final, almost-satisfying click.

"It's... it's us who's family, isn't it?" he whispers. "We're related, aren't we, Ki?"

Kiara crumbles before him then, as if he'd pushed over that stone statue of a girl and watched her fall to the too-hard tiled floor. "Yes," she cries, catching herself on her bed and sitting down. Her iron grip on the book remains, as if some of her strength was still hiding away somewhere. "I – I didn't know how to tell you."

Lucas just stands there, lost for words. After a moment that's silent save for Kiara's crying, he whispers: "But... but how?"

Kiara sniffles, wiping her nose on her sleeve and scoffing almost angrily. "Remember your uncle?"

Lucas hesitates. He did remember his uncle, the one who was a killer, a dictator, a horrible, rotten man. His uncle, who had ruled over this country and single-handedly brought its demise.

His uncle, George Henderson.

"No," he whispers, suddenly feeling that nausea that Kiara had written about in her journal. Without thinking, he crosses to sit next to her, their shoulders touching. She flinches away from the contact. "Ki-"

"It's true. I'm so sorry, Lucas."

"You're sorry?!" Lucas almost shouts. He wrenches Kiara's hand free from her journal, holding it tight. Her skin is clammy and too hot. "You do *not* get to be sorry for this, Kiara. You have nothing to be sorry for."

She hiccups out another sob. "You have every right to loathe me. I've been sleeping in the same room as you for days and keeping this horrible secret."

Lucas shakes his head. "Not horrible. It isn't horrible if it means we're family."

She finally – *finally* – meets his gaze. Her ebony cheeks are stained with salty tears, and Lucas finds himself wanting to cry, too. "It isn't a good thing, Lucas.

My father... I can't even bear to think about him right now."

"Then don't," Lucas urges. "Don't."

He rises, taking the journal from her and tossing it half-heartedly on her desktop. She watches, agape, as the book lands, like Lucas had just desecrated the very object that was holding her hostage.

He turns to her again, fighting as hard as he can to remain steadfast under her tearful gaze. If she can't be strong, he will be for her. If she can't think or speak or function, he'll do it for her.

With a sad sort of smile, he motions around the room. "I cleaned. Did you notice?"

Part Fifteen: The Cancer

Peter

"Good afternoon, darling!" Nurse Butters calls as she enters Peter's room.

"Hello," he rasps.

The older woman hesitates, hands frozen in unbuttoning her coat. Her eyes imploringly search Peter's face and he grimaces. "Peter. Not doing well today, I'd guess."

"No," Peter replies, his hand coming to his throat instinctively and rubbing it gently. The action makes his body ache.

"Any throat pain?"

He nods, clearing his throat for the billionth time.

She steps back and writes something down. "What have you eaten today?"

Peter's stomach growls and he clutches the white sheets underneath him. "Nothing."

"Good," the nurse replies, "and has there been any-?"

Peter's stomach grumbles again, but this time it leaps into his throat and he bends over towards the conveniently-placed trashcan to his right. When he sits back up, wiping his mouth, Peter catches the kind-eyed older woman staring at him with a concerned expression he knows all too well.

His heart hammers in his chest and he doesn't know why he's nervous. Then he follows her gaze to the trash, noticing his vomit is flecked with blood.

"I'm going to get the doctor," she responds, her voice not holding the cheerful tone it usually has.

She exits, and after a minute, Doctor Charles comes in with nurse Butters on his heel. He looks almost businesslike, a far cry from the nonchalance he normally radiates, which makes Peter more scared than before. He drops his bag on the table and grabs Peter's chart for the day, taking the nurse by the arm and pulling her closer.

As they speak in hushed tones, Peter studies the two for lack of anything else to do. Charles is taller and balding, and his skin is olive, like Peter's own. The nurse, on the other hand, is short and round, and her skin is dark and smooth. Her hair is much darker than Kiara's, and it's cut down to her chin in thick curls. Watching them work together, Peter notices that they keep making eye contact with one another every so often and just studying the other person.

They'd be cute together, he won't lie.

"Okay, Peter. Here's the deal," Charles says, grabbing a chair and pulling it up to Peter's bedside. Nurse Butters stands vigilantly behind him. "We're going to have someone on your PR team put out an official statement."

"Saying... what?" Peter asks, fingers fidgeting in the sheets again.

"Saying that you've officially entered stage two."

Ah. Peter swallows, feeling bile rise in his throat. "Okay," he responds, hating the way his voice cracks. "What does this *really* mean?"

The doctor hesitates. "Well," he begins, "your symptoms are going to change. You will still have the fever, and the headache, but those take a backtrack for-"

"The coughing and puking up blood," Nurse Butters finishes with a cringe.

"Exactly," Charles says. His eyes scan the tabletop to his right, looking at the vials there, some older than others but all failures nonetheless. "We're trying as hard as we can to find something to help you, but something is seemingly halting any medicinal cures we inject. I have something new we can try, but I left it in my office."

The doctor leaves, shutting the door quietly behind him and leaving Peter alone with nurse Butters.

She paces the room, casting wary glances at the boy. After a second, Peter can't handle the silence any longer.

"Stop," he snaps. She halts in her tracks and stares at Peter, open-mouthed, and he's immediately flooded with guilt. "I'm sorry."

The woman sits beside his bed, taking Peter's hand and cradling it gently, forcing him to look at her. "Peter, may I tell you something?"

He nods. That hurts, too.

"When I was about twenty-five, I had met an amazing man from my sector. We were married, and I was expecting our first child together. But then he got sick," she pauses, taking a deep breath, "and he died within the first two weeks of this sickness."

Peter wishes he were strong enough to say something to her. Instead, he squeezes her hand.

"So I was left alone. *Pregnant* and alone. But I powered through. I went back to the house we had bought together and lived alone, refusing help from anyone who offered it because I was *determined* to make it on my own. And then I had my son," Peter's chest tightens, and he wonders how she's telling this story with barely any emotion. "He was named Adam. And he was the most beautiful child you've ever seen. He got a bad case of pneumonia. Poor thing was wailing day and night, and I couldn't do anything to help. He passed away too."

Peter nods again, feeling his stomach sink in sadness. He wants to – he *can't* – say anything.

She continues as if in her own world, or maybe a few years in the past. "I enrolled in medical school soon after that. I never wanted another mother to suffer the way I had. And then years passed. I had no friends, no children, no husband. And I watched four particularly spunky kids overthrow the entire government and then lo and behold *I* end up with one as my newest charge. One kind and caring, with a good head on his shoulders. I know, Peter, that you're feeling lost. And alone. I know that feeling. I want you to know that *I* am with you, always. No matter what you go through."

Peter detaches his hand from hers and wipes his eyes, which are threatening to spill impending tears. He clears his throat to ask for help, but he doesn't need to. She reaches up and wipes his other cheek for him. "Thank you," Peter whispers, meeting her dark brown eyes. Her irises are almost the same shade as Kiara's, and Peter sniffles at the near sight of his best friend.

"Don't thank me," she whispers back, taking his hands again. "I'll get you through this."

Peter closes his eyes for a moment, letting himself relax in the safety of her nearness. In his head he sees Kiara and Diana laughing over breakfast, he sees Lucas joking around at a meeting, he sees Cameron reading on the couch. Peter reopens his eyes and looks around the office, this place he knows so well, this empty room that used to be filled with such joy and stress and sadness but is now up to the brim in sick, stale air.

Peter sniffles, fighting that recurring emotional overwhelm. "I don't want everything to end right *now*," he whispers, pushing the words out with force.

"I know, darling, I know," she says, crossing to him and wiping his cheeks with her thumbs. "I can't imagine what you're feeling."

Before Peter can respond or react, the woman wraps him in a hug, allowing him to muffle his sobs in her shoulder. "Shh, dear. Shh," she whispers in his ear. Peter grasps at her sleeves like a toddler being torn away from their mother but he can't bring himself to detach his grip on the woman. It's safe to cry here, it's safe.

"Peter. Peter, dear. Look at me," Ruth says, pulling away from him and holding him by his shaking shoulders. Peter nods, lip quivering, and she continues. "I cannot look you in the eye and tell you that I have answers, because I don't. But if I can give you one piece of advice, I would tell you that as long as you continue to *hope* that you can get out of here and continue to love those people, then those same ones who you think of all day are standing outside these walls thinking of you as well." She gives Peter's shoulders a squeeze. "So don't let their thoughts go to waste. Keep fighting."

Peter nods rapidly, blinking away the last of his tears. Then he starts to cough, pulling up the corner of his bedsheet to cover his mouth for a good ten seconds as his body shakes.

Charles comes back in then, pausing as he takes in Peter's appearance as the boy tucks his bedsheet back under his quilt. "Please tell me you haven't been crying, dear boy," he says, glancing briefly at Ruth. "I don't know if I can handle all these emotions."

Nurse Butters chuckles, passing the doctor a sterilized needle which he sticks into the vial of medicine he's holding. After a quiet moment, Peter feels the familiar pinprick of a needle in his right arm. A split second later the pain is gone, and he glances up to see nurse Butters taping a gauze pad on the spot.

"Let's see how we do with that, my boy," the doctor says, grabbing a notebook and parking himself in the cushy chair against the wall. Usually, the doctor stays for the rest of the day after Peter is given a new trial, just to monitor his reactions and symptoms. Charles glances up at Ruth. "Thank you for your help, Ruth," he says, smiling kindly at her.

The nurse smiles back, but instead of leaving, she takes a seat on the foot of Peter's bed. "Actually, I think I'll stay. Perhaps Peter wants more company."

Peter is sure he looks as surprised as Doctor Charles does, but they both say nothing as the nurse smiles approvingly and makes herself comfortable.

They sit in that comfortable silence for a long while, nearly an hour, until Charles gets up and examines Peter from head-to-toe, eyes roaming his arms, face, and, upon request, the inside of his throat as he sticks out his tongue and says 'ah'. Charles nods to himself, sitting back down, but as he does, Peter feels his hand clench and his gut churns.

Nurse Butters has the trash can under Peter's chin before he even realizes he's throwing up.

Peter looks back up to see both adults looming over him, Charles writing adamantly in his chart and Ruth reaching for a tissue, which she uses to wipe Peter's chin and mouth. It comes away bloody.

"It didn't work," the older woman whispers, her voice slightly dismayed.

Peter meets her forlorn gaze and then quickly must turn back into the trash can.

"We don't know that just yet," Charles says, but his tone isn't much happier than the nurse's was.

"We do, Charles," she replies, turning entirely to face him. Peter watches his eyes travel her face. "This one hasn't worked, so send it back to the team and tell them to find something else." Once again, the doctor looks taken aback at the fire in her voice. "I will not let Cameron back in here seeing Peter look this forsaken. So, Charles, we *are* finding a cure."

After considerable hesitation, Charles nods. "No, I – um, of course. I'm sorry, Peter, that this one hasn't worked."

Peter says nothing – just coughs into that sheet again.

"We'll leave you be, Peter. Ring for us if you need anything." Charles goes after a long moment of no noise besides hacking, gently taking Ruth by the arm and leading her out of the room. Peter groans and leans back against the pillow, once again pushing his bloodied bedsheet corner under his too-hot, scratchy quilt. When he closes his eyes, he's writing to Cameron.

Part Sixteen: The Cancer

Peter

Dear Cameron,

I wish I could give you better news. I've entered stage two of the sickness; added symptoms are a horrible cough and vomiting, most of which is just blood.

I haven't left my bed all day today or yesterday, but luckily Ruth and Charles make good company.

How are you? I hear from Charles that you guys are three days out from being back in the world. What kind of stuff are you getting for work?

Please tell me about every boring thing you've been doing. I need to be able to picture normalcy outside of this office. And I need to picture your face, surprisingly enough.

How are Lucas and Diana? Have they made a public announcement yet? When they do, please tell me if they're holding it on the steps so I can watch. And how's Ki? Still kicking everyone's asses, I assume.

Oh, also, can you include a picture of yourself in your response so that I can put it on my bedside table? I'm picturing the one from our first photoshoot with Lucas, where you're in that dark-green shirt.

I guess there's nothing else. I'm feeling pretty awful today, definitely worse than yesterday. But I love you, and I miss you more than anything. I can't wait for the day I can open my door and you'll be on the other side of it.

Yours, Peter

Part Seventeen: The Scorpio

Cameron

Dear Peter,

You know, for someone so reserved, you seem to have quite the dramatic flair in your writing. I like to read the notes you've put in the margins of these books and bills, and I can practically hear your voice.

It's the worst thing ever, Peter, to imagine you sick all by yourself. But I know nurse Butters and Charles are taking good care of you. I always knew I liked them, even if Charles and I butt heads sometimes.

All in all, I'm still doing good, despite worrying about this cute boy all day and night. You might know him, he's kind of a celebrity.

I don't have any symptoms still, thankfully, and I've been mostly working but also attempting to reorganize the office since I realize three days in there alone makes you way more of a slob than I thought. I've been going over a few cases that were pushed up by the country's courts, but nothing too serious. Sometimes, when I'm passing your way towards the bathroom, I sort of listen by the door. Not being creepy, obviously, but just to hear your voice. I haven't so far yet, though. Lucas and Diana are prepping for their conference as we speak, and it'll be on the steps on Sunday at one-thirty. Kiara is still a badass as far as I'm aware, but things are awfully quiet on her and Lucas' side of the hall.

Peter, when they open that door, I'll be waiting on the other side. Promise.

I love you.

Cameron

Part Eighteen: The Aries

Kiara

"What was she like?" Lucas asks, tossing Kiara's stress ball back to her.

She catches it from her bed, one-handed. "Who?"

"Your mother," he replies from his own cot on the other end of the room. "What was she like?"

"Oh," Kiara mumbles, "I don't know. She died the same day she had me."

Lucas frowns. Kiara had come to the realization that they frowned the same, too. "Well, in your mind you still know her, Ki."

She can almost feel her chest tightening around her knit-together heart. "I don't think I know what you mean."

"She's your mother, no matter what. Who is she to you?"

Kiara swallows, and she's surprised at how fast words bubble from her lips. "She'd be quiet, I think. Quiet, but not in an angry way like I am. I like to think she'd be very kind, too."

"My mother was that way," Lucas adds at the perfect lull. "Empathetic almost to a fault."

Kiara chuckles, but not happily. "I guess *we* get our personalities from our fathers."

"No," Lucas immediately interjects. "We might think that, but deep down we aren't like them one bit."

Kiara nods, wishing she could agree with him or even hear him at all.

"What did she look like?" Lucas asks, voice soft as if he knew the turbulent thoughts rampaging through her head. "In your mind, what does she look like?"

"She's got dark skin like mine, obviously. Maybe even darker than mine, I think. That seems right in my head. She would have been pretty, with hair that curls so tight, the way I always wished mine was like. Dark eyes, the same as ours." She hesitates. "But I don't know how a woman like that would ever fall in love with someone like Henderson."

Lucas shrugs. "How could a woman like Anastasia Rutherland fall for my father?" he rebuts her.

Kiara sighs. "That's true, I guess." She can't help but smile very slightly as she meets Lucas' gaze.

The prince's eyes, those same dark irises, hold a determined shine. "We would have helped you, Ki. When your mother died, we would have made a home for you in Alynthia."

Kiara feels an overwhelming urge to run and hug him, but she resists. Quietly, she speaks. "I've got a home right here."

Part Nineteen: The Scorpio

Cameron

"I'm just bored."

Ms. Miller's automatic voice huffs out a sigh on the other end of the phone. "Cameron, you in particular were given a hellish pile of security work to do. All this clearing of medical staff and such is not light work."

"I'm done with it all."

"There's no way."

"I *am*. I worked all night, and woke up at six in the morning upright at my desk."

Cameron's office looks very different from the others: papers are strewn across the floor, coffee cups and empty food boxes litter the surfaces, and the potted plant that had been there since Oliver Hill had worked in the room was drooping quite sadly.

Only today had Cameron recalled that his phone was, in fact, still hooked up to the rest of the system, and Ms. Miller had been his second call after Peter, whose phone must've been removed because when Cameron dialed his number, all that came over it was a long buzzing tone that was eerily similar to the sound looping through Cameron's head.

"Well, what have you been doing since then?"

Cameron makes a face. "*Funding.*"

Ms. Miller barks out a laugh and Cameron groans. "Sorry, sorry, it's just... funding?!"

"I know, that's what I said."

"I can't ever picture you in funding."

"That's what I tried to tell Barbara, but-"

"She didn't care."

"No, she did not."

They're both quiet for a moment, and then they begin to laugh. It's a strange sight, Cameron laughing, because he hasn't for what seems like forever. And it feels good. In fact, if he could, Cameron would feel like this forever. But it quickly fades as he catches sight of his closed door, reminding him once again that Ms. Miller wasn't in the room laughing with him, she was across the hall, on the phone, and that's where she'd stay for the next three days.

He clears his throat. "Um, Miriam, I'm gonna go. I've gotta clean this place up a bit."

"Alright, darling. Hang in there."

Cameron doesn't respond, instead hanging up the phone and rising to his feet. Without another word, he grabs the little cup of water from his desk, turns towards the plant, and dumps it into the soil.

Part Twenty: The Taurus

Diana

It's the middle of the night, and Diana is asleep.
Maybe. She could be.

She's lying in bed, green eyes fixated on the ceiling.

Dinner that night had been delicious, and yet Diana had eaten it slowly, methodically, at her desk.

It wasn't that she was sick, in fact, she felt good considering she hadn't left her office in what, four days? It was that the salad she was eating was Peter's favorite, and something had struck her tonight sitting there alone.

In her mind, she pictured her best friend, who – according to the regular updates Charles had been giving – was slipping away day after day. She could picture Peter wasting away, with nothing to look forward to except the infinite worsening of sickness.

Peter might not make it out.

And what would she do if that happened?

The question had been plaguing her ever since, and she couldn't get the nagging little query out of her brain. Even here, in an in-between sleep state, it haunted her.

It seemed like nobody else had thought about that fact yet. Or, if they had, they weren't paying it any mind. But Diana couldn't stop envisioning Doctor Charles leaving Peter's room, with tears streaking his face, having to tell the world outside their Capitol building that their Secretary of Education would never open another school, or hold another infant for a magazine photo.

She couldn't stop seeing Kiara and Lucas, chests hitching at the news, shutting themselves in their rooms to mourn alone because they felt as though they couldn't face the world. To Diana's dismay, that was one familial trait that the two of them shared.

And Cameron. Cameron, who Diana knew was so truly, deeply in love with her best friend. Cameron, who would never give himself the time to grieve and would throw himself into his work and run himself ragged until he too faded just as Peter had.

But the one part of the problem that Diana couldn't see was what *she* would do.

When Maya had died, Diana had lost the ability to function. She sat there in the Capitol all day, right on the stone tile, while Barbara and her friends flitted around her, trying to help. She had only gotten to her feet in order to dress herself for the funeral. It had taken days for her to eat a full meal, or to take a shower, or to start a conversation with someone.

That all-consuming grief strangled the air from her lungs, it weighed on her shoulders, it pulled at limbs and prodded at her skin. Some days, it still did. Most days.

But something told her Peter would be different. When Maya was alive, she urged Diana to continue, no matter what. But Peter was the person she could go to if she needed a rest, a break, a respite from the world around her. So if he was *gone*, would she ever come off that break? Would she ever get to go back to the real world?

Could she *ever* recover?

That grief, the one that pulled and poked and choked, that pushed and burned and kicked – would it just get worse? Would it kill her, too?

Diana climbs out of bed with a sigh and crosses to the window, sock feet padding across the floor. She's in her blue pajama pants and a white shirt that was once Lucas' but was now very much hers. She unlatches the lock with one hand and pushes the window outwards, allowing it to swing on its hinges and grant the cold night air entry into her warm room. Diana leans against the sill, propping her elbows on the brick, and tries to focus on just the sting of the night air on her face, nothing more, not even her thoughts.

"Good morning. Or should I say good night?" a raspy voice asks from a window down.

Diana turns with a jump to see Peter, leaning out his window the same way she was. His dark curls were blowing off his forehead with the gentle, biting wind, and his face was turned up towards the moon. The pale light made his features more defined, made his hazel eyes glow. He looks almost angelic, and Diana can't help but wonder if he's just a figment of her imagination.

No, she *knows* she's imagining him. Or dreaming. Either way, she's glad he came to visit.

With a small smile, Diana turns back towards the view of the empty Plaza. That was another beautiful part of this dream: the space looked serene, and still. "Either works."

Peter closes his eyes, unmoving. "I miss you."

"I miss you too."

"I miss you more now than I did six years ago."

"Me too. I think now that I've found you, I don't want to let you go."

He opens his eyes and turns towards her. "You won't have to."

How could you know that? "How are you feeling?"

A shrug. "Not fantastic."

"For lack of a better adjective."

He coughs out a laugh. "Well, I'm stage two."

Diana grimaces, recalling the notice she had been given that was still sitting on her desk. "Yeah, I knew that much."

"I haven't eaten since yesterday morning."

She glances at him nervously. "Because-?"

"I can't keep anything down. Ruth says it's the disease. But I've been getting proper vitamins through my IVs and stuff, or whatever. I dunno, really. They could be poisoning me and I'd never know."

Diana chuckles. "I'm sure they aren't."

"No, Charles has been taking good care of me."

She smiles, turning to face him. "I like him a lot."

"Me too. He... he's become like family to me these past couple days," he turns to Diana. "But I miss my *real* family, though."

She smiles, which quickly dips into a frown. "We miss you too."

"How's Cam?"

"Okay. He's been awfully quiet with the rest of us. We got a letter or two at the start of the lockdown, but it's been radio silence since. The only reason we know he's alive is because he calls Miriam every once in a while."

Peter looks down and sighs, clasping his hands and resting his forearms on the windowsill. "He writes to me a lot."

"Yeah?"

"Yeah. But now it feels like we're sort of going around in circles. The only things I want to tell him, to show him, can only be done in person. I want..." he laughs sadly and looks up at the stars again, "I want him with me."

"We all want him with you."

They fall quiet. Diana reaches out her right hand, and without looking, she feels Peter hold out his left. They're far away, but close enough so that the tips of their fingers barely brush, close enough that she feels the ghostlike heat of his touch as their fingertips pass through one another's in a spectral dance.

She knows this isn't real. But she really wishes it were.

The sensation alone – the feeling of his phantom nearness – is enough to make Diana want to cry, but she focuses on the stars and the breeze and the inky blackness of the night that might not be true, ignoring every emotion that threatens to tear through her calmness. If she let herself cry, would she wake up?

Peter breathes deep, and Diana pretends she doesn't hear the rasp burrowed in the inhale. "I love you, Diana."

Diana swallows and blinks rapidly, trying to clear her eyes. "I love you too."

When he goes, she sleeps the rest of the night without any more dreaming.

Part Twenty-One: The Libra

Lucas

Lucas wakes up with a groan as the door slams shut, and he burrows his cheek into his too-hard mattress, throwing a pillow over his head. Kiara's footfalls – he'd grown to recognize them – cross the room, then move closer.

"You snore," Kiara says from over him.

Lucas peeks out, squinting at her. "So do you."

Kiara chuckles airily, jerking her head over to the desk. "Breakfast is here."

Lucas sighs in delight and sits up, letting his blanket and pillow fall away as he rises and perches on the edge of Kiara's desk, still clad in his pajamas. She wrinkles her nose at him from her bed but says nothing.

They sit in silence for a moment, with no noise besides the scratching of Kiara's pencil in her journal and the muffled sounds of Lucas' chewing. Then an idea strikes him.

"Hey, have you thought about the coronation?"

Kiara looks up, eyebrows raised in an expression that says *what the hell are you talking about?* "What coronation?"

Lucas swallows and shrugs. "Yours. Being the niece of the King of Alynthia makes you a princess. But you haven't been crowned."

Kiara's face goes grimly neutral, the same way it always did when they talked about her – *their* – families. "I don't really want to have one. I'm not... I'm no princess."

"No, you're not, because you haven't been crowned," Lucas replies sarcastically.

Kiara rolls her eyes, although she smiles. "Don't be rude."

Lucas picks around his breakfast tray a bit more, pushing the orange slices to the side with a wrinkle of his nose. Kiara hops up and sits on the other side of the desk, gladly taking them off his hands. "It could be fun to plan. Besides, if you decide to work just with the public and stuff, you can make this one of your first big events. You wouldn't even have to go to Alynthia for the ceremony," he pauses. "Probably. I'm not the most well-versed on those rules."

Kiara shakes her head. "It just seems like a bad idea. Putting the least publicly inclined American in front of two countries and sticking a crown on her head? Recipe for disaster."

Lucas points a finger at her. "You forget Diana."

Kiara laughs. "You're right, she's worse than me. But my point still stands."

Lucas tilts his head. "You don't have to decide right now. But... maybe it wouldn't hurt to look into."

Kira nods, albeit slowly. "Alright. Let's look."

Part Twenty-Two: The Cancer

Peter

Peter groans as his eyes flutter open.

Well, less of a flutter and more of a fracture, because they're so crusted over with mucus that his eyes can't really "flutter."

"Here's a cold compress, Peter," Ruth says as she passes him a damp towel.

Peter dabs the towel over his eyelids, clearing away the gunk. With a wet cough, the remaining cobwebs clear from his throat.

When Ruth speaks, her voice surprisingly light and lilting. "Your symptoms have been much the same. As for the public announcement, there has been an outpouring of support. Not only for you, but for Cameron as well. And Diana. And the others. It seems our people are far more empathetic than I once gave them credit for," she grins at him, her white teeth sparkling. "I'm assuming you played a hand in that all those months ago."

Peter just coughs again, pushing himself up a little straighter to hack the bloody mucus into a napkin. Some gets stuck in his throat, and the retching doubles in intensity as Ruth hurries over.

"Don't you dare die on me. Not while Charles is out of office."

Peter looks over at her. When he finally speaks, he only manages one word. "Where?"

She pauses, pulling tighter the rubber gloves she had donned for her cleaning and delicately taking his soiled tissue. "He... he had a meeting today with a psychotherapist from Alynthia. A Mr. Inesh Mahra." Peter grimaces, and Ruth sees. "He'll only be here to help, Peter. We fix your body; he'll help fix your brain."

Peter just rolls his eyes.

"Charles-" she seems to catch herself, but Peter notices the blush darkening her skin. "*Doctor* Charles is going to be back at some point later," she watches Peter's smirk grow. "Don't, you. God, even your silent teasing is unbearable."

Peter smiles. For the first time in a while.

Part Twenty-Three: The Scorpio

Cameron

"I'm going to throw myself out this window."

"Please don't," Ms. Miller's voice responds over the phone. "That's a bad look for the country as a whole."

"I will. If I have to spend one more day here, I will."

Cameron slouches against his seat. He had been on the phone with Ms. Miller for over an hour, wandering the room aimlessly to burn some calories. Or just to stifle some of his boredom.

He knew he wasn't keeping the Libra leader from work. She would've let him go forever ago if she had anything to do. Anything *pressing*, at least. Besides, he had nothing to do, because he had lost the security file he was supposed to be going over that had all his NDA information for their guards. Oops.

"Cameron, what are you doing right this second?"

He looks around. "Um, nothing. Dinner's coming in thirty. Why?"

"Go to your window."

So he does, pushing the shutters open with a creak. He pushes the phone receiver a little further into his collarbone, nestling it between his ear and his shoulder. "What-?"

"Secretary O'Connor!" someone shouts from across the street. Cameron looks to see a young boy, standing a little way away from the back entrance with an older woman. With his shout, a handful of other people turn to see Cameron leaning out his window, confusion gracing his features. The boy breaks away from who Cameron can only assume is his mother and runs to the base of the window. "Mister O'Connor! Hello!"

Cameron whispers into the phone, fighting to hide his smile. "Thanks, Miriam."

"Of course, dear. I'll talk to you soon." The line goes dead, and Cameron drops the phone to the floor.

"Hey, kid!" he hollers out the window. "What's your name?"

The little boy grins. "Joshua!"

"It's nice to meet you, Joshua."

The kid chuckles, putting a hand in front of his face to shield the sun. When he notices the placement of his hand right above his eyebrow, he straightens his posture and turns the gesture into a salute. Cameron, with a proud smile, salutes him back. "We miss you, Secretary O'Connor," Joshua says in a melancholy voice.

"I miss everyone as well. But I'll be out in..." he thinks for a moment, "twenty-nine hours."

The boy grins again, and Cameron notices one dimple appears in his cheek. "Good! I... I hope I'm just like you when I grow up."

Cameron's heart swells with pride, and he nods firmly. A year ago, the thought of a little kid turning into a liberal, emotional, gay Scorpio would've disgusted people. But now, this kid had someone to look up to. And Cameron could only be grateful that it was him. "Thank you, Joshua. That means more than you could possibly know."

Part Twenty-Four: The Aries

Kiara

After seven days, they had one more medical clearance and then they were out.

Kiara had packed all her belongings that morning, and now she was waiting patiently, seated on the front of her desk, staring at the door.

Lucas was by her side, his stuff just as neatly set aside as hers. She was pleasantly surprised at just how well-versed the prince was in folding his own clothes. She knew now that it was a product of her aunt's teachings.

Kiara refused to think about what her world would look like when she got out. She was certain things would be different when she told everyone, especially the nation. How different, she didn't know. But that was an issue for later.

Five minutes pass in silence.

Then someone knocks on the door, and Doctor Charles pokes his head in, smiling brightly as the two hop off the desktop. "Ah, Your Highnesses!"

Kiara can't help but cringe.

Charles helps himself into the room, and it's only then that the relief of the present moment sets in. Charles gets right to work as Lucas and Kiara share an impatient look, with the doctor holding out two thermometers. "You know the drill."

Kiara and Lucas stick the thermometers under their tongues in tandem. Small clips are hooked on their pointer fingers and blood pressure cuffs are squeezed, then the cousins answer a round of questions.

"Coughing? Especially any blood coming up?"

"No," they reply.

"Chest pain or shortness of breath?"

"No."

"Weight loss or loss of appetite?"

Kiara snorts. "The opposite for this guy," she jabs a thumb in Lucas' direction.

"Shut up," Lucas groans, his accent thick.

"Well," Charles says as he takes one final note and smiles at the pair, "I'm giving you two a clean bill of health."

Suddenly, Kiara hears a clatter from across the hall, and a high-pitched squeal. She assumes Diana and Cameron have already reunited, and she can't fight her smile.

Then, the door flies open. All the way, so fast it slams against the wall.

Cameron is on the other side, and he holds his arms out, his freckled face splitting into a wide grin. Kiara runs into his arms, and he lifts her off her feet, laughing in her ear.

"God, I missed you," he says as he sets her down, "so *freaking* much."

Kiara grabs his forearms to steady herself. "I could say the same. How has security funding been?" she can't keep the playful grin off her face, despite everything.

He rolls his eyes and laughs. "You're lucky I missed you so much, or I would be very mad that you asked that."

"Hey, careful, you two!" Lucas hollers. Kiara and Cameron turn around to see Lucas and Diana, arms slung giddily around each other, at the doorway of the president's office.

"Ki!" Diana shrieks. Kiara loves seeing her so happy. The two girls embrace each other, grinning like idiots and jumping around so energetically they bump into the wall, sending Diana sprawling on the ground.

"See, girls, this is why we can't have nice things," Lucas says with a laugh as he helps Diana to her feet. He kisses her on the head and crosses to Cameron, putting out his hand. "Good to see you again, Cameron."

"For God's sake, you two, just hug already," Kiara says, threading an arm through Diana's. "You act like you're just boring coworkers."

Lucas and Cameron share a look, then laugh, wrapping each other in a strong hug.

Diana turns to Kiara. "We get to sleep in our own beds tonight."

Kiara sighs blissfully. "Yes, yes, we do." The two girls embrace again, and suddenly, everything hits Kiara like a slap in the face, all her giddiness rushing out of her in one fell swoop as she looks at her best friend who had, only days ago, given her the worst news.

Kiara pulls out of the hug, spotting Cameron there, still smiling at the two girls.

Without thinking, she speaks. "Cameron," she begins, desperate to rip off the bandage, "I need to tell you something."

Diana's eyes fill with worry, and Cameron looks confused. "Okay? Are you alright?" he asks.

Suddenly, Kiara's eyes well with tears. And yet, she forces onward. "Cam, Cornelius told Diana before we left last month that George Henderson had a wife, who died in childbirth. But the daughter survived."

Cameron's cheeks pale. "Kiara, you're not saying-"

She nods, swallowing the bile in her throat. "I'm Henderson's daughter," Diana takes her hand, and Kiara continues. "And Diana only told me right before I quarantined with Lucas, and I needed time to process it, and I didn't know how to tell you, especially not over the phone. But that doesn't mean I'm any less sorry for keeping it from you."

A soft hand – Diana's hand – wipes tears from her cheeks, and Kiara realizes she's crying. Cameron is still stunned, and Lucas' face is neutral, so neutral that Kiara can't tell what he's thinking. All her conversations with him from the past week feel so small against this wall of grief.

Before she can continue, Lucas crosses the distance between them in four long strides. For the most fleeting moment, Kiara worries that he'll hit her, or storm right past. After all, what else should she expect? But then he does something even more surprising.

He hugs her.

It's not just a hug, though – it's an anchor, with Lucas' strong arms holding her tight. Immediately, Kiara hugs him back, letting herself cry into his chest. Suddenly, all those turbulent emotions dissipate, and Kiara can only think of one word.

Family.

Lucas holds her for a long moment, until he whispers, "Our dads really suck, huh?"

Kiara chokes out a laugh, then nods, sniffling as she pulls away. "Yeah, they do. Thank you, Lucas."

Lucas holds her at arm's length, and suddenly two matching pairs of dark eyes connect, ones that had met countless times before. While he cradles her safely, Cameron finally speaks. "Listen, Ki. I cannot even imagine what you're going through, but we're here for you. You're part of *our* family."

"And family looks out for each other," Diana replies, her voice soft.

"That they do," Cameron says, moving to the pair with Diana in tow. He nudges Kiara with a joking smirk. "So, *princess,* what do you say?"

Kiara shakes her head, but she can't fight a small smile. Even so, she feels that clenching darkness creeping around her insides. "I don't know what to do," she whispers.

"You don't need to do anything," Lucas states firmly. "Time will give you more peace than your brain ever will."

Diana chuckles. "Whatever that means."

Kiara nods solemnly, forcing it all away for just one more moment of peace.

Lucas reaches over and gives Diana's shoulder a squeeze. "Hey, you. Press conference is in two hours."

"Oh, right!" Diana says. She turns to Kiara. "Are you going to be okay?"

Kiara forces a smile, looking into bright green eyes and wondering how they all survived their childhoods without each other. "I'll be okay."

"Oh, Cameron," Lucas says, holding up a finger and disappearing into Kiara's office, returning a few moments later, "this is nice, by the way."

He's holding a magazine, a traditional tabloid that he and Kiara had pored over themselves already. On the cover is a large photo of Cameron hanging out his window, with a little boy on the cement below him. Both are smiling, and both are saluting one another. The contours cast from the sun over the Capitol dome give Cameron a long, God-like shadow. His hair looks almost aflame, and the look in the child's eyes is nothing short of utter adoration.

Cameron takes the magazine from Lucas and smiles, gazing affectionately at the photo. Under his breath, he whispers, so quiet Kiara is almost certain nobody was meant to hear. "Thanks, Joshua."

Part Twenty-Five: The Taurus

Diana

"Okay," Diana says, coughing somewhat dramatically, "that's good."

She waves her hand to clear the cloud of hairspray away as her two hired dressers for the day take a few steps back, away from the vanity promptly set up in her bedroom. One of them is Hayley, the senior guard, who was the perpetrator of the hairspray assault.

"What do you think?" Hayley asks, gently taking Diana's arms and tugging her over to a standing mirror. She claps excitedly as Diana studies herself.

The outfit made for today was a knee-length dress made of a thick, dark purple fabric, covered in a matching coat with black faux fur trim around the wrists. Without a word, the other dresser takes hold of one of Diana's feet and slips on a black heeled boot, repeating it with the other foot. She's handed a pair of purple gloves, and she pulls her hair out of the way to allow them to clasp a string of pearls around her neck. Diana bends down and lets the older of the two attendants fasten a pearl barrette in her hair, which has been curled and left draped across her shoulders.

"It's stunning," Diana whispers. She turns to the two women. "Thank you so much."

"Wow," Lucas says. Diana turns to see him standing in the doorway, in a black suit with pearl cufflinks to match her jewelry. He's grinning wider than Diana has ever seen him, and she smiles back instinctively as her cheeks get warm. "You look..." he trails off, wringing his hands together.

"Showstopping?" Diana asks, striking a flamboyant pose.

"More so," he says, confidently crossing to her without ever breaking eye contact. He gathers Diana in his arms and leans down, and Hayley and the other girl take that as their cue to leave, shutting the door quietly behind them. After he pulls away, the prince smiles down at her. "Monroe, I've never been more in love with you than I am right now."

"Not even when I beat you up that one time?" Diana asks, straightening his tie, the same color as her dress.

Lucas' hands drift to her hips, and he smirks sarcastically. "You joke, but..."

Diana laughs. "Okay, okay," she pulls him by the hand to sit on the foot of her bed. "Lucas, what do you think people will say?"

"About us?" he asks, twining his fingers through her own.

Diana nods.

Lucas swallows. "Well, I think that maybe some people might think it's strange. But it doesn't matter to me."

"It really doesn't matter what people will think of you? What about the monarchy?"

He laughs out loud. "The monarchy can be damned, but really, it doesn't matter. Monroe, the only reason we have to do this at all is because the one match people never imagined were a president and a prince. But it happened, and they deserve to know. The whole world is finding out today, and whoever is angry about it will just have to get over it."

Diana shifts her weight on the duvet, looking up at him. He meets her gaze, and Diana watches his dark eyes lighten a little with the sun filtering through the window. Lucas smiles and small, barely-there wrinkles appear in the creases of his eyes, permanent history of a happy childhood. After another second of staring, he chuckles. "What are you looking at?"

Diana shakes her head a little, grinning back at him. "Nothing. Just that if we... had kids-"

Lucas' eyes widen considerably,

"-they would obviously be next in line for the throne, after you. But what about America?"

He's quiet for a second. "Okay. Theoretically, we have a choice. Either we can go the way of a democracy, and nothing really happens unless the kids decide to run for president. The second option is they enter the Alynthian line of succession, and they go after me. Or after Kiara, depending."

Diana nods. "That's true."

Lucas continues. "But obviously, kids are a big 'if,' considering if they're anything like you-"

Diana interrupts. "You'd be *blessed* to take care of them?"

He grins, his nose scrunching ever so slightly. "-I'd have my hands full with such crazy brilliance. That's what I was *going* to say, obviously."

Diana considers something, then speaks. "What would you *want* to do?"

Lucas sighs in an almost blissful way. "I do want kids. Always have. But..."

Diana clutches his hands harder, unable to keep her brow from creasing in worry. "But what?"

Lucas shakes his head, looking down at their joined hands. "My father – and my uncle, I suppose – aren't exactly the best men. Far from it. And I can't help but wonder if-"

"No," Diana interrupts, dipping her head and forcing him to meet her gaze. "Lucas, you have the kindest heart and the strongest will. You aren't anything like those two. Promise me you won't ever think that of yourself again."

Lucas smiles gently. "Okay. I promise."

Diana leans forward and kisses him tenderly, parting her lips and cupping his face with her hands. Lucas pulls back and smiles. "I believe we have a public announcement to make, Monroe."

Diana grins. "I believe we do."

Part Twenty-Six: The Cancer

Peter

Peter is practically vomiting up his stomach as Ruth gets him ready to watch Lucas and Diana's press conference.

The nurse is scrambling to help him pull a shirt over his head while also simultaneously pushing his bed towards the window as he dry-heaves into a trash bucket. It's one thirty-four, and Peter can hear the crowd chattering on the Capitol steps as well as the hum of news cameras and lights.

"I'm doing my best, I'm doing my best," she whispers, almost in reassurance. She maneuvers Peter in front of the window, all situated in a nice polo shirt, and brandishes a comb. "Let me fix your hair."

Peter peeks through the drawn curtains as Diana and Lucas, dressed to the nines, are stationed with two bodyguards plus Barbara in front of a microphone. Peter can't see Cameron, Kiara, or the other Congress members, so he assumes that they must be off to the side or waiting indoors. Ruth leans over and pushes the window open a crack, and Diana's voice drifts into the room.

"-Prince Lucas and I have been in a romantic relationship since late October," she says, looping her arm through his in a gentle but obviously romantic gesture as the hand holding a bundle of index cards falls to her side.

The crowd falls silent. Peter watches Diana shift her weight nervously as Lucas leans over and whispers something in her ear.

And then the mass of people starts to clap. Men, women, children, newscasters, journalists, reporters, *everyone* begins to applaud. Diana does a little jump, the one she does when she's overcome with joy, and Lucas grabs her arm, pulling her into a huge hug. Cameras flash, and Peter watches grins spread like wildfire across all the faces in the Plaza.

"Oh, yay!" Ruth squeals from where she's watching next to Peter.

He flops back against his pillow with a huge sigh, a sigh of relief. Closing his eyes, feeling a slight weight lift from his tight chest, Peter lets himself settle for a moment.

The room falls quiet, and Peter hears Ruth draw the curtains and shut the window. Suddenly, Peter's body begins to quiver, and something doesn't feel quite right. His eyes fly open and he grabs Ruth's wrist as his stomach sinks.

"Ruth," Peter whispers, his voice hoarse and his mouth flushed with the metallic taste of blood, "get Charles?"

She rushes out without asking questions and returns a few agonizing moments later with Charles.

"What's wrong?" he asks, voice frantic.

Peter swallows down bile, feeling his heart begin to pound with fear. "My-" he can't continue, his anxiety shoving at his insides and causing the entire world to feel much too overwhelming. Ruth pushes the trashcan into his arms just in time.

"Stop," Charles interrupts, voice firm. He examines Peter's face, eyes, and the charts at the foot of the bed, and then sighs. "Shirt off, please."

Ruth pulls Peter's shirt over his head with shaking fingers. "What are you doing?" she asks, her voice breaking.

The doctor doesn't respond, instead, he takes a hammer-like instrument from his bag and begins hitting Peter's rib area gently. While he does this, Ruth lands a stethoscope on his chest.

Finally, Charles leans back. "There's a lot of tightening around the liver area. I think the disease on top of his Wilson's diagnosis is causing liver failure."

Ruth nods, all business. Somehow, the lack of emotion on her face makes Peter less nervous. "What do we do?"

"We're going to have to take him in for a transplant, as soon as possible. The lab is in the south wing of the school building. He's going in today, if I have anything to say about it. Ruth, make the pre-op quick."

"How long do I have?" Ruth asks.

Charles shakes his head. "An hour. Maybe two."

"I've got all his recent scans. It's just a matter of finding and assessing a donor. I need a healthy B-positive."

As the two prattle on, Peter is flushed with that familiar yank into sleepiness. As he closes his eyes, a memory of his and Cameron's time in Sector Five flashes through his head.

"This is the pediatrics ward," the hospital director says as he leads Peter and Cameron through the halls. They're trailed by a cameraman, and a few journalists, as well as their bodyguard team.

They come to a stop in a big lobby, where beds have been set up to hold the overflow patients. "Who are all these?" Peter asks, pointing to a small line of kids in beds by an operating room.

"They're waiting for transplants. Unfortunately, we're understaffed and underprepared for such a number, so they

may not get the care they need. We can only hope that their organs will heal on their own," the man responds.

Peter frowns. "How bad is the wait?"

"About six weeks, as of now. But for them, it gets longer by the day," he replies.

"Wait, why does it get longer?" Cameron asks. Peter tries and fails to look away from the furrow in his eyebrows.

"Because adults who have more money are able to buy their way up the list. Families who can afford it get their kids in sooner than families who have less."

Cameron raises one eyebrow. "That's ridiculous," his tone is bitter, and low, and it causes a knot to form in Peter's stomach.

Peter nods his agreement. "Yeah. It isn't fair."

The hospital director shrugs. "There isn't anything we can do. At least we're helping some people."

Peter nods slightly, studying the beds of sick children. "At least you're helping some people," he whispers. But the words feel forced and untrue even as he says them.

Part Twenty-Seven: The Aries

Kiara

"Oh, shit," Kiara whispers into the phone receiver. "Okay, thank you Miriam. Yes, I'll tell him."

She hangs up the phone and looks up, where she's met with the confused faces of Diana, Lucas, and Cameron. Diana and Lucas are still in their press conference outfits, while Cameron is in sweatpants and a shirt Kiara has an inkling is Peter's.

They're stationed at their kitchen counter, pizza boxes on the surface in front of them. Kiara is standing by the elevator door, next to their home phone.

"What did Miriam want?" Diana asks, using one hand to cradle a pepperoni slice and the other to remove one of the pearl clips from her hair.

Kiara swallows, glancing at Cameron, who's stopped paying attention and is now refilling his solo cup from a liter bottle of soda. He pauses, almost noticing the silence, and looks up, meeting Kiara's eyes. "What's wrong?" he asks.

Kiara opens her mouth to respond, but no words come out, instead, she almost chokes on her air and starts coughing. Diana rushes to her side and whacks her on the back, holding Kiara steady by her shoulders. "Woah, Ki! What's going on?"

Kiara takes a deep breath, clearing her throat. She stands up straight again and squeezes Diana's hand, still clutched in hers. "It's Peter."

The three collectively intake a sharp breath. "What happened?" Cameron whispers. He stands up, putting his stuff down, and closes his eyes, as if steeling himself for something terrible. "What happened?" he repeats, voice still soft and full of fear.

"He's going in for a liver transplant. Something happened, I guess, but it was Peter who realized something was wrong. I don't know. Miriam didn't tell me a lot, just that Ruth wanted us all to know that they were in the operating room," Kiara looks over at Cameron, who's seated again and chewing his lip in thought. "I'm sorry," she whispers.

"No, it's... don't apologize, it's not like it's your fault," he replies, leaning back against the counter. "God. I hope he'll be okay."

"He will be," Lucas replies, almost too fast. When the other three stare at him, he clears his throat and continues. "What I mean is... we've got the best doctor in the country looking after him. The operation will go well, I'm sure of it."

"Lucas is right," Diana adds, "he's gonna be fine."

Cameron nods, looking at the floor, definitely only half-convinced. He gets up from the table, heading down the hall. "I'm gonna go to bed."

"It's seven o'clock," Kiara responds.

But he's already gone.

Diana slouches so fast, it's almost like she was waiting for Cameron to leave to melt out of her cheerful facade. "God, what do we do?" she asks, crossing to the couch and slumping into the pillows.

Lucas and Kiara follow her and sit. "There's nothing we *can* do," the prince replies. "Poor Peter."

"Poor *Cam*," Kiara adds. "He must be so scared."

Diana buries her face in her hands. "I just... I wish there was something we could do to help, besides just sit and wait."

"About that," Kiara says, jumping up and grabbing something off the end table by the front door, "I spoke to Barbara. She wanted to offer me and Lucas an extension of our jobs."

She tosses the piece of paper Barbara had given her to the prince, who catches it and unfolds the page. "What is this, Ki?" he asks.

"She said that if we want to give a piece of our daily PR work to Diana-" Kiara glances at Diana, who grimaces ever-so-slightly, "-if she wants, obviously, you and I could take jobs in the lab. Going over test results, helping work through trial meds, and making public statements. She figured that a Citizens' Liaison should be helping the public more, and that you're probably bored of politics for a country that isn't even yours."

Lucas considers, then nods, smiling a little. "That actually sounds nice."

"I like it too," Diana interjects. "We've got to get you back out there, Ki."

"Excuse *me*," Kiara says sarcastically, "are you implying that I don't *positively love* all my desk work?"

Diana laughs. "When you turned in your annotated bill files to me yesterday, there was a full-page caricature of Mr. Boone in there."

Kiara throws up her hands defensively. "It was a four-hour meeting! What was I *supposed* to do?"

"I dunno – *focus*?" she responds with a chuckle. "Anyways, I like this idea. When does Barbara want you to start?"

Kiara grins and plops down to Lucas' right. "As soon as possible."

Lucas turns to her and smiles. "Teammates *again*. First quarantine buddies, then cousins, now this."

Kiara nods, holding out her hand for a high-five. "They can't handle this duo."

Diana groans. "I didn't even think of the fact that you two are gonna drive me *insane* working as partners."

Lucas latches onto Kiara's hand and pulls her to his side, a mock expression of shock falling over his features as he wraps his cousin in a loose headlock. "Monroe, I will not let you sit here and disrespect Kiara and Lucas Enterprises. You may be my girlfriend, but she is my *business partner*."

Diana and Kiara burst out laughing, and Kiara had forgotten how good it felt to be happy.

Part Twenty-Eight: The Libra

Lucas

Lucas lies awake, counting his breaths and letting his head empty itself of all of his pre-routine thoughts.

He waits one minute, then two, then three.

Finally, his alarm beeps at six o'clock, the piercing noise breaking the room's comfortable, warm silence. Lucas punches the 'off' button and rolls out of bed, flicking on the lamp that rests on his bedside table as he heads into the bathroom.

He brushes his teeth and washes his face, running a comb through his thick hair. Arms raised, he pauses and stares at himself in the mirror, at the four long white scars in his left arm.

Without warning, his father filters into his head. What was he doing right now? Is he awake, getting ready for the day just like Lucas is, or is he still sleeping, in the room he used to share with his mother? Lucas wonders if Cornelius has ever thought about his son the same way the prince was thinking of his father right now. Maybe he's changed.

But maybe he hasn't.

The hardest thing for Lucas to realize when he left was that his father might *not* change. He could go back to Alynthia someday, and it would all be exactly the same.

When Lucas grows up, the plan is to go home eventually. He needs to be there for when his father passes, so he can take his crown. But after the coronation, everything becomes one big, tangled mess.

Diana can't be queen. She could in title, but not in duties. President *and* queen might be hard. And does

Lucas move back there forever? What happens to his friendships with Cameron and Peter? What happens to his new cousin, and where does she even fit into all of this?

Lucas pulls on a polo shirt and khakis and then ties on his work shoes. As he's strapping his watch to his wrist, his bedroom door creaks open.

"What are you doing up?" Diana asks, rubbing her eyes. A blanket is draped over her shoulders, and she's wearing a long shirt that used to be Lucas' before it mysteriously disappeared from his drawer.

"Morning, Monroe," Lucas says, keeping his voice low so as not to wake Cameron, who's probably still asleep, "Kiara and I have to be out of here by six-thirty. First day at the lab."

Diana nods and yawns, crossing to Lucas' unmade bed and snuggling under the covers where he had lain before. She closes her eyes and Lucas sits next to her, putting his hand on her shin, déjà vu spinning through his head from when they'd been in a similar position in an Alynthian bedroom. He leans down and kisses her on the forehead, lowering his voice to a whisper. "I love you," he whispers. "You gonna stay here until you have to get up?"

She nods, keeping her eyes closed. "Seven."

Lucas reaches over to his alarm clock, turning the dial to seven. "Okay. There's an alarm."

She opens her eyes slowly and rolls over on her back, meeting his eyes. Lucas fights that flush of warmth as she looks at him with a hooded gaze. She takes Lucas' right wrist in her hand. "Where did you get this?" she asks as her thumb traces the circular watch face and then naturally moves to the scars on his palms. She had gotten very good at ignoring the scars her power had caused.

Lucas runs his fingertips along the watch. "Both Rutherland men have exactly the same one. Gifts from my mother."

Diana smiles lightly. "That's really nice." She brings Lucas' wrist to her mouth and kisses the top of his hand, her soft lips pressing down on his skin ever-so-gently and yet not gently enough. She releases him and lays back down, snuggling into the sheets, and Lucas gets up and grabs his jacket off his desk.

When he turns around, Lucas pauses for a second to admire the girl in his bed. She's nearly sound asleep, and her blonde hair is matted from the pillows he'd rested on previously. She sleeps on her side, cradling the corner of the pillow in her hands. Lucas pulls his jacket on and kisses her on the cheek. "Bye, darling."

Diana opens her eyes again, smiling gently. "That was a bad kiss."

Lucas chuckles, then leans down and kisses her a little more urgently on the lips, cradling the back of her head. He pulls away after a long moment and studies her face, his thumb tracing her lips. "Better?"

She smirks. "Much." As he rises and crosses to the door, she whispers: "Goodbye, Lucas."

Lucas shuts the door gently behind him, unable to keep the grin off his face.

Part Twenty-Nine: The Aries

Kiara

A coffee lands in front of Kiara. "Thanks," she says to this mysterious gift monger.

"You're welcome," Lucas responds, taking a seat across from her.

They're in the schoolhouse, the basement specifically, where a large medical lab has apparently been for months – the first iteration of Peter's plan to build a hospital. The room is dimly lit, with lab tables sitting against the walls and a large round table in the center covered in papers, vials, and medical instruments, most of which look somewhat like torture devices. According to Barbara, the lab was used for power studies and transfers when the school-aged children received them, before its Peter-led revamp. Kiara was actively trying not to think about how many of those experiments her father had been present for, and how many of those had resulted in the patient not walking out.

"Morning!" Doctor Charles exclaims as he enters, trailed by another doctor, a man dressed in the same white coat as Charles but with a familiar royal crest embroidered on it. Kiara doesn't know who he is, but Lucas jumps up, grinning excitedly.

"Inesh!" he shouts, running into the doctor's arms. Kiara is suddenly struck by a wave of jealousy for her older cousin, the one who came from a place that loved him.

"Ah, Prince Lucas!" the man says with a laugh. He pulls back, holding the prince at arms' length. "My, you've grown!"

"Lucas," Kiara interrupts, "gonna introduce me?"

Lucas smiles and nods, motioning to her. "Right. Kiara, this is Inesh Mahra, the best psychotherapist in Alynthia. He's a family friend, has been since I was a little kid. Inesh, this is Kiara, Citizens' Liaison of New America," Lucas hesitates, giving Kiara a look that asks '*should I?*' but Kiara shakes her head gently.

"Nice to meet you," Kiara says, holding out her hand. The doctor shakes it, and she studies his face. He's tall and tan, with black hair and brown eyes. Quite handsome, she thinks, and definitely younger, no older than his mid-twenties. She feels her cheeks warm without warning as she pulls her hand away a little too fast.

"Likewise," Inesh responds, speaking with the same posh, foreign accent that Lucas does. He looks around the lab, nodding approvingly before looking back at Kiara and Lucas. "So, Charles and Barbara roped you kids in with us?"

"Well," Kiara begins, "we aren't exactly sure what it is we've been roped into, actually."

Charles chuckles good-naturedly. "You're looking at the boots-on-the-ground health advisory team for Peter Simon. Ruth is our nurse, I'm the physician, Inesh is our psychotherapist, and you two are our community leaders."

Kiara quirks an eyebrow. "Surgeon? Public representative?"

"I like her, Charles," Inesh says with a grin.

"Well, I'm a trained surgeon. Besides, a public representative... that's you, isn't it?" Charles replies.

Kiara shrugs in a manner of relenting. "Sounds good to me."

"Can we start?" Lucas asks. "Charles, maybe a tour?"

Charles smiles and nods, waving them through the various parts of the lab. Turns out, the space was beginning to transform into a hospital, which was originally Peter's own idea, but the construction had been stopped quickly when he had fallen ill. After almost an hour of explaining tests and machines, Charles hands Lucas a bundle of papers and Kiara a little trinket that has markings of different colored lines. "What are these?" she asks.

Charles motions Lucas over to a lab table, where he sits. "Lucas' papers are Peter's test results, along with some other randomized patients from Sector Five. His job is to go over them and look for trends in both that may match. Kiara, I need you to test these trial medicines and pass off which ones make the cut to Doctor Inesh, who will then approve them for Peter's trial use, or not. Both of these things will help us get to work on updating our pandemic response."

Kiara nods and gets to it, unscrewing the caps of the medicine vials and sticking the thin, pen-like instrument into them. The thing blinks red if the medicine isn't usable, and green if it is. She doesn't know how the hell this little thing *knows* that, but hey, she isn't one to really question modern medicine. All the little vials are unlabeled, so Kiara has no idea what's in them or *what* this thing scans.

"How's it going?" Inesh asks as he walks up to her.

Kiara motions to the two bottles she's finished and the forty-ish she has left to do. "How do you think?" she shakes out the pen with a frustrated huff. "This stupid thing takes so long to scan."

Inesh chuckles under his breath. "Yes, I designed that particular instrument rather quickly, right before I flew over here. It makes sense if it takes a while to work."

Kiara freezes where she's in the middle of another scan, and she looks up at him sheepishly. "Sorry. I didn't know it was your invention."

The doctor laughs aloud now. "No, it's refreshing to meet someone who is so vocal about their opinion. Very American, and very much to your infamous stereotype."

Kiara laughs bashfully and shakes her head. "What do you mean?"

"Oh, well," he says, picking up another one of the scanner wands and beginning to help with the job, "you four are *everywhere* in Alynthia, especially after the revelation about the president dating Lucas." He motions stealthily to the prince, who seems to be engrossed in his work. "In fact, on the private helicopter I took here, one of the supplied magazines had *your* face on the front."

Kiara scrunches her nose. "Weird."

"Weird, but very, very cool," he responds. "It's not often someone holds so much power at such a young age."

Kiara shrugs, nodding. "Yeah, you're right, I guess. I like being able to use it for good, unlike-"

She pauses, stopping herself, but the doctor just laughs again. "Cornelius, you can say it. I love him, I really do, but he can be... "

"A maniac?" Kiara finishes. Although she hadn't been picturing Cornelius, she wasn't about to disagree.

"I was going to say controlling, but you're close enough."

Kiara pauses and looks at the work they've done so far. Together, they've completed almost half of the vials. Inesh nods, wiping his hands down his coat. "Very good," he says, turning to face Kiara. "Lunchtime?"

She nods, and sits next to Lucas after accepting Inesh's hand of aid to help her hop down from her tall stool. Lucas looks up from his papers, which are spread across the table so far that there's no more countertop showing. "Yes?" he asks, looking way more frazzled than how Kiara left him earlier.

"Lunch at the cafe?" she asks, pulling her wallet from her bag. "On me."

"Sure," Lucas responds. He hesitates as he stands. "Actually, could we run a quick errand afterwards? I need your help with something."

Kiara glances at him warily. "Um, sure," she replies carefully, "let's go, then."

As they head for the door, both grown-up doctors wave from their table, where they're eating out of brown paper bags. "Back in an hour?" Charles asks.

"Back in an hour," the pair echoes at once, letting the lab doors swing shut behind them.

Part Thirty: The Libra

Lucas

"Okay, this way," Lucas says, leading Kiara through the Plaza.

"Lucas, where are we going?" she asks, weaving through throngs of people to keep up with him.

Lucas stops short outside a storefront, causing Kiara to slam into his back. "Here!"

She detaches herself from their entanglement and studies the building. "Wait, the jewelry place? Why?"

Lucas holds out his right wrist, pulling up his sleeve just a little to reveal his watch. "I need a new watch."

Kiara grabs his wrist, flipping it over and studying the silver timepiece. "What, why?! This thing is *sweet*. Is it broken?"

Lucas grins and pulls his arm away. "Not broken. I just need to get something quickly. I ordered it this morning."

So, they enter the store, where they're met with bright mood lighting and rows of glass displays. The shopkeeper, a tall, ginger woman, looks up as they enter. "Ah, Prince Lucas! I'm so glad you called," she says, pulling out a black velvet box and setting it on the countertop. "Here is your order." She opens the box, and Kiara and Lucas lean in to get a better look.

Inside is a wristwatch, like the prince's, but gold. The band is a little thinner than his, but the actual watch face is the same. The store owner takes it out and flips it over, revealing the engraving in the underside of the watch.

Bugger off, darling. -LR

"What does it...?" Kiara trails off. "Oh. Oh, Lucas, that's for Diana, isn't it?"

Lucas grins at her. "Yeah, do you think she'll like it?"

Kiara shakes her head and grins in the exact same manner. "She'll love it."

Lucas breathes out a huge sigh of relief. "Thank God. You know her better than anyone, and if anyone would tell me it's a stupid idea, it would be you."

Lucas digs a handful of bills out of his pocket, passing them to the shopkeeper. Kiara's eyes widen at the amount, but she doesn't say anything. The owner counts it out, smiles, and pushes the box towards him. "Thank you, Your Highness. I hope to see you again soon."

"Of course," Lucas replies. As he turns to leave, he hesitates. "Actually, ma'am, could you make another? Same style as mine this time. Silver, without the engraving."

"For what?" Kiara asks.

Lucas lowers his voice as the shopkeeper nods and begins ringing up another watch. "The watches are a Rutherland tradition. I'm getting one for my cousin."

Kiara smiles gently, and Lucas would swear she blinks back tears. "That's really thoughtful, Lucas. How can I thank you?"

He claps her on the shoulder, shaking a laugh out of her. "No need."

Lucas crosses to the counter, chatting about a delivery date for the new watch. After a moment they exit the shop, and Kiara chuckles. "With the amount of cash you just handed her, she could make those watches for every person in America."

Lucas elbows her playfully and laughs, cradling the box in his right hand. "Oh, shut up."

She gingerly takes the box from him and cracks it open, studying the watch again as she speaks. "In all honesty, though, it's really sweet." She hands it back to Lucas and looks him in the eye. "You know, we all had our reservations about you. Me especially. But I don't think Diana could've found anyone better, and *I'm* glad Peter, Cameron, and I got another friend out of it." She pauses. "I'm glad I have a family."

Lucas stops walking and stares at her. She shrugs under his gaze, and he laughs in response, taking her by the arms. "Kiara, that's like... the nicest thing I've ever heard you say," Lucas pulls her into a hug, which she slowly and hesitantly returns, "thank you."

Kiara pauses, giving him a little squeeze, and then pulls away. "Don't thank me, you idiot. We're gonna be late."

Lucas smiles and nods, following her back to the lab. But all he can think about is how the once-terrifying Citizens' Liaison isn't really so bad after all.

Part Thirty-One: The Scorpio

Cameron

Cameron is sitting at his desk, flipping through a book, when Ms. Miller enters.

"Morning," he says, putting the book down on the tabletop. He looks back up at her with the best smile he can muster. "How are things going?"

She pauses, eyebrows knitting together. "Cameron, what time do you think it is?"

Cameron hesitates. "I got here at... six, I think," he shrugs, confident now, "so it's like, nine? Maybe ten."

Ms. Miller points to the clock over the door. "Three-thirty." She sits in one of his office chairs, making herself comfortable. "Also, you have to be in at eight. Why were you here two hours early?"

Cameron rubs his eyes, sighing. "Sorry. I just... had to distract myself."

She reaches over his desk, touching the corners of the framed photos that sit there, one by one. She takes one between two fingers, turning it around so Cameron can see it. It's of Peter and him, not an official portrait, instead of them at home, doing dishes. They're stationed in front of the sink, and Peter is holding a sudsy plate while Cameron is wielding the scrubber as what seems to be a threatening weapon. Both of them are soaked, and both of them are laughing.

Cameron smiles gently when he studies the photo, the bright shine of Peter's eyes and the crease of his own dimple. Ms. Miller catches his expression and her gaze softens. "Oh, Cameron."

Cameron looks back up at her, and her sympathetic look makes his eyes begin to water without his permission. He rubs his eyes, shaking his head and rapidly getting up as he places the photo facedown on the desk. "I'm fine. I just... misplaced my portfolio for today's meeting-"

She stands, grabbing his shoulders so Cameron has no choice but to look at her. "*Cameron*. You missed the meeting. That's why I came by, to make sure everything was okay."

Cameron pauses, but she nods in an unspoken permission, so he lets his shoulders slump and he leans on the desk, refusing to meet her gaze. "God, I'm sorry. I'm really throwing a wrench in the whole 'organized democracy' thing, huh?"

Ms. Miller sits back down, shaking her head gently. "Nobody blames you. I can't even begin to fathom what you're going through."

Cameron sits in his chair as well, rubbing his hands over his face and sighing heavily. "That's the thing. One day I feel so angry at... well, at *everything*, but the next, I'm so sad I can't even get out of bed. And the *next*, I'm so scared out of my wits that I can't even hold a pen."

She nods, seeming to contemplate his words. "I'm scared too."

Cameron pauses, looking up at her. "You... you are?"

"I wouldn't lie to you, Cameron. Of course I'm scared. In all my years of working in the government, I've never seen it endangered in such a way. Of course, you four put it in danger when you overthrew it, but..." she trails off, and Cameron laughs. "We all love Peter. But unfortunately, there's nothing *we* can do. It's up to Charles and the medical team."

Cameron nods. "Yeah. I know. I just... I just *miss* him, is all. It's like everyone thinks I'm just scared for his health, which I obviously am, but I know that if anyone can overcome this, it's Peter. I just feel like someone has removed a piece of the puzzle, you know? Like, everything I do has been altered now that he's not here."

She nods, and something in Cameron knows that she really does understand. "That would explain the forgetfulness."

Cameron snaps his fingers and points at her. "Exactly! Peter normally would come get me before meetings, since he's right across the hall. But now that I don't *have* that, I'm not used to doing it on my own."

Ms. Miller chuckles. "No, I see your point. But worrying about him is *normal*. So it's okay to let yourself just feel sad, or scared, or angry, and not throw yourself into all this work to distract yourself."

Cameron nods, looking down at the desk. "Thank you, Miriam," he whispers.

She reaches over and pats his hand. "Don't thank me," she replies. She glances at her watch. "When is his operation?"

Cameron sighs, slouching deeper in the chair. "Seven tonight. According to Charles, they're gonna do some scans and stuff while they've got him in the lab."

Ms. Miller considers, tilting her head. "Well, that's good. Maybe we'll see something on the scans."

He nods. "That would be nice. I'm only hoping his operation goes fine."

"That too," she replies. She stands and dusts herself off. "Alright, dear. I'm off. Please, Cameron, remember you can talk to me *whenever* you need to."

Cameron smiles. "I will."

She leaves, and Cameron pulls out a pen and paper from his desk drawer. A date and a stamp later, he begins drafting a letter for Peter.

Dear Peter,

T-minus sixteen hours until your operation. Are you feeling any better? Are you nervous? I sure am. But I know that you'll be okay.

Also, I have a hunch that you're scared. All I can say is thank you, I guess. You going through with this means that I might get to see you again. So, coming from a completely selfish place, thank you.

Anyways, I just wanted to write and say that I miss you. Kiara and Lucas are in the lab, trying to help Charles and this Alynthian psychotherapist, Inesh. Have you met him? He seems really nice. Diana is doing her normal thing, and I think she's pretty insistent on helping organize the pandemic response for Sector Five.

My job at the moment is funding, which, as you know, is a nightmare for me. I can barely look at big numbers, much less be in charge of where they go. I'm supposed to figure out the most efficient way to channel funds into the hospitals down south, and I've been at it for almost three days now.

You're probably resting. Please, please, *please* write if you can, and tell me how your operation goes. I'll ask Charles, but I want to hear it from you too.

I love you. A lot. Probably too much, but I don't care.

Love, Cameron

Part Thirty-Two: The Cancer

Peter

The entire American government stands around a large table.

    Nobody, not one person, says anything.

    At the head of the table is Diana. Then, the chairs work counter-clockwise: Cameron, then Peter, then Kiara, then Barbara Oswald, Ms. Miller, Mr. Boone, and finally, Ms. Brewer.

    All eight of them stand behind their chairs, hands resting on top of them in a uniform stance. Kiara's fingers are skimming the leather upholstery, Cameron is picking at the stitching, and Diana is just staring at the ground.

    "Can we sit?" Diana mumbles, casting a look at the four adults.

    Barbara motions to the chairs, pulled out from the table and waiting to be occupied. "You're the president, dear. You tell us."

    Diana pauses. Then she sits.

    Instantly, as if they'd been practicing *for this moment, the seven others follow suit, in perfect unison.*

    And then, when the scraping of chair legs ceases, everything is quiet again.

    Finally, Cameron clears his throat. "What's the first order of business?"

    "Um," Diana begins, "I... I don't know."

    "We should start by re-analyzing the zodiacs," Barbara interjects.

    "Why?" Kiara asks.

    "Well, you need a way to split people up, correct? So why not redo what we've already got?" The older Aquarius

responds. Her hands are folded perfectly on the tabletop, as if this were any regular Congress meeting.

"But *we* shouldn't *split people up*," Diana says, "that defeats our whole mission."

"But what are *we* if not our signs?" Mr. Boone questions.

Everything goes quiet for the third time.

Peter thinks about what Boone was insinuating. Their whole lives have been defined by their signs. What was Diana if not a Taurus? What was Kiara if not an Aries? What were Cameron and Peter if not the Powerful Ones of Sector Three and Five?

"Well, now we're the president," Kiara says, somewhat hesitantly and finally breaking the stifling silence, "and the Citizens' Liaison, and the Secretary of Security, and the Secretary of Education. I mean, we're still our signs, sure, but shouldn't we take this new change to attempt to be more than what we used to be?"

They all nod, letting her words sink in. "I agree," Ms. Miller says. They didn't know Miriam very well yet, other than that she used to be the Libra leader.

"Me too," Ms. Brewer, the old Sagittarius leader, adds. "The point of these kids being here is that they've proven themselves to be better leaders than the ones we used to have. And, upfront, their titles are higher than ours. So who are we to disagree with them?"

Peter glances at Diana, who's smiling softly. "Thank you. And for the record, I might be higher up in title but doing this is going to take everyone. Not only are we our jobs, but we're our strengths, too." She turns to each of the others as she speaks. "Ki, you single-handedly drove away America's biggest enemy. Cameron and Peter, you guys were the first groundbreaking Powerful Ones. Barbara was the one who convinced us to keep going. Ms. Brewer, Ms. Miller, and Mr.

Boone all agreed to accept a new change. So yes, we're all certain signs and titles, but we're also colleagues," She shuts the ledger that had been placed in front of her. "Let's get to work."

Peter opens his eyes slowly to see the worried faces of three adults.

One is a woman, short and bigger, with dark skin and hair. The other two are men, one who looks vaguely familiar and one who doesn't. The shorter one is balding and fair-skinned, and the taller, younger one is handsome, with dark hair and a well-kept beard. All of them are in lab coats, and all of them are standing over him nervously.

As his eyes refocus, Peter notices that the woman, her dark eyes trained on the foot of the bed, is clutching onto the older doctor's hand. His body suddenly floods with relief, and then something clicks into place as he realizes he *knows these people.*

"Ruth?" Peter asks, groping for the woman's free hand.

She looks up at Peter and gasps, squeezing the man's fingers. "Charles, he's awake!"

The doctor- *Peter's* doctor- looks up and grins when he makes eye contact with the boy. "Of course he is. Peter, son, I knew you could do it."

The other man comes closer, smiling gently down at Peter. He looks around twenty-five, maybe even younger. "Nice to see you're awake, Peter. You've been asleep for three days, and you gave us all a bit of a fright. I'm Doctor Inesh Mahra," the man speaks with an accent, one that sounds like Lucas' but is slightly less opulent, like he learned to talk *outside* of a palace.

Peter smiles as best he can, craning his neck to look around. He's in a dimly-lit basement, no, a lab, in a roll-away hospital bed. They're the only four people in the room. Peter is dressed in his now-familiar hospital gown, and the inside of his elbow and wrists are peppered with IVs and other instruments. He goes to shift his weight when a jolt of searing pain ricochets through his entire spine.

"Ah!" Peter hisses, his voice hoarse.

"Woah, woah, calm down," Charles says as he jumps from his seat and helps Peter readjust. "You had surgery a few days ago, Peter, so let's not go running a marathon, okay?"

The nurse stands up, resting a gentle hand on Peter's arm. "You're still sick, honey. But we think the spread has slowed, just a bit, since the infected organ has been replaced. We've bought ourselves more time. *Valuable* time."

Just then, the double doors at the front of the room swing open and two people in more white coats walk in, laughing and talking to each other. They catch a glimpse of Peter and both freeze, their faces slowly breaking into large grins.

"Peter!" Kiara and Lucas shout at the same time. They both start towards him, when Inesh holds out his hands.

"Stay back, guys, he's still sick," he says.

Lucas and Kiara freeze, too obliviously happy to even care. "Peter, we miss you!" Kiara says. "And I have to tell you something really important-"

"Okay, you two out," Inesh says, pointing to the door, "we don't stand a chance of getting through to him if he's distracted by the lot of you."

"Okay, okay," Kiara says, taking Lucas by the arm and waving to Peter. They're both still smiling, something Peter hasn't seen in a while. "Bye, Peter."

Peter wishes he could respond as the doors swing shut behind them. He looks at his nurse, who's gazing down at him somewhat sadly. He wonders if his face looks as melancholy as hers.

She wipes at her eyes. "I'm glad the operation went well."

Charles, always the opposite image of Ruth, smiles at Peter. "You've got the coolest scar as well."

Ruth reaches down, unbuttoning the front of his gown. Sure enough, a decent sized scar sits right where the incisions were made.

"It'll fade a bit, but to a degree, you'll have it forever," Charles says. He sits at the foot of Peter's bed, gently pushing his legs to the side. "Alright, Peter, let's talk business. So, like Inesh said, it's been three days since you've been... well, conscious," Peter nods, and he continues. "A brief update on our Capitol business, yeah?

"Your friends Kiara and Lucas, as you just saw, are beginning to help Inesh and me down here in the lab and have filled out our advisory board. Your beau and the president have been at the Capitol, making sure everything else runs smoothly. Diana is in charge of pandemic response for Sector Five, so you don't need to worry about that."

"And how are cases overall?" Inesh asks. Peter assumes he hasn't been briefed yet today.

Charles tilts his head. "Well, that's the thing. As of now, we've noticed that although the cases aren't lessening, they're climbing at a considerably slower rate than before."

"That's good," Inesh states plainly.

"Yes. Which is why we've got three test vaccines for you to try."

Peter flips his arm over as best he can without shaking the already-there needles and holds it out in Ruth's direction.

She laughs. "Not right this second, dear. You still have a little ways to go in the healing process before we start sticking you with unknown medicines. We've decided to send them to Sector Five first."

"And this is your new room for now," Charles states. "We've got a separate, *actual* hospital room that we'll station you in, so that Kiara and Lucas can come back to work."

Peter just smiles weakly.

All three doctors pause, giving Peter a weird look. "Is everything all right, Peter?" Ruth asks. "You're especially... cheery today."

"As cheery as he can be, more like," Inesh says.

"Cheery is good," Charles starts, "because *not* being cheery means you're thinking, which is-"

"Bad," Inesh finishes. He grins when Peter looks over at him. "Don't get me wrong, I'm not saying you should shirk away from your emotional journey, but spending all your time thinking about how you're cooped up isn't going to help."

Ruth nods. "Well, sure," she says, "I like that."

Charles claps his hands together, rising to his feet. "Alright, my boy, let's get you situated in your new room."

So, Peter is unhooked, unplugged, and wheeled into a new room. This one has white walls, bright fluorescent lights, and a bed with *clean sheets*. Ruth comes over and hooks her hands under his armpits. "Alright, Peter. We're gonna stand you up now, alright?"

He nods, and she hoists him out of bed. "Ah," Peter groans as he feels the strain on his whole body, like gravity had multiplied tenfold. Both men rush to steady him as he shakily plants both feet on the ground.

Inesh and Charles release him after a moment, but Ruth doesn't, moving her hands from his underarms to his wrists. She backs up on her right foot, and Peter follows her, without even thinking about it. They're six steps away, five.

Ruth pauses, glancing up at him. "Good?"

Peter lets out a shaky breath, then a spitty cough.

"Where does it hurt?" she asks, lowering her voice a little.

Peter sighs and moves his hand in a general waving motion over his abdomen and chest.

Ruth doesn't reply, instead she continues to back up towards his new bed. After what feels like forever, she turns around, allowing the back of Peter's legs to hit the bed frame. His knees buckle, and he closes his eyes as he falls back.

The mattress catches him and Peter sighs with relief.

He sits in silence as Ruth helps him under the covers, propping one of the pillows behind his head. Once he's situated, the three adults gather at the foot of the bed. Nobody speaks, and Peter closes his eyes against the searing lights that are implanted in the ceiling.

He hears the shuffling of feet, and then a shadow falls over him. He opens his eyes to see Inesh standing next to him. He holds an envelope out in Peter's direction. "For you. Came in on the day of your operation, but you were out cold."

Peter nods gently. When he looks up, he realizes that Charles is looking down at his feet, fingers twitching nervously at his comforter. Something tightens in Peter's chest as he studies the man's upset gaze.

"Charles," Peter rasps. "Stay?"

The doctor looks up as the other two nod, shuffling out of the room. After a second of silence, he clears his throat. "What's going on, son?"

Peter fingers the corner of the envelope, letting the smooth edge calm him down. "Charles, will I get better?"

The doctor sighs, pinching the bridge of his nose. "Yes."

"Don't lie."

Charles shakes his head. "I... yes. I will make sure of it."

Peter coughs again, harder this time. "I said-"

Charles interrupts, and he sounds almost mad. "I'm not lying. I wouldn't lie to you, not on purpose."

The two stare at each other, and Peter can't help but swallow against the bloody lump rising in his throat.

Charles wordlessly passes him a handkerchief. "Your first session with Inesh will be after Kiara and Lucas. Try to get some sleep."

When Peter is done reading his letters, he does sleep, and he talks to Cameron.

Dear Cameron,

Sorry it took so long to answer. According to my personal medical team over here, I was out for three days. The operation went well, but I'm still sick, obviously. Charles is hoping that in replacing my liver, we slowed the spread at least long enough to try out some new medicines. The Wilson's makes it harder, I guess.

For the record, I love the idea of you being in the security funding department for the time being. I can't imagine how bored you are. I remember when Barbara was first letting us test the waters before we chose our jobs, and I tried funding for like, two days, but then felt like I'd rather poke my own eyes out. So, if that's the effect it has on me, I don't even want to know what's happening to you.

On the upside of things, I got a new room. I'm in a spot right off the lab, beneath the school where the hospital construction was started. Kiara and Lucas are working there now, apparently, and I got to see them briefly. They've got the lab coats and everything. The downside of the new room is that I'm further away from the Capitol. It's weird, because I still felt sort of... connected to everything when I was there, but now, I'm relocated and just... away. It's a hard feeling to describe.

Yes, I've met Doctor Inesh. He's super nice, and apparently very good at his job. I think what Charles isn't telling me is that he needs help with me, more help, so now Inesh is on full-time too. Maybe that's good, I don't know. My first therapy session is after Kiara and Lucas'. They didn't say anything about you and Diana, so I wonder why he has to talk to them.

Anyways, I'll talk to you soon. If these new medicines work in their trials with the Sector Five patients, and then work with me, I might ask Charles if I can start to have visitors.

I love you the most.

Part Thirty-Three: The Taurus

Diana

I know I put it somewhere, Diana thinks as she opens, closes, and then re-opens her desk drawers. She'd lost a file – a few, actually – and she could have sworn they were in her office. Maybe she'd left them at home.

"Come in," Diana says in response to the sudden knock at her office door.

Lucas pushes the door open and grins at her. "Good *morning*, Monroe," he says, wiggling his eyebrows.

Diana can't help but be confused, but the lost files are immediately forgotten as she looks upon Lucas' face. "Good morning?"

Lucas crosses to her now-disorganized desk, placing something in front of her. It's a medium-sized jewelry box with a smooth, velvet top and sides. He backs up, sitting in the chair against the wall. "Do you know what today is?"

Diana studies him. He's dressed up a little more than usual, in tan khakis and a white button down with a light-blue crew neck over it. *He looks handsome.* "Um..." she reaches for the calendar on her desk, flipping through the pages, "what day is it again?"

He smiles, raising one eyebrow. "January twentieth."

Diana thinks for a second, staring into his dark eyes. After a moment, she gasps. "Four months!"

Lucas claps his hands together once and nods. "Four months."

Diana leaps out of her chair and he meets her halfway as she's pulled into a strong hug. He laughs as she buries her face in his chest. "Rutherland, why didn't you tell me?!"

Lucas kisses the top of her head. "I just did, didn't I?" he runs his hands down her sides, then back up so the heels of his palms press against the side of her chest. The pressure makes Diana almost giddy with warmth.

She nods and pulls away, holding him by his forearms. Her eyes search his face, and his lips curve up into a confused smile. "Monroe, what is it?"

Diana says nothing, instead taking his face in her hands and kissing him gently. He leans into the contact and smiles against her lips. She pulls back and leans her forehead against his. His lips are glossy and she can't help staring at them. "I love you, Lucas."

He chuckles, his fingers playing in her hair. "Wow, first name."

"First name," she whispers back, but the words get lost as she presses her lips against his again.

"Well, *Diana*, I love you too," he pulls away, grabbing the jewelry box and placing it in her hands, "now open this."

Diana cracks open the black velvet box and gasps as she gets a glimpse of the item inside. She opens it all the way and looks up at Lucas, swallowing the lump that's rising in her throat. "Lucas, this is beautiful," she whispers. She grabs his wrist, pushing up his sleeve. Diana compares the two watches, realizing that they're almost exactly the same. Same, but different, unique but similar. Just like the two of them were.

"Read the engraving," he says, his voice soft.

Diana removes the watch from its box and flips it over, eyes following the engraving on the back. She takes a deep breath and then holds out her right wrist. "Help, please."

Lucas laughs but he doesn't protest, taking the wristwatch from Diana carefully and latching it onto her arm, his thumbs brushing her skin almost tantalizingly. When he's done, he runs his thumb along the face, bringing it up to his lips and kissing it softly. He drops Diana's hand and places his index finger under her chin, tipping it up so she's looking him in the eye. His gaze is shining with emotion. "Here's to many more months, right?" he asks.

Diana smiles and leans in to kiss him again. "To many more."

Part Thirty-Four: The Aries

Kiara

"Nope," Kiara says, tossing the file she's holding towards Lucas. He nabs it out of the air and sighs, dropping it onto the growing pile to his left.

"Are any of these results giving us *anything?*" he asks with a groan.

Kiara buries her face in her hands, propping her elbows on the lab table and saying nothing and yet it answers Lucas' question all the same. She never thought she'd admit it, but she'd much rather be elbows-deep in speech drafts.

"Afternoon," Inesh says as he and Charles enter. "Anything in your results?"

"No," Lucas and Kiara say at the same time. They'd gotten scarily proficient at speaking at once.

The doctors had given them results from the three medicines they had tried in Sector Five. The job was to go through and see if any of the patients' charts were showing differences. And so far, the trends were all the same: nobody was getting better.

Charles sits down next to the prince, grabbing the first chart off the top of the stack and skimming it. He nods towards Inesh, who has taken a seat next to Kiara. "They're right, Inesh. No one is improving."

The other doctor nods, seemingly ignoring Charles and instead grabbing a different chart and beginning to read it. He stands up and begins to pace the room, bringing a finger to the paper and tracing the trendline.

"What are you-" Lucas begins.

Inesh cuts him off by halting in his tracks and holding the chart out triumphantly. "This trendline."

"What about it?" Kiara asks.

He passes Kiara the chart, pointing enthusiastically at the line skirting across the page and bringing the two closer together. "Kiara, explain that trend right there."

Kiara clears her throat, sputtering a bit. "Um, well... it's going up."

Inesh grins. "And then what?"

Kiara's eyes widen as she finally sees what he's seeing. "And then it's flattening."

"And then it's flattening," he repeats, his voice rising. "Which means?"

"Which means this person's symptoms aren't *worsening*," Lucas mutters, sitting up straighter. His head snaps up to look at Inesh. "Which means that this antidote *is* working."

"Wait, wait, let's not get ahead of ourselves," Charles says. He taps the table in front of Kiara, who pulls her gaze from Inesh's glittering eyes. "Kiara, if this is working, how did you two miss this data?"

"We just weren't looking in the right place," Kiara says, feeling a little shell-shocked about this new revelation, "we were looking for *declines*, not for *flatlines*."

Charles turns to Lucas, who nods rapidly. "She's right, Charles. We were looking for a decline in symptoms. We thought that the antidote would *heal* these patients."

"It *was* supposed to heal them," Charles says, rising and turning to Inesh, "so they haven't worked as planned."

Inesh shrugs, still smiling. He grabs Doctor Charles by the shoulders. "So? Charles, do you see? They *have* worked. Maybe not in the intended way, but they *have*."

"Okay, wait," Kiara says, shuffling the charts around so she has about seven spread out in front of her. "What you're implying is that the treatment isn't healing them, it's instead *halting* the worsening of their symptoms?"

"Exactly," Inesh says. "Although we manufactured this particular treatment to stop *and* heal the disease, this is only executing the stopping part."

"So we need something else," Lucas supplies. "We've stopped it, but it's not like the patients are recovering."

"Alright, listen. We're gonna put a pin in that for the next three days," Inesh says, speaking dramatically with his hands. "Monitor everyone's charts, especially the ones with flattened trends. Kiara, you're going to make a speech about the new pandemic response. Charles and I can call the president."

"Okay," Lucas says, jumping up and racing to the phone, "I'm gonna call Barbara and have her get in touch with Sector Five to implement whatever it is that we decide to alter."

"Perfect," Charles says, brushing his hands down his pants, "if the trends continue to show the treatment halting symptom increase, we're going to continue administering it and then test it on our dear Peter."

Kiara whoops loudly, overcome with the joy that this *crisis* might have a real ending. "This is great."

"Yes, ma'am," Inesh responds, clapping her on the shoulder. "It might be just barely a glimmer, but there is a light at the end of the tunnel."

They all fall silent.

Until Lucas begins to laugh. "Sorry, sorry," he says, wiping tears from his cheeks, "but that's, like, the most Inesh thing you've ever said."

The doctor laughs too, a big, booming sound, and he crosses to Lucas, wrapping his arms around the prince's shoulders in a familial hug.

Kiara looks at Charles. "What else do you need me and Lucas to do?"

The older doctor grins. "Go home. Find Diana and tell her."

"Okay," she says. She grabs Lucas' arm. "Let's go, Trust Fund."

Lucas nods, detaching himself from Inesh and waving as the two of them exit the lab. When they get outside, Lucas breaks away from Kiara, jogging ahead, much to the disdain of their bodyguards. He whoops loudly, pumping a fist in the air and drawing the attention of more than a few people.

"Lucas!" Kiara shouts, laughing despite herself.

Lucas turns to face her, his white teeth flashing in the afternoon sun. "Race you home, Kiara? Last one there buys dinner."

Kiara grins. "Fine." She jogs closer, now in step with him. "Ready, set, go."

Part Thirty-Five: The Scorpio

Cameron

What a concept sleep is, right?

You feel like you can't get enough of it when your alarm goes off at six in the morning. You feel like you never want any of it when you're racing through the halls of a palace at midnight with your best friends.

But it always comes. It's your body's way of telling you it's gotta get some rest. But that only works if your brain is willing to slow down and relax too.

And Cameron's sure as hell is *not.*

Whatever little imp is piloting the upstairs is running a *freaking marathon.*

Cameron rolls over onto his back and stares up at the ceiling, rubbing his eyes. He moves his foot and hits a soft lump.

Cameron sits up to see he's unconsciously kicked his blanket into a pile at the foot of the bed. He sighs and tugs it up past his waist as the door creaks open.

"Holy shit," Diana gasps as she sees him, jumping nearly a foot in the air.

"Sorry," Cameron mumbles. "Didn't mean to scare you."

She crosses to the bed and sits, her fingers playing in the fabric of her navy-blue pajama pants. "I assume we're both in here for the same reason."

"What could you possibly mean?" Cameron asks sarcastically.

Diana scoffs, pushing his legs over and getting under the covers. Cameron reaches for her hand and she doesn't resist, giving his a gentle squeeze. She turns to face him. "Cam, people don't sleep in their boyfriend's beds when they're not there just for kicks."

Cameron sighs. "Yeah, you're right." He uses his free hand to tug at the pillowcase under his head, sending a waft of Peter's cologne across the sheets.

"So, what's wrong?" she asks.

"I just miss him, is all," Cameron whispers. "How about you? Why are you here?"

Diana huffs. "Same reason. I feel like I need to speak to him, not even about anything important, even just the weather, or something. I've got to hear his voice, I've got to see his face. I... I miss my *friend*." Her voice breaks, and she clamps her mouth shut.

Cameron swallows hard, saying nothing and letting her cry. He clears his throat against the tears welling in his eyes. "Diana?" he asks, feeling a single tear roll down his cheek.

"Yeah?" she asks, voice thick with emotion.

"Can you stay here for the night?"

She nods. And then she chuckles, a weak, gentle sound. "For what's left of it, at least. We're up for work in three hours."

Cameron groans, covering his face with his hands. "I can't, I'm too tired."

She laughs. "Me too."

Cameron closes his eyes, rolling over so his cheek presses into the pillow. He breathes him in, and smiles despite himself. If Cameron pretends hard enough, it's almost like he's there. "Goodnight," he whispers.

"Goodnight," Diana replies.

But Cameron thinks she knew he wasn't talking to her.

That morning – later that morning, more like – Cameron is sitting in his office across from Inesh Mahra. Cameron had spent the past forty-five minutes explaining the entirety of his life in the most abridged manner possible, while Inesh raced to write it all down.

"So, your mother," Inesh says slowly, "she's still alive?"

Cameron's heart thuds. "Um-"

Thankfully, Inesh interrupts with another question. "Wait, actually, scratch that. I starred this interaction with Peter here. Something about mixing powers?"

"Our powers are compatible, like our zodiac signs are. So when he and I are together, our powers amplify."

Inesh is either genuinely fascinated or a really good actor. "Interesting. So now that he's gone from you, do you feel the separation more deeply?"

Touche, Cameron thinks. He walked right into that one. "I... well, yeah, I guess. I lean on the others, but Peter and I-"

"-Are connected." Inesh finishes.

"Exactly."

"When you picture life with Peter, what does it look like?"

Cameron smiles immediately, reflexively. "It's serene. Quiet and peaceful, just like Peter himself is. He's good – the best, actually – at slowing life down for me."

Inesh chuckles. "I understand that. I felt the same way about my father."

Cameron watches as the man's eyebrows knit together just barely, and he wonders if Inesh was always so proficient at masking his own emotions. "That look isn't great, Doctor Mahra."

Inesh barks out an awkward laugh. "I suppose I should've known you of all people could pick up on that, huh? My father died when I was young. But I find that even thinking about him is enough to slow me down, like you said. It just takes practice."

"I'm sorry," Cameron says gently. Then, he pauses. "What do you mean, though, about slowing it all down?"

Inesh shifts a little in his seat. "Well, Peter is the anchor for you when you need to tamp down or control your anxiety. But when Peter is absent, you must develop a way to use that same sort of strategy on your own."

Cameron nods. "How do I do that?"

Inesh flips to a new page and poises his pencil. *Just like Diana,* Cameron thinks. She never wrote her notes in pen. "What are three things Peter makes you feel when things get slower?"

"Calm," Cameron starts. "Quiet. Grateful."

Inesh listens, nodding. He's looking at his notepad, and Cameron feels shockingly unembarrassed. "Does he do anything in particular to make you feel that way?"

"Sometimes we do something quiet, like reading. Or we'll talk through whatever it is that's making me anxious."

Inesh smiles. "Well, there you go. Your mind associates these feelings not only with Peter, but with these actions, too. So, I'll challenge you to read or journal next time you feel anxious. Picture Peter with you or address your writings to him."

Cameron nods, then points to the three underlined words on the page resting in Inesh's lap. "Can I hang onto that?"

Inesh rips out the paper and passes it over to Cameron with a wide smile.

Part Thirty-Six: The Cancer
Peter

Peter crumples a letter in his fist with a groan, tossing it blindly towards the wall. But, ever the athlete, it hits Charles instead.

"...Yes?" Charles asks, slowly turning around to face him and putting down the bloodwork he had been reviewing. He bends down and picks up the crumpled ball, throwing it back at Peter.

Peter snatches it from its landing spot on his blanket, thrusting it out towards the doctor. Charles reads aloud, quite uncomfortably: "'Dear Peter, it's still me, the lab is good, but Cameron is still staying in your room'-" he cuts himself off. "Why is Kiara telling you about all their sleeping arrangements?"

Peter sighs, his breath much quieter and filled with sadness rather than frustration now. "I'm not there," he croaks.

"Not... in your own bed?"

Peter looks up, meeting his eyes. "With *him*."

The doctor sighs, rubbing a hand over his face and setting the letter down. "Peter, you're *sick*-"

"*Yeah*," Peter snaps back. The man looks taken aback and somewhat hurt, so he turns his gaze down and tries to muffle his cough.

"Peter, I know that being sick is awful-" Charles starts.

"Being hungry is pretty bad, too," Ruth interrupts as she enters the room. "God, I remember how much your sorry ass *groaned* when we had to put you on liquids for the first time."

Some of the tension seems to dissipate. "Good morning to you too, Ruth," Charles says. His voice is fond, and Peter swears he blushes.

The woman smiles. "Hello, Charles,"

Peter swears, if he dies in this lab, he will die *knowing* what the hell happened there.

"What's been happening today?" Ruth asks, clearing her throat.

"Oh, Peter is telling me about Cameron's new development," Charles responds. Peter glares at him, and he shrugs. "It's true."

"And what would this 'new development' be?" The nurse asks as she begins unloading her bag.

"Cameron has been sleeping in Peter's room. According to Kiara's letter, he hasn't been in his own bed in days."

Ruth ponders his words for a moment, too long, actually. Then she turns to Charles. "Doctor, a word in the lab? Inesh is here too."

Charles rises, buttoning his coat. "I don't know what I'd do without you, Ruth."

The woman laughs, a loud guffaw that sends a blush creeping over Charles' cheeks. "I don't know what you'd do without me, either."

Part Thirty-Seven: The Aries

Kiara

"Would you say you're quick to anger?"

Kiara can't help but huff out an uncomfortable laugh as she crosses her arms. "No."

Inesh, seated in the chair across from her, sets his notepad on his knee and mimics her crossed arms. "What would you say your predominant emotion is?"

Kiara waits a moment, listening only to the ticking of the clock in the room. They were in Kiara's office, where she had been pulled from work by a very insistent Barbara and an even more insistent Charles to have a psychotherapy session with a stranger.

"Kiara?" Inesh asks, raising a well-groomed eyebrow. "Did you hear me?"

"Happiness," Kiara says too fast.

The two lapse into another silence. "This will only work if you're honest, Kiara."

"I am being honest."

"Let's shift gears," the doctor says, once again picking up that godforsaken notepad. Kiara makes a silent vow to burn that thing someday. "Tell me about your childhood."

Kiara's eyes immediately narrow. "Did you ask Lucas this too?"

She has to give him credit – Inesh matches her attitude quite easily. "Lucas grew up in a neighboring orbit, Miss Kiara. I know lots about his childhood, but nothing about yours."

Kiara takes a deep breath. "I didn't have a childhood. Not in the normal sense. I don't know my parents – I never did. None of us do. I grew up at school like every other kid, then I moved. Just like everyone else."

Inesh's dark gaze could cut Kiara's skin. "Do *you* think you're like everyone else?"

Kiara feels her resolve slipping. "I – what kind of question is that?"

"The kind that I would like you to answer."

She laughs again, more openly mirthlessly. "I don't like therapy."

Inesh smiles, kindly and honestly. "You don't need to like it. But I'll tell you, Kiara, that we've been here thirty minutes and something is keeping you in this chair. If you want to go, you can go."

There's a long stretch of silence. "Do you... have a family?" Kiara whispers, plucking at the chair's upholstery.

Inesh smiles. "My mother and two younger sisters, yes. The girls are twins, and they're thirteen now. Anvi and Anika."

Kiara can't help but mirror his infectious smile. "Grateful and complete."

Inesh looks both impressed and mildly stunned. "Why am I not surprised that you know Sanskrit?"

"I like languages. It helps me understand things – people – better."

"What does your name mean?" he asks. Kiara likes the low, gentle tone his voice takes on. It makes her feel infinitesimally better.

"Depends on who you ask. Some say it means 'dark,' others say 'bright.'"

Inesh smirks. "Coincidental, isn't it?"

They're circling right back to the topic Kiara was fighting to avoid. Lacking any and all tact, she changes the subject harshly. "And your parents?"

Inesh's smile falters for a millisecond. "Just my mother, Jiya. My father is dead."

"Oh," Kiara whispers. "I'm sorry, I didn't mean to be-"

"It's okay," Inesh replies, "It was a long time ago, now. He was part of the Alynthian navy, and he and his crew died on a routine mission. A faulty torpedo launch."

Kiara breathes deeply in tandem with him. "How old were you?"

"Fifteen. The twins were only three."

Kiara shakes her head. "I'm really-"

"Don't say sorry. It isn't your fault."

Kiara swallows. "I don't know what else to say."

Inesh leans forward a little bit more, setting his notepad on the ground next to his chair so he's fully focused on Kiara. "You lost people too. It's not a solitary experience for just me."

"No, but..." she hesitates. "But I didn't lose family."

He pauses, then speaks very gently. "I heard about Maya Monroe. And about Lawrence Kerrigan."

Kiara's heart thumps dangerously against her ribcage. "Right. That, uh, that makes sense."

"When you lose someone, your brain often-"

"Anger," she interrupts.

"Pardon?"

She blinks rapidly against the hot tears in her eyes. "You asked what my predominant emotion is, and it's anger. It has been since the revolt."

Inesh doesn't react. Kiara doesn't know if she wants him to or not. "Who are you angry at?"

"My – Henderson," Kiara splutters, furiously swiping away a burning tear. "Angry at him, at the people who opposed us, at Cornelius and Kerrigan and..."

She cuts herself off with a sob, and she shakes her head as Inesh speaks. "'My' what?"

"Huh?" she asks, even though she knows. Inesh doesn't continue, just stares at her.

She doesn't want to say a word, and yet, she wants to tell this kind-faced, kind-hearted stranger psychotherapist everything. She wants to process everything and unstitch herself a little bit at a time until her grief isn't choking her. Until her father, Kerrigan, Cornelius, and all those nameless faces didn't have their hands around her throat and weren't watching the life drain out of her.

She wants to tell Inesh everything.

Instead, she gets up and leaves.

Part Thirty-Eight: The Libra

Lucas

Back at the lab, Kiara and Lucas are reviewing charts.

What else is new?

There's no noise besides the buzzing of the fluorescent lights and the shuffling of papers.

Charles and Inesh are seated across the room, both wearing what Lucas considered semi-ridiculous goggles, hunched over a vial of medicine held up in a metal structure. Neither speaks, working in practiced, professional quiet.

A few more moments pass in dead silence.

Finally, Kiara groans. "God, Lucas, could you stop it?!"

Lucas jumps nearly a foot in the air and turns to face her. "What?!"

She buries her face in her hands as if she was nearing her wit's end. His cousin had been suspiciously and gratingly silent all morning. "Licking your finger every time you turn the page."

"What does that have to do with you?"

"Nothing, it's just *annoying*."

Lucas raises one dark eyebrow. "Then no."

Kiara turns her whole body to face him, looking more than a little offended. "I'm sorry, you aren't a prince here."

Lucas stands, his stool scraping against the floor. "No, but I'm still a royal, nonetheless. That puts me ahead of you at *most* political functions-"

"Well, I'm royalty too, you ass, or did you forget that my father is-"

"*Barely* royalty! If your father hadn't been a total idiot, you might've been able to-"

Kiara rises to meet him, getting right up in Lucas' face. "I swear-"

"Both of you stop, now!"

Kiara and Lucas turn to see Inesh on his feet, Charles hovering over his shoulder. He looks... well, angry, a far cry from his normal nonchalance.

He clenches his fists and talks again, looking between the two teens as he speaks. "You two are best friends. You need to get it together, if for these patients' sake over anyone else's. We're a team, and it's time you two started acting like it."

Inesh hesitates before he speaks. "Sounds like they're more than best friends, Charles." He looks warily at Kiara. "Royalty?"

Lucas and Kiara share a guilty look. "Um, Kiara is my first cousin," Lucas mumbles.

"What?" Both doctors gasp.

"Your... father, Miss Kiara. That's who you were referring to in our session," Inesh says in a low voice.

Kiara nods, feeling her stomach twist as it always does when she thinks about her family. "George Henderson is my dad."

The two men stare at her, and Kiara plays that familiar game of trying to guess how much they now hate her. "Wow," Inesh says after a moment. "Well, that doesn't change who you are, Miss Kiara, you know that."

"Huh?" she whispers.

Charles nods. "You've spent your life trying to be better than your family. You *both* have," he corrects, looking at Lucas, "but you don't have to do that here."

"Thank you," Kiara and Lucas mumble at the same time.

"Now, Lucas, apologize to your cousin, please," Inesh says with the wisp of a playful smirk.

Lucas glances back at Kiara, shifting his weight nervously. Without looking at her, and instead averting his eyes to the linoleum floor, he whispers: "Sorry, Ki."

She nods, Lucas can see it out of his peripheral vision. "Me too. Really."

"Good," Inesh affirms, re-seating himself. "Now, do either of you have anything for me?"

Kiara and Lucas both sit simultaneously, digging through their papers. "Nope," Kiara says finally. "No more flatlines, no declines, nothing."

Charles groans, rubbing a hand over his face. He looks more exhausted than normal, and Lucas tries to suppress his worry that Peter may be getting worse. "Dammit. I wanted to bring good news to Peter this week."

They all fall quiet. Then, Lucas gasps. "Wait a minute."

Kiara looks over at him, fear flashing ever-so-briefly through her brown eyes. "What is it?"

Lucas grabs her by the arms. "My uncle."

"Your what?"

"George. He might have known."

Kiara thinks for a minute, then her eyes widen. "He might've known about the disease, you mean."

So Lucas, without any word to a very confused looking Charles and Inesh, races out the door, through the deserted school hallways, and into the Plaza.

It's dark outside, and Lucas has the fleeting thought that they've been in the lab for countless hours. He pushes it out of his mind as he takes off running through the empty Plaza, towards the Capitol. The air is cold, colder than normal since Lucas forgot his jacket back in the lab. There isn't a soul around, and the dark night sky is cloudy, without a trace of a star.

All the windows of the Capitol are dark, and a chill runs up Lucas' spine as he wonders what sort of strange things could be lurking in the dim halls of the old building. With a huff of exertion, he takes the big front stairs two at a time, reaching the front door and tugging on the handle.

It's locked, obviously.

"Shit," he whispers to nobody in particular, walking a little further down the length of the building. He fits his fingers in the small cracks in the wall, letting the cool stone calm his racing heart. He gets to a first-floor window and casts a look over his shoulder. "Let's hope no tabloid sees this, Lucas, or your American tour is going to be *really* short." With that, he hoists the window all the way open, unceremoniously leaping into the room.

He lands on his feet, quickly turning and shutting the window behind him. The room is pitch-black, darker than it was outside, and something about it feels unfamiliar. Lucas fumbles along the wall, hands searching for a light switch, and when he finds it, he flicks it on.

His subconscious was right: he's never been in this room before, and he blinks rapidly to let his eyes adjust to the warm light. It's a storage room and a messy one at that. Papers are strewn over an old, decrepit desk, dusty books sit crooked on the shelf, and an ornately carved mahogany cane leans against the wall in the corner, hidden amongst large piles of folders and other miscellaneous objects. The place looks as if no one had been in it for months at least, but then Lucas' eye catches on the door handle, to the exit that leads into the hallway: the lock is twisted from the outside, signifying that the room wasn't a storage closet at all.

It was an office.

Henderson's office. Lucas was in the right place.

Lucas swallows against the lump in his throat. He shouldn't be here, he knows it. And he didn't even really know for sure if this was his uncle's office or not. But then he sees the faded map of Sector One lying on the desk. He sees an old, black-and-white photograph of twelve people sitting on the windowsill. He sees a red blazer hanging over the back of one of the chairs.

Slowly, Lucas crosses to the desk. His footsteps scuff loudly across the battered rug on the floor, and he winces even though he knows no one is around to hear him. He picks up the picture, smooth edges cool against his fingertips, and studies the people in it. It's obvious this is the Board of Zodiacs: well-dressed, stern expressions, posing in front of the Capitol building. But looking closer, Lucas realizes there aren't just twelve people, there are fourteen.

Two teenagers stand on either end of the line: one boy, one girl. The boy is tall, and blonde, and his hands are clasped behind him. His smile is alarming: on the surface, he looks happy, almost excited, even. But paired with the unsettling gleam in his bright eyes, to Lucas the grin looks... sinister. Just like his own father's.

The girl is young, too. She has dark hair that's down around her shoulders, and she's wearing a skirt and long-sleeved sweater. She wasn't smiling, but her neutral expression and barely-raised eyebrow seemed familiar to Lucas.

"Barbara?" he whispers, running his index finger over the photo and leaving a dust trail in its wake. His finger moves to the other boy. "And... Uncle George," he puts the picture back down, turning in a circle to study the room again. Then he spots that mahogany cane, propped in the corner. He glances back down at the picture, then back to the cane. Then at the picture and then at the cane once more. The man in the photograph who's holding the cane isn't George, nor is it the tall blonde man whose hand is clasped on George's shoulder. It's held in the firm clutches of a tall, skinny, dark-haired man standing behind Barbara.

So why would Orion Oswald's cane be in George Henderson's office?

Lucas was no stranger to New American politics. Diana had told him that she and the others had had to do an Alynthian deep-dive when they first found out about the country, since Lucas' father had a knack for secret-keeping. But New America was different. They blasted their power across the world, across the sectors, hammered it into the minds of every citizen. So Lucas had spent many homeschooled days going over American history when he had finally been told of their existence: each member of the current BoZ, the first and last names of all Twelve Founders, and geography of all the sectors. He knew when he met Barbara Oswald that her father was the first Aquarius leader, and he had passed the gauntlet to Barbara when she was forty-one and he was in his early seventies. Not long after, Orion had died, although nobody knew how.

Lucas had seen pictures of his father with Miriam Miller's mother as a young boy, before he had fled the country. Barbara and George had been thirty-six when Ms. Miller was born, which Lucas knew was the largest age gap in the current BoZ.

But he hadn't known that George and Barbara had grown up together. They must've even been close, if Orion had given George his cane.

It isn't why he came, but Lucas' curiosity gets the better of him, and he crosses behind the desk, pulling open one of the drawers. With a plume of dust, it slides open, and inside it is a tied stack of letters. Lucas gingerly removes them, pulling at the red ribbon that bound them together.

He takes the first one from the top and begins to read the long, scrawling cursive.

Dear George,

I wish I wrote to you with better news. The doctors were right, the cancer has come back. It appears I don't have much time left.

So, with this most likely being our last correspondence, I must leave you with a difficult message.

You are not the heir to the Aries Zodiac.

Do you remember, twenty-seven years ago, when we met with the others in the Oswald's basement? The day the betrothal was canceled? I certainly do. That was where we found out all of the Twelve Founders were one of each sign. That is where young Barbara gave us this ridiculous idea in the first place.

But it seems we were lied to, my boy. It seems one of the Twelve Founders was not being truthful about their astrological alignment.

The Oswalds are standing in the way of your ascension now, George. They will stop at nothing to undo what you and I have worked for. So I urge you, do not let them win. Take matters into your own hands- define that as you must.

And whatever you do, don't let Barbara Oswald win.

I read a very interesting book yesterday, "The Ram and The Waterman", it's down in the archives, a delightful children's book. I know you may think yourself too old, but if you're going to do one last thing for your dear father, allow yourself to enjoy the tale of a man who lived by the water with his pet ram. It's quite fulfilling.

Love, Father

Lucas moves to place the letter back on the stack as gingerly as he can, but something makes him hesitate. He can't help but feel confused, but not about the letter. He's mostly wondering why there's a cold pit settling in his stomach, why the hair on his arms were standing up, and why it suddenly felt like he was being watched.

Moving his gaze around the room, Lucas wonders how much proof of Kiara's existence was here, or if she'd even want to find it at all. What other secrets had his uncle been hiding?

Lucas carefully folds the letter, tucks it into his back pocket, and heads back towards the window, forgetting entirely about his mission. Something was telling him to leave, telling him not to be alone, shouting at him to show everyone this letter.

As he walks back through the dark Plaza, he pulls the letter out and reads it again, then again. Every time, when he reaches the piece about the book, a chill runs down his spine.

You are not the heir to the Aries Zodiac.
But it seems we were lied to, my boy.
Define that as you must.

He gets back to the lab, pushing open the doors. Kiara and the doctors are waiting, and Inesh quickly jumps up to greet him.

"Lucas!" He says, gripping Lucas' forearms and giving him a little shake. "What did you find?"

Lucas swallows, then holds up the letter. "This."

Charles and Kiara glance at each other, then wander over to the prince. "What is that?" Charles asks, taking the letter and skimming the page.

"A letter. From Damian Henderson to George," Lucas says, pulling himself from Inesh's grip and taking the letter back. He doesn't fail to note the way Kiara's whole body seems to stiffen. His next words are just for Kiara. "Apparently, your father isn't the rightful Aries leader."

"We need to talk to Barbara," Charles says, tone stiff.

"No!" Lucas shouts, causing all three to look at him as if he had three heads. "I mean, I – I dunno. She's mentioned in this letter."

"That doesn't mean she knew what was going on," Kiara replies.

"I know. But-"

"Lucas, this isn't up to just you to solve," Kiara says, voice soft. She gently removes the letter from his grip and looks up at him, her dark eyes meeting his darker ones. "We're your friends. Your *family*. So if there's something to fix, we're gonna do it together."

Lucas sighs with relief, as if he'd hoped she'd say something like that. "Okay. Okay. Call Barbara."

"Lucas, it's almost one in the morning. We need to go home."

Both doctors nod. "We all need rest," Charles says, "and I need to check on Peter, too."

"Tell him we say hello," Kiara says as she hands the letter back to Lucas. "Let's go, Trust Fund."

The pair walk back to the apartment in silence. Lucas watches Kiara walk, a few paces in front of him, like she was rushing to get out of this big vast space. Something was bothering her, he knew.

"What's wrong, Kiara?" he asks as they pass the fountain in the middle of the Plaza.

She sighs without turning around, in fact, Lucas thinks he notices her pace speed up. "Henderson's wrong."

"Why? Besides everything."

She stops in her tracks, and Lucas slams into her back. She turns around, and Lucas's eyes widen at her cheeks that are streaked with tears. "He hurt me, Lucas. When I was twelve. And I..." she chokes out a sob, and Lucas grabs her forearms to steady her, "and I think he did it because I was his daughter. Did Diana tell you that's one of the reasons I joined her? Because I'd never be able to live with myself if he continued that way. Did she tell you that the biggest goal in my life is to kill him? To watch him... suffer?"

"No, I..." Lucas doesn't know what to say, "I know he hurt people. But not you."

"Well, he did. And I don't know..." she trails off, looking up at the sky, "I don't know what to do now. To know that he's my..."

Lucas says nothing, instead just wraps her in his arms, hugging her tightly. Kiara grips at his jacket, her fingers fitting in the folds of the fabric. It's the first time she's ever really hugged him back, and Lucas hopes it's comforting her at least a little. "Have you told the others?"

"They know that it happened," she whispers. Lucas fills in what she isn't saying: that they didn't know she was still suffering this badly. That they didn't know how horrible she really felt.

Lucas pulls back, putting his hands on her shoulders. "I'm not going to try to comfort you like Diana or Peter would. I'm going to help you get vengeance, no matter how."

Kiara huffs out a bitter laugh. "You don't think I'm crazy to hate my own dad?"

"No," Lucas replies instantly, "in fact, I know exactly how you feel."

Kiara looks at him, wet eyes glittering. She doesn't speak; she doesn't need to. Lucas just nods at her, silently ensuring that he would be there for her. Without another word, he straightens his jacket and continues back towards the apartment, his cousin at his side.

Part Thirty-Nine: The Taurus

Diana

Around noontime, someone knocks on Diana's office door.

She's already seated, with tea and crackers set on the table between herself and the other chair up against the wall. "Come in!"

The Alynthian psychotherapist, Inesh Mahra, opens the door. He smiles politely. "President Monroe, it's good to see you."

Diana returns the smile as he sits in the open chair, a notepad resting open on his lap. "Please, call me Diana."

Inesh nods, glancing down at the small chicken-scratch notes he's put at the top of the page. Diana's heart thunks, *and she swallows before speaking again. "I, uh, had tea made. It's an Alynthian brew that Lucas likes, so I thought it may remind you of home."*

There's that same tight, unreadable smile. "That's very kind."

Diana can't hide the nervous wobble in her voice. "So, how do we start?"

"Well, I'll leave that up to you. Today is just a beginner session, which means we'll get to know one another and start to unpack any longstanding issues."

Diana nods, even though she's mentally scrolling through the endless list of things that Inesh might deem 'longstanding issues'. After a moment, she motions to his notepad. "What did you write down?"

He holds it up with a chuckle. "Just some notes on you, actually. Simple things like where you grew up, your family, and your career."

"Right," Diana whispers. "Find anything interesting?" She tries to joke, but her unnerved tone makes it fall flat.

Inesh seems to sense her silent discomfort. "I did want to speak about your relationship with your mother and your sister. Were the three of you close?"

Diana steels herself and prepares her most diplomatic politician's answer. "Well, I wasn't close with my mother. She was a Gemini, and we lived separately, but I visited my older sister once a week. We were much closer and remained that way until her death."

Inesh says nothing, just listens. "And what happened then?"

"Um- what do you mean?"

"When she died. You said you remained that way until *her death*. When it happened, were you still on good terms?"

The question feels too pointed, too much like an attempt at digging up something that had been long buried. Diana fights back a familiar wash of thorny grief. "We... we had fought a few days earlier, but it wasn't that bad-"

"Do you wish you had done something different?"

A tense silence falls. Diana's breath catches when she inhales, but she tries to ignore the darkness creeping into her ribcage. "I wish I had apologized," she whispers, "but it's too late."

Inesh nods. "That day... later on, did you think about that? When you made it inside the Capitol, when you made it in here," he motions around the office, "did you think about her?"

Diana sniffles. "I didn't think about anything else. I didn't until the Inauguration."

Inesh's dark brown eyes seem to analyze every part of her timidity. "When you were sworn in, what did you think about then?"

Diana's reply is immediate. "America."

She doesn't realize, but that silence had fallen again as she had been sucked back into the day she was inaugurated. It's only broken when Inesh speaks softly. "Did you ever think about yourself?"

Diana starts to speak, starts to defend herself, then pauses. "I..."

Inesh interrupts, but not rudely. When he speaks again, his gaze on Diana's is understanding, but also imploring, like he saw a different version of the president than every other stranger saw.

"Do you ever think about yourself?"

Diana wakes up at the sound of the elevator door sliding shut. She glances at her clock, which reads one in the morning in glaring red numbers. After her therapy session earlier that day with Inesh, she was surprised she had slept at all. Reality, though, had a way of crashing back into her.

A few minutes pass, and Diana hears two people mumbling to each other outside the door, a girl's voice and a boy's. Then, her door shuts gently, and she feels a weight settle next to her, the mattress caving slightly with the weight of another person. She rolls over, looking up at Lucas.

"Hey, Monroe. Didn't mean to wake you," he whispers as he glances up from untying his shoes.

Diana stretches and sits up, pulling her hair from its elastic and letting it fall over her shoulders. "It's okay. I couldn't really sleep, anyways." She glances over at him to see that he's staring at the wall, expression vacant. "Hey," she says, placing a hand on his back, "what's wrong?"

Lucas turns to look at her, eyes roaming her face. Diana could tell he was feeling a lot, from the dark look in his eyes, the worried crease of his eyebrows, the slight purse of his lips. But he doesn't say anything, instead, he leans down and kisses her tenderly. When they pull away, Lucas leans his forehead against hers. "Nothing to worry yourself about, Monroe," he whispers, pulling her even closer and gently kissing her forehead.

"I *am* worried, Lucas," Diana protests as she pulls herself away. "Talk to me."

"It's nothing, really. We can talk in the morning."

"It *is* the morning."

Lucas chuckles, resting his forehead against hers. After a beat, he sighs and speaks. "I've never been stressed like this before."

Diana's mouth dips into a frown, and she takes Lucas' hands in her own. He looks at her, but not really *at* her. "What do you mean?"

"I just... this is the first real job I've ever had. Being Crown Prince took work, but not like this. *Lives* hang in the balance of our daily decisions, and I'm not sure if I can handle pressure like that."

Diana places her hands on either side of Lucas' face, rubbing her thumbs to warm his cheeks, still cool from the night air. She can't tear her eyes away from his, and she doesn't want to. "You *can* handle this, Lucas. I know as well as anyone else that no matter what you do, you'll always work hard for others, especially the people you care about."

Lucas smiles, leaning into Diana's touch. Wordlessly, he takes her hand from his face and presses a gentle kiss in the center of her palm, slowly tracing two letters there, and his electric touch makes Diana shiver.

Lucas seems to notice that, based on the way his gaze flits to hers and he leans in and kisses her again, and Diana's heart pounds at the urgency in the way he pulled her so close their chests touched. Instinctively, her hands weave their way through his hair, pulling near the back of his head. Lucas' breath catches, and he pulls away, looking her in the eye as Diana slumps back against the pillows. The two stare at one another, both breathing heavily. Diana is nervous and she doesn't know why, and she fights the urge to place a hand over her heart in an effort to keep it from leaping from her chest.

"Di..." Lucas trails off, eyes skimming the length of her body. "Diana," he says again, voice hard and almost questioning.

"Yeah?" she whispers, reaching forward and threading their fingers together.

Lucas glances down at their hands before looking back up at her, swallowing hard. "I want... I..." he huffs, chuckling at himself and averting his gaze.

Diana laughs, pulling him towards her. "Use your words, Lucas," she says, even she knows what he wants because she wants it too: an escape, even a momentary one, in the arms of someone who was safe.

Lucas uses his free hand to brace himself against the headboard with a gentle *thunk*, and his eyes bore into Diana the same way they did when they first met. Diana tilts her chin up to look at him, and she grins when his familiar smirk flashes across his face. "You're impossible, Monroe."

With that, he leans down and their lips meet again. Diana lets go of his hand and pushes his jacket off his shoulders, watching him shrug out of it. He unbuttons his shirt, pulling it off, and lowers himself onto Diana again. "Now we're a little more even," he mumbles against her lips, motioning to her long pajama shirt.

Diana smiles, pulling away from him, and he sits back on his heels, tilting his head. "Is everything okay?"

he asks, putting his hands on either one of her legs. "Do you want me to stop?"

"No," Diana says hurriedly, "I just... I've never seen you like this before," she whispers, eyes traveling across his torso.

"You've seen me shirtless," he protests with a laugh. "In fact, I've been shirtless in your bed *before*."

Diana groans and laughs. "Can you stop talking, for once?"

Lucas shrugs one shoulder, and the movement sets off butterflies in Diana's stomach. "You asked me that back in Alynthia once, and instead I told you I was in love with you. So I'm not sure how well that worked out."

Diana smiles softly. "I would say it worked out pretty well for me, at least," with that, she tugs him back towards her.

Lucas' hands work at his belt, and he kisses Diana in such a way she gasps as one of his hands makes its way under her shirt, traveling upwards. "Is this fine?" he whispers in her ear.

Diana wishes she could say something witty, or form words at all, but instead she just nods rapidly, leaning her head back against the pillow as Lucas' touch sends a shot of flame through her whole body, the heat landing in the bottom of her stomach. Lucas shifts against her, his hips connecting with hers, and Diana's whole body lights up. "Lucas," she whispers, pulling a lip between her teeth.

He looks down at her, and his dark eyes are filled with something so heated that Diana has never seen before. "Yeah?" he whispers, cupping her cheek with his hand as his fingers slow their movements.

"I want you," she whispers in response, barely believing that those words were coming out of her mouth, barely believing that the prince she once couldn't stand was now undressing himself in her bed, barely believing that that same prince was pressing feather-light kisses to her bare stomach.

Lucas looks up, smiling gently as he moves back to kiss Diana's swollen lips. The warm breath of his whisper makes Diana's stomach do cartwheels. "You've got me, Monroe."

Part Forty: The Cancer

Peter

Dear Cameron,

I'm not doing well, really.

I can think of something I really want to say to you.

I know you're probably going to completely ignore this request. You're gonna write back and claim that I'm crazy, but I really, really need you to listen. This isn't easy to say, so it does me a lot of good hoping that you'll take this seriously.

If I die here, I need you to promise me something.

And don't say I won't die, because right now it's looking like I might, which isn't a great realization to come to, but it's something I'll have to make peace with, I suppose. See, the hardest thing about knowing you're going to die is that your whole life goes away, but that's not what's bothering me. I've lived so much in just eighteen years, I've done so much. I've helped so many people, more people than I ever thought I would.

The tricky thing for me is that I'm going to die alone. Alone, in a hospital bed, because my body failed even though my brain was completely fine.

It makes me think about Maya. I miss her a lot these days, and I can't think why. In fact, I should be missing Maya the least out of everyone, but I miss her the most, next to you. I guess I think a lot about how she died, which is a little weird, but let me explain.

Maya died protecting us. By us, I mean our whole country. And she did it voluntarily. She knew what kind of danger she was getting into, and she did it anyway. I don't know if I've ever told anyone this, but I was the only one who watched it happen. Kiara was fighting another guard, she didn't see until a few seconds after. Diana might've, but actually, I watched her look over at the guard when he fired the gun, so she didn't, not really. And you had fallen, so you were looking at the ground.

But I watched the whole thing. I watched Maya, I watched the bullet like it was in slow-motion. And do you know what she did when you dropped that shield and fell?

She smiled. She knew what was coming in that next second, and she faced death with a smile because she knew that it wasn't you in her place.

I don't say this to make you guilty, because I know you sometimes still feel that way. I say this because it made me realize something. Maya smiled when she got shot because she knew she was dying to save you. And while I watched the whole thing, when I saw Maya fall, when I saw Diana with her, something in me didn't make me run over to Maya, to help her. I went to you.

It wasn't some romantic, suspenseful thing, I just remember going over to you and rolling you over, pulling you to your feet. But when you did that, rolled over, I mean, I remember seeing your big gray eyes and the only thing I could think was "thank God it wasn't him."

Isn't that weird? The woman who was practically like my big sister got shot right in front of me and my first thought was "thank goodness it wasn't that Scorpio who I barely know."

It could've been love, then. Probably not. Maybe that's when I realized I felt so much for you I couldn't have lived with myself if you'd been killed instead of Maya.

Which brings me to my one request for you.

If I die, I want you to move on. Maybe not right away, you can assuage my ego a little bit. Wallow for a time. But not forever, okay? Get over it, in the nicest way possible. Work, but not as much as you have been. Be nice to yourself, and to the others. Don't blame yourself. Go and fall in love again, get married, start a family. Do all the things you want to do with me, but with someone else.

Don't get me wrong, Cam. This hurts more than you can possibly know. The idea that I might make you so upset that you can't go on makes me feel like such a terrible person, and sometimes I'm glad you can't see me because I know it would hurt us both too bad. And I want nothing more than to live a long, stress-filled, happy life with you. But this is the hand we've been dealt, Cameron. So... I'm sorry. It was my fault. It was my idea to go to Sector Five. I put us at risk, I got myself into this, got all of us into this.

I'm sorry, Cameron.

All my love, Peter

Part Forty-One: The Libra

Lucas

Lucas wakes up four hours later, when Diana's alarm goes off.

He groans loudly and frankly, quite obnoxiously, and reaches behind himself to punch the off button.

"Wake up, Monroe," he mumbles, shaking Diana's shoulder and planting a kiss on her jaw.

She rolls over, and Lucas' heart skips a beat at the way the white sheet is pooled around her shoulders, her blonde hair splayed against the pillows, her bare skin shinily defined in the morning light. She rubs her eyes and smiles at him, and when she speaks, her voice is groggy. "I'm awake."

Lucas lies down again, propping himself on one elbow to look down at her. "I can see that," he kisses her forehead. "Should we... talk about last night?"

She closes her eyes for a breath, then opens them again, meeting his gaze. "What about it?"

Lucas shrugs, trying to look nonchalant. "I dunno. I... had fun."

Diana smirks. "Fun, huh?" Her tone is teasing.

Lucas sits up, burying his face in his hands. "God, I'm sorry. I'm so bad at this."

Diana scooches closer, reaching one of her hands over to rest at his waist, the other taking him by the shoulder. Lucas swallows as his body alights the same way it did last night. "Just tell me how you're feeling, Lucas."

Lucas looks down at her, running his fingers gently through her hair to untangle it as best he can without hurting her. He speaks without meeting her gaze.

"Okay, fine. I feel like I am very in love with you, and last night simply reiterated that. Also, I already knew you were absolutely gorgeous, but..." he breathes out through puffed cheeks. "This is hard. You're stunning, okay? And... and I liked knowing that you were completely mine, and that I could do those things to you, make you feel the way you did. And I know we're young, but... but I don't regret it."

He swallows to stop himself from blabbering on and finally looks down at Diana. Her green eyes are piercing, and he releases a shaky breath. After a long moment, she speaks.

"See?" she says, smirking mischievously. "That's much better," when he scoffs playfully and laughs, she grabs his hands. "Lucas, look at me." He does, and she continues. "I agree with you, about not regretting it. In all honesty, I think I've wanted that for a really long time, and it was... it was perfect, Lucas. I feel safe with you."

Lucas' gaze softens, and he cups her cheek, smiling when she tilts her head into the contact. "Di, I don't think you know what you do to me."

She sits up, pulling the sheet with her to cover herself as she shoots Lucas a wink. "I think I know perfectly well."

After they've showered and gotten dressed, Lucas and Diana exit her room, meeting Kiara in the hallway.

"Morning," Kiara says, her voice barely above a whisper. "Be careful with Cam."

Diana glances down the hall, where Cameron is sitting at the counter, head in his hands. "Why, what happened?"

Kiara tilts her head, studying the ginger-haired boy with a creased brow. "He got a phone call from Ruth earlier. Apparently, it was... not good news."

"Well, what did she say?" Lucas whispers.

Kiara shrugs. "I don't know. I saw him listening to her, and it was a long call. Then he just started to cry."

Diana's expression melts into one of pity, and she heads down the hall without another word to Kiara or Lucas. "Hey, Cam," she says, brushing her hand along his back as she passes him.

He looks up at her touch as the other two file into the room. "Hi."

Diana sees his eyes are puffy, and his freckled cheeks are red. He rubs his eyes as Diana leans on the counter in front of him. "Everything okay?"

He looks up at her, and Diana notices his strawberry-blonde eyelashes are wet right as he bursts into tears.

Lucas is the closest one to him; he grabs Cameron's arm out of instinct and Cameron leans into him, forcing Lucas onto the stool beside him and wrapping Cameron in a hug. Kiara sits on the other side of Cameron, running her fingers across his back in a soothing motion. Diana grabs his hands, forcing him to look at her.

"Cam, hey," she whispers, remembering when she whispered the same way to young Katie before the Battle of Zodiacs. "Talk to us."

Cameron huffs out a laugh, one that sounds almost manic. "He's not improving. He's getting worse."

"Oh, no," Diana whispers. "Oh, Cam. I'm so sorry."

Cameron scoffs. "I'm just... angry. I don't know why, I'm angry at him."

"That's okay, though," Kiara says. "It's okay."

"And I'm *sad*. I need to see him. I've said it before, but now..." his voice breaks, "now it might be my last chance."

Diana nods slowly. "I hope not."

"None of us do," Lucas mumbles, patting Cameron on the shoulder.

"I just don't know what to do," Cameron cries.

Diana squeezes his hands. "Cameron, did it ever occur to you that you don't *need* to figure out what you would do? I know it's hard to hope now, I know it is. But it will be so much easier to confront your fear of this if you try."

Cameron wipes his nose, sniffling. "I know. And I will try. For Peter's sake, if nobody else's."

"Exactly," Lucas says, voice exponentially cheerier than the other's, "and things at the lab are going okay. So before you know it, he'll be better."

"He hasn't responded to any of my letters this whole time," Cameron mumbles.

"Maybe he can't write back," Kiara responds. "They're probably doing a bunch of tests, and we know he's weaker than normal."

Cameron pulls himself out of everyone's grip and stands, brushing himself off. Like someone flipped a switch, his cheeks are dry and his expression is neutral if not mildly peeved. "We have a meeting with the others soon, right? So let's just go."

He turns to the elevator as Lucas glances nervously at Diana. Kiara just shrugs. "He's not wrong."

Fifteen minutes later, the eight are seated on the Congress floor.

Barbara Oswald clasps her hands on the tabletop. "Alright, Your Highness. What do you have?"

Lucas pulls the letter from his pocket. "This," without a word of explanation, he begins to read, and when he finishes, he looks up at the rest of them.

Diana and Cameron look confused. Barbara looks mildly angry, her face twisted into a scowl. The others are just staring at Lucas as if waiting for him to continue.

"I just don't get it," Lucas says. "I don't understand. I know what's behind this country. I know that George went after Damian because he was the oldest son." He passes the letter to Barbara as she thrusts out an open palm. "And what does this book have to do with anything?"

They all fall silent. Diana puts her hand out to Barbara, and the older woman passes her the letter. Diana reads it once, then twice, and then her eyes widen. "Wait." Her voice is shaking.

"What?" Lucas asks urgently. "Did you figure something out?"

"I... I think so," Diana swallows hard. "Just... follow my thinking for a minute," she glances at Barbara briefly before continuing, but the look is too quick for Lucas to decipher what it might mean. "He says that George isn't the heir."

"Right," Mr. Boone affirms, the tone of his voice egging her on.

"And then says someone in the original twelve lied about their sign," Diana glances around, raising her left eyebrow, "and then gives *Barbara's* name, telling Henderson to not let her get in the way."

"We *did* read the letter, Di," Kiara says.

"Just listen," Diana commands. "The book title is 'The *Ram* and The *Waterman*.'"

The table falls silent.

Then, Ms. Brewer gasps.

Lucas' eyebrows knit together.

Diana drops the letter. "Oh my God." She knows she's right.

Cameron reaches over and takes Barbara's hand.

Lucas looks over at Barbara as a single tear rolls down her cheek. "Diana," she whispers, turning her head almost mechanically towards the president, "are you suggesting that George Henderson killed-" her voice cracks, and Diana gasps: it's the first time she's seen Barbara Oswald cry.

Steeling herself, Diana nods. "I'm saying your father was the liar. He was the Aries, and George Henderson killed him for his spot on the BoZ."

"Do you have any proof besides your word?"

Lucas swallows. "I do."

All eyes turn to him, and his heart begins to pound. He runs his sweaty hands down his pant legs under the table, fighting the urge to clench his fists. "When I was younger, I had flashcards with pictures of all the Twelve Founders. And in the picture of Orion Oswald, he always carried a cane. And... that cane was in Henderson's office."

"You're certain? You're certain it was his?" Barbara asks, tone growing frantic.

"Mahogany, carved with a willow tree," Lucas affirms.

Barbara shakes her head. "I... I hope you're wrong. Because if you aren't, that means that the Board of Zodiacs was built on a lie. That means George Henderson started his whole career as a murderer, and he put himself in a position that was rightfully my father's. And-" she swallows hard, "and that means the day my father went missing, the day I went back to North Carolina and searched our entire house for him, he was here, being bludgeoned to death by his own cane."

Nobody speaks. Then, Diana reaches across the table and taps Lucas' wrist. "Rutherland, take us to the office."

So Lucas rises from his seat, leading the other eight to Henderson's locked office in silence, the only sound being the reverberation of eight pairs of feet off the walls. Wordlessly, Cameron comes forward and unlocks the door, pushing it open to reveal the musty office.

Lucas crosses to the corner, pulling the cane out of the piles of junk. He holds it up to the light of the window, and a collective gasp ripples through the room.

The head of the cane is stained with blood.

"You were right," Lucas says, looking over at Diana.

Mr. Boone interrupts. "Someone find that book."

So the eight tear the office apart: overturning papers, yanking open drawers, shuffling books around on the shelves. After a moment, Miriam speaks. "I found something."

The others look over as she holds up two photographs.

One is a faded, dusty ultrasound image, with a small baby barely visible in the swirling black-and-white print. The other is a picture of a newborn, nestled in a small incubator bed. In the baby picture, no adults are present, beside whoever was behind the camera. The infant is tiny, with dark skin and a crying, creased brow.

Reginald frowns, breaking the tense silence. "Whose baby is that?"

Lucas looks over at Kiara, at the same creased brows that are in the baby's photograph. Before he can speak, he watches Ms. Miller read the bottom of the ultrasound image, where tiny text sits. After a moment, her eyes widen, and she looks back up, over the top of the image.

At Kiara.

"March thirtieth," Miriam whispers, now reading aloud the date on the back of the baby picture, "Kiara Joan Henderson."

Nobody speaks, and Ms. Miller's whispered words seem to cut a fissure in Kiara's resolve, for one single tear slips down her cheek. Lucas and the other teenagers are sharing guilty looks, and the four adults in the room look completely shell-shocked. Even Barbara's normally unshaking expression is one of fear and blatant disgust.

Kiara crosses to Miriam in three long strides, taking the photos from her hand and tearing them in two with one strong pull. "Ki!" Diana says, racing to her, "stop!"

"I hate him!" Kiara wails, dropping the shredded photographs as she and Diana land shakily on the carpet. Kiara sobs for a moment as the others stand there, frozen. "He should've let me die in that stupid hospital!"

"Kiara," Barbara says, finally speaking, "enough."

Kiara looks up at her, agape, and then her dark gaze turns vicious. "You don't get to tell me how to grieve."

"I'm not," Barbara begins, taking her forcefully by the arms and pulling her to her feet, "but this sick man has tried to take everything away from you. He has tried to break you down *again*. Do not let him."

Kiara swipes angrily at her eyes and nods, looking in turn at the others in the room. "You all must hate me, too. You must think I'm disgusting."

After a long beat where Lucas fears the other adults might turn tail and flee, Victoria Brewer shakes her head. "No," she says, voice firm, "we think you're strong."

"You are not your father," Miriam whispers, taking Kiara by the shoulders. "You aren't his actions."

Kiara breathes deep, then meets Lucas' eyes. "Lucas is my cousin," she whispers.

"Yes, we connected those dots," Barbara replies, glancing at Lucas. "What a tangled web this family tree is."

Kiara ignores her, pushing her shoulders back as if to shove away the terror that was taking hold. "We aren't here to talk about me, we're here to get justice for Mr. Oswald. So let's find that book." No one moves, and Kiara raises one eyebrow. "Is there something you're all waiting for?"

Everyone scatters and the nervous chatter resumes as the hunt begins again.

Lucas crosses to the windowsill, but trips over a lump in the rug. He looks down, and when he sees the rectangular outline, he drops to his knees, rolling up the rug at the corner.

"Lucas, what are you-?" Diana bends down next to him, then gasps, "You found it."

Lucas holds up the dusty, thin book, wiping the grime from the cover. "'The Ram and The Waterman,'" he reads. "This is it."

Barbara takes it from him, and stares at the cover long and hard. Wordlessly, she passes it to Cameron. "Read it, please."

He opens the book, clears his throat, and begins to read. "'Once upon a time, there was a man who lived by the sea. On his birthday, at the end of January, his wife gave him a ram as a pet.'" He looks up. "Should I go on?"

Everyone nods.

Cameron tilts his head and continues. "'The ram grew quickly, accompanying the waterman to and from his journeys to the sea. And the waterman grew old. After many years, the ram was bigger and taller than the frail old man, and one bump of the ram's horns would send him tumbling.'"

"I'm sensing a metaphor," Diana mumbles.

"'The man died on a cool, early-April day, when the ram was outside in his pen. And from that day on, the ram was wild, answering to nobody but himself, in charge of his life for the very first time. The end.'"

"That's it?" Miller asks.

But Lucas' eyes are stuck on Cameron, whose mouth is agape and face has gone paler than normal. "Cameron?" Lucas asks. "What is it?"

Cameron swallows. "There're... there're pictures."

Diana's chest rises rapidly. "Of what?"

Cameron swallows. "Orion Oswald."

With that, he turns the book around. Taped into the pages are photographs.

One shows Orion Oswald, crouched against the bookshelves of the office, hand thrown protectively over his face. His eyes are full of fear, with a glint of rage behind them. The second is of Orion crumpled on the floor, skull caved in and face covered in blood. Lucas kicks himself for thinking that the blood wouldn't come out of his perfectly-pressed white shirt. The third and final picture is the same spot, but the body is gone: in its place is the matted, blood-stained carpet and the cane, leant against the bookshelf.

Cameron hands the book to Barbara, slumping against the bookshelf. When he catches Lucas' disgusted glance, he looks down at the rug beneath his feet and grimaces, leaping away from the carpet and the shelf.

"So it's true," Barbara whispers without tearing her eyes from the page. "George killed my father and took his title."

"Oh, God, how horrific," Ms. Miller whispers.

"Barbara, you're... you're really an Aquarius though, right?" Diana mumbles.

"February thirteenth," Barbara says solemnly.

"But didn't you know your father's actual birthday?" Kiara asks.

"He told me it was January twenty-fourth," she replies. "I guess I won't ever know his real one."

"But what about your old house?" Diana asks. "Could something be there? A birth certificate, maybe?"

Barbara shakes her head. "A group of protestors burned it down a few years after the Twelve Founders put themselves in office. Anything once there is gone now."

"It doesn't matter either way," Lucas says, "but now we can charge Henderson, right? Put him on trial for murder?"

Diana shrugs. "What good would that do?"

Lucas gapes at her. "It would put him in jail, no?"

Mr. Boone shakes his head. "Sorry to tell you this, Lucas, but..." he sighs, "murder wasn't exactly the biggest deal when the BoZ ruled."

Lucas' eyes widen as he looks around the group. "What? Who else?!"

Kiara, Barbara, Ms. Miller, and Ms. Brewer raise their hands. Diana casts Lucas an apologetic glance, mumbling: "I don't actually know if I killed Joaquin Garcia or not."

"And none of *us* are rotting in jail," Kiara mumbles.

Lucas hesitates. "So... what do we do, then?"

Barbara shrugs, laughing bitterly. "There isn't anything we *can* do. George is gone. My father is dead. The government has been remade, so what's the point in vengeance now?"

Lucas glances over at Kiara, whose fists are clenched almost as hard as her jaw. "I don't think you guys understand. My uncle is *alive* somewhere. What if he comes back? What if he-?"

Barbara interrupts, holding up a well-manicured hand. "Your Highness. With all due respect, George Henderson remains the *least* of our issues right now. He's been gone for months. But in this country, we have a secret heiress daughter, a dying Secretary of Education, and a sector that still remains isolated because of an incurable disease. Henderson is not causing any issues right now."

"He killed your father!" Lucas practically shrieks, throwing his arms up in frustration. "He tried to kill all of you, the day of your revolution! He led that backwards government you had for *years*!"

"We were all part of that backwards government, Mr. Rutherland," Barbara argues, her tone hard and emotionless, "so does that make us just as bad as Henderson?" Lucas' mouth drops open, but Oswald continues. "And these three kids here broke more laws than any rebels in American history, including your own father. So does that not make them as corrupt as Henderson?" She sighs. "I'm not saying he isn't an evil, twisted man. If I had my way with him, he would be dying a slow and agonizing death, and he'd never hurt another person again. But he is no immediate threat."

Everyone is quiet. Until Kiara speaks.

"Do you know something, Barbara?"

Barbara glances over at her, and Lucas swears she could see tiny cracks begin appearing in her hard porcelain expression. "What?"

Kiara looks up from where her eyes had been fixated on the floor. Her gaze is hard, and angry. Lucas remembers people in Alynthia describing those eyes: the ones that belonged to the girl who defeated George Henderson with nothing but a knife clutched in a bloody hand in front of the whole country. "I'm not going to tell you exactly how horrible he is. You of all people already know. But *nobody* has hurt me the way he has. Not the guard who attacked me during the Battle of Zodiacs. Not Maya when we found out she lied to all of us. Not those stuck-up nobles in Alynthia – not my *uncle* – who didn't even give me a second glance. *Henderson* hurt me the worst. My own father. So I apologize if I'm not going to sit around and wait for him to strike again."

Barbara looks somewhat taken aback, but she crosses her arms over her chest. "We aren't getting anywhere standing around and arguing about it. But I'll give you this, Kiara. If you think you can be discreet, and controlled, I don't see harm in trying to track him down. But I need your word that you won't do anything rash."

Kiara takes a deep breath and raises an eyebrow. Then she nods. "Fine."

Barbara seems to relax a bit. She waves her hands, corralling everyone towards the door. "Let's go, then," she turns, looking over her shoulder at the place in the old rug, the spot on the bookshelf, the shredded photographs, "and pray we never have to come in here again."

163

Part Forty-Two: The Cancer

Peter

Two loud knocks sound on Peter's door, and then Ruth pokes her head into his room. "Hello, darling."

The nurse enters fully, shutting the door behind her. She seats herself at the table in the corner, putting a pillow into a clean case as she speaks. Peter watches her fingers work around the fabric. "Another letter came for you."

Peter bites his lip and looks towards his hands, which are folded in his lap.

"It's from Cameron."

"Throw it," Peter replies instantly, letting the sentence get swallowed by a cough.

Ruth sighs in frustration, letting the pillow drop from her hands. She levels a stern gaze at Peter. "No."

Peter glares right back. He doesn't say anything—he can't, really, but he doesn't have to.

"I won't throw this one away, just like I didn't throw away the other two," Ruth's expression turns pitiful. "My dear, just read them. Please."

Peter crosses his arms, and his whole body aches. "No," he coughs out.

Ruth reaches into her jacket pocket, pulling out three letters. She fans them out in front of her like a hand of cards. "They're *right here*," she says, drawing out her words as if she were a peddler in the street, advertising her wares.

Peter tears his eyes away from the envelopes, looking at the cluttered table even though the sight of Cameron's familiar scratchy handwriting makes his heart ache. "I don't *want them*," he replies, mimicking the nurse's tone to the best of his ability.

"Yes, you do."

Yes, you do. "No."

"Fine, *I'll* read them to you."

"No!" Peter nearly shouts. Ruth pauses from where she's opening the first letter, finger poised threateningly under the envelope flap and eyebrow raised teasingly. Peter finally relents, sighing heavily and holding out his hand with a weak effort.

Ruth grins and crosses to him, gently handing the stack of letters over. "Would you like me to-?"

Peter just nods.

The nurse grins and leaves, throwing Peter a wink as she shuts the door.

Peter sighs, heart hammering in his chest as he stares at the letters. Was it really worth it? Sure, he didn't want to hurt Cameron, but he also didn't want to hurt *himself*. Reading these would just make him more upset.

He thinks, as his fingers work in removing the first letter.

Fingers shaking, he removes the paper from the envelope. Ruth has done him the liberty of opening all of them, for his shaking fingers would be unable to do it themselves. The paper is dated from a few days prior.

Dear Peter,

I was bored this afternoon, so I've decided to make a list of all the things I want to do with you when you get better.

1. Get a portrait with Finnigan (he misses you so, so much)

2. Go to Sector Three with you (I miss that place, surprisingly enough)
3. Have a twenty-four hour reading date (books of your choosing)
4. Stargaze (I've never done it before)
5. Properly ask you to be my date to a formal event (I regret how we agreed to go to Lucas' ball together)

There's more, obviously, but I don't want to risk writing it on account of someone else potentially opening this letter before you, so I'll leave it to your imagination. Feel better soon, superhero.

Love, Cam

Peter sighs, then he puts the letter aside and reaches for the other envelope. It's dated just that morning, mere hours ago. Peter swallows, steeling his nerves before opening the flap.

Dear Peter,

This isn't where we intended to be, huh?

I'm writing this very, very early in the morning. I can't sleep. So I'll paint you the picture.

I'm in your bed, and you're not with me, and Finn doesn't come in here anymore for some reason. He stops right at the threshold, sleeps against the doorframe.

When I got that call from Ruth last night, I told Diana. She told me I needed to have hope, so I did. I did, for a little while. I imagined what it would feel like to hug you again, to touch your hair, to see your smile. But then it went away.

I cried when I thought of you and didn't feel happy anymore. Before this moment, I would get that anxious, bubbly happiness when I thought of you. Now my heart starts to pound and I feel sick inside. Not because I don't feel the same way for you, in fact, whoever said "absence makes the heart grow fonder" was onto something. It's that now, my fear, my sadness, the big empty space you left outweighs the happiness I feel when I think of you.

Every time I write to you and get nothing back, you leave me over and over again. But we can start over, if you get out. I'll do anything, Peter. Anything to make it perfect. Just please, don't leave me.

We didn't even get a proper goodbye. The last thing you told me was to leave, so I didn't get sick, and the last thing I said was "fine." I think about that a lot. I think about all the things I wish I could've told you right then, so that it would make this moment easier.

I remember when we stayed watch together, out in the woods. You were mad at me that night, and I can't really remember why. But I think I saw you for the first time that night. I think I realized what you were going through. The difference between you and the girls is that when I met them, they flat-out told me their problems. But I met you, and somehow, you were a whole puzzle to figure out, and I liked it. I liked seeing pieces of you fit together and make sense to me, and I liked that you showed me those parts of yourself.

You were a riddle, a whole book to read, a character that I hadn't yet seen developed but now I do. And before I could tell you that, you disappeared.

But part of me still thinks you'll be back, Peter. And I'm not going to stop writing to you, even if now it's more of my existential crisis rather than how my workday was. You don't have to answer, but know that every time you don't it makes me feel like you're getting more and more gone, and I don't like the idea of you fading away on your own.

A whole bunch, maybe all, of astrology is based on stars, right? Well, the Scorpius constellation is in the Southern sky. Yours is in the Northern sky. We're pretty far away, considering our signs are compatible. I did more research on your constellation, because it's really pretty. Apparently, it's the 31st largest constellation in the whole galaxy. It has ten named stars, and two stars have known planets. It covers 506 square degrees of the sky. Scorpius is near the center of the Milky Way, and it's the 33rd biggest. I like learning about the stars. I think I'll be more mindful of them from now on.

Be safe, superhero.

Love, Cameron

Peter swallows, heart hammering. This is what he wanted, right? He *wanted* Cameron to take this seriously. He *wanted* the fact that he might die to be acknowledged.

So why did this hurt so bad?

He didn't feel like crying, surprisingly. He figures he really can't anymore, unless he's crying because he's happy, which didn't happen often.

Someone knocks on the door, and Charles enters.

"What's wrong, son?" he asks, setting his bag down and shrugging out of his coat.

Peter holds up the bundle of papers with a teary shrug.

Charles nods, his mouth set in a tight line. "Everything okay?"

Peter shrugs one shoulder again, then shakes his head.

Charles sighs, removing a needle from his bag. "I have a new trial for you. Inesh and I perfected it yesterday. And as for Sector Five..." Charles pauses, and

Peter looks up towards him. The older man is frozen in his place, looking at his patient with nothing short of an apologetic expression. He swallows as Peter quirks an eyebrow. When Charles speaks again, his voice is low, as if trying to make it impossible for Peter to hear him. "They're going away, actually."

Peter's breath seems to evaporate from his lungs. Slowly, he takes a deep, raspy breath. "Really?" he croaks.

Charles shakes his head as if trying to change the subject. "I... they're stopping. The infected people are starting to get better."

Peter swallows. Somehow, he feels both excited and disappointed, and this clash of emotions takes up his insides. His shaky hands are sweating.

"A little over one hundred thousand infected are left."

Something takes flight in his stomach: could it be hope? He motions to the medicine in Charles' hands. "Was it that one?" he manages.

Charles grins and nods. "Yes, sir," as he prepares the injection, he continues to rattle off statistics. "It's shown the best results of the men there so far. It seems to be the best for those who weigh the same as a regular adult," he waves a hand down the length of Peter's body, "although you've lost fifteen pounds since you got hospitalized."

He sticks the needle into Peter's right arm just as Ruth enters. She beams when she sees the open letters on Peter's bedside table.

"Hello, darling," she says, stationing herself at Charles' side.

Peter smiles gently at the pair as Charles tapes a gauze pad on his prick spot.

"How is this going, Charles?" Ruth asks. When she passes the doctor to get to the table, she gently brushes her fingertips across his back. Peter's eyes widen and both of the adults notice. "What's wrong?" Ruth asks.

Peter smirks as he regains a little bit of authority over his own body, shaking his head in a dismissive motion.

"Okay, Mr. Simon. Symptom check?" Ruth asks, pulling out a pen and clipboard from absolutely nowhere.

Peter nods, and Ruth winks at him. "Headache?" Another nod.

"Last time you ate a decent meal?"

Peter looks at Charles, who hesitates, humming low in his throat. "Two days ago," the doctor replies.

"And have you been feeling hungry at all?"

A shake of the head.

Charles chuckles as he seats himself on the tabletop. "Boy had me running back and forth from the tap for more water. Make note that he's been thirsty."

Peter smiles at him as Ruth continues. "Any vomiting?"

Shaking head, weaker than before.

The nurse nods, writing quickly. "Finally, any body aches?"

Peter shifts around a bit, as much as he can. He responds a moment later with a decisive nod.

The adults share a glance. "Where?" Ruth asks finally. Peter points to the sore spot.

"It could be something with your lungs," Charles says nonchalantly, "but don't go panicking just yet."

"Huh?" Peter mumbles.

Charles holds up a finger, digging through his bag. He holds up a device with three different colored tubes. "This is a spirometer. It measures and monitors your lung conditions. It can show us whether or not your airways are constricting, causing the aches."

Peter nods, and Charles instructs them through the test, breathing long and hard into the tube on the device. After a few minutes, Charles pulls Ruth aside.

Peter leans his head back against the pillows, staring up at the ceiling. He thinks about Cameron, about his letters. He misses Finnigan, he thinks, as his fingers trace paths through the sheets.

The adults reconvene with him a moment later. "Just as we thought," Charles says, "your lung airways are constricting. Nothing urgent, though. Narrowed airways don't let as much air come in or go out of your lungs, which limits the amount of oxygen that enters your blood and the amount of carbon dioxide that leaves your blood," Charles puts the device back into his bag. "We're going to put you on oxygen, and then set you up with some steam treatments to relax your lungs a bit. If it continues to escalate, we'll look into an operation."

Peter nods. Ruth sits on the edge of his bed, taking his hands in hers.

"Peter, don't be afraid. This is relatively normal for this stage of the disease." She studies his eyes, frozen on the foot of the bed. "Peter, dear," her voice is growing more and more concerned. "What's the matter?"

Peter swallows. "My stomach."

Ruth pushes against his stomach. "Is it a nauseous feeling?"

He shakes his head. "It's tight." He tries to speak again, but can't. His tongue feels swollen and his throat is constricting, like someone had their hands around it.

Charles' eyes go wide. "He's having an allergic reaction. To the medicine."

The medics snap into action as Peter chokes: Ruth yanks back the bedsheets, revealing Peter's bare legs poking out from his hospital gown. Charles overturns his own bag, then Ruth's, letting the various tools clatter to the ground. He shuffles frantically through the objects as Peter sucks in a sharp breath, wheezing as he exhales. He grabs at Ruth's arm as his vision starts to blur; she violently waves the doctor towards them.

Charles appears, handing Ruth a long cylindrical object. Peter only realizes it's an epinephrine injector when the nurse sends it plummeting into his thigh. She holds it there for a few seconds, then removes it and begins massaging the injection spot.

Peter manages to take in a few quivering breaths of thin air, and he lets his vision slowly creep back to him. He groans as another wave of tightness overtakes his chest, a reminder to never hope too much.

Charles looks at his watch. "Do you need anything, Peter?"

Peter shrugs, grogginess overtaking him. "Finn."

The doctor glances at Ruth. "Who?"

Ruth sighs as she rises and begins writing something on a fresh piece of paper. "His dog."

Charles' face breaks into a smile. "Oh, yes. I remember him from the magazine pictures."

Peter nods, closing his eyes. As he sits in darkness, he begins floating downwards with a mechanical whir. He knows it's just Ruth lowering his bed. He listens as their voices float through the room.

"You get the oxygen for this afternoon," Ruth says, voice growing distant as she steps away from the bed. "And this," the sound of a paper sliding over the tabletop piques Peter's attention, although he doesn't open his eyes.

"First, I'll go to the lab. I'm going to see if there are any more trials I can get my hands on, and I'll meet you back here in, say, five hours?" Charles responds.

"Sure. And check the ingredients this time, please. I'm thinking it's an amoxicillin allergy."

They are quiet for a moment, and Peter hears Charles begin to shrug his coat on, zipper sliding.

Right as he's just fading into sleep, he hears Charles speak again. "And... we're still on for dinner tonight, correct?"

Ruth smiles, Peter can hear it in her voice as she settles in the chair in the corner. "Absolutely."

Peter falls asleep with a little smile on his face.

Part Forty-Three: The Aries

Kiara

"It just doesn't make any sense," Kiara complains as she swivels around in her stool again. She'd been spinning for almost an hour, reviewing charts with Inesh and Lucas. It was a couple hours after lunch, maybe two in the afternoon. They'd been in the lab since nine that morning.

"What doesn't make sense is that you've been spinning in that chair for an hour and you haven't thrown up yet," Inesh responds, handing Lucas a chocolate-chip cookie, ones that Ms. Miller had sent down to the lab.

"Thanks," Lucas replies from his seat on the floor. He's sprawled out like a starfish, lying on his stomach. "What doesn't make sense is that this medicine trial was healing *other* people, but not Peter."

"What doesn't make sense is that he had an allergic reaction to this, but nothing else," Kiara says.

The others nod. "At least now we know what *not* to include in the trials," Lucas responds.

Inesh crosses to the center lab table, picking up the folder Lucas had brought in that morning after he had spent all night digging in the Archives. "And these charts are helpful, but not for Peter. If they were marked, besides what Lucas has done so far, it would be ten times more useful."

Lucas stands, stretching his arms over his head. He crosses to Inesh, pointing out a few charts in particular. Kiara gets up and goes over as well, hovering at Inesh's right side. "These were interesting. I think it might be for Powerful Ones. You see how the line here starts to flatline, then decline, but this second one just keeps going up? I think that's a Powerful One's infection, and the declining one is just a normal, healing person."

"But it doesn't show us how to *heal* the Powerful One," Inesh argues.

"Doesn't it? I mean, not explicitly, but it shows that whatever healed this person didn't work on the Powerful One," he turns to Kiara as she continues. "So this disease is and has been incurable, which means the Powerful One must've died from this, considering how steep that incline is. Is there anything about past Powerful Ones in the archives?"

Kiara nods slowly. "Yeah. A book, with names, but no personal biographies or anything. Maybe there's something from when Lee's books got moved, when you took the office."

Inesh shrugs, putting the chart back onto the gleaming white table. "It doesn't hurt to check. When do you go to the Capitol next?"

Kiara and Lucas exchange a look. "Whenever we can. Originally, we were supposed to give Diana only a portion of our work, but now she and Cameron have been doing it all so we can be here."

Inesh turns to the two of them, bracing himself against the tabletop. "You can go now, if you want. And you can always take on less work here if you have to."

"No, I like it here," Lucas says, "I like that we're helping the Cancers."

Kiara nods. "And Peter."

Inesh grins at them, teeth almost as white as the fluorescent lights. "I'll see you both tomorrow, at noon. Take the morning off, sleep in. If we need you for an emergency, we'll call."

Lucas grins widely and gives Inesh a quick hug. "Thank you, Inesh. We'll bring the book in tomorrow, along with whatever else we find in the archives."

Kiara grabs another cookie from the tray on the table as she leaves, stuffing it in her mouth and tossing a two-fingered salute to Inesh. He salutes her back and laughs. "Until next time, Miss Kiara."

Kiara pokes her head into Diana's office a little while after the cousins leave the lab. "Hey, anything you need me to do?"

Diana seems anxious- on edge, really. "No." She deflects the question. Kiara knows she's lying.

She sits down on the edge of Diana's desk, peering over the messy surface. "What's wrong?"

Diana sighs, rubbing the crease between her eyebrows. "Unrest in the Northeast. They need money, food, shelter. And I can't figure out how to get that for them."

Kiara nods, letting the problem seep into her skin and get her gears turning. "Did Cameron try anything while he was doing funding?"

"No. It wasn't an issue until now, because now there's a union on strike."

Kiara hums. "What are their terms?"

"Higher minimum wages, mostly. Plus, they want more help with the environment, like a team who can assist with the winter conditions when they worsen or people who will improve the buildings to withstand them."

Kiara sighs. "I didn't realize how fragile it was over there."

Diana laughs glumly. "Not just there. Obviously there's anger in Sector Five, but we've also got gangs of angry Geminis who are hung up on Maya and Oliver, and a whole bunch of Henderson supporters who-" She catches herself at the last second, but it's too late.

"What?" Kiara asks incredulously. "Supporters? Of... no, you can't be serious."

Diana shakes her head with a tired sigh. "Just rumors, for now. I put people up in Sector One and around there after Henderson fled, which you know, but they're coming to me now with an increase in... whispers, I guess."

"What kinds of whispers?"

"Just ones that miss the old ways. When Aries, Leo, and those people were on top. George gave that world to them, and they want it back."

Kiara scoffs. "They want hierarchy and elitism back, is what you mean."

Diana hesitates, then nods. "I'm sorry, Ki."

Kiara tries to tamp down her building rage. "No, I am. We should have been here to help you more. It's not fair for you to do all this on your own." She takes Diana's hand, then notices another piece of paper that stands out from the rest. "What's that list?"

Diana picks it up: it's written in her familiar writing, and it's a list of various file numbers or names. "Just some stuff I need to reprint. I think it's the stress, but I keep losing my files and bills."

Something there is strange, but Kiara can't quite place it. "Weird," she mumbles instead.

Diana just shrugs. If she's worried, or suspicious, she isn't letting on. "I'm sure it's nothing."

Part Forty-Four: The Cancer

Peter

Peter wakes up as Ruth and Charles re-enter his room. and he blinks groggily.

"How was your nap?" Ruth asks with a small smile.

Peter shoots her a thumbs-up, rubbing his eyes with his other hand.

Charles approaches, beginning to hook him up to oxygen. Peter groans as he adjusts to the tubes in his nose.

The airy sensation sends tingles through his body, but he will admit that it does make life infinitesimally easier.

Charles chuckles. "Perfect, if I do say so."

After a few minutes of acclimation, Ruth wanders over. "Feeling fine so far?"

Peter nods. It's true: his breathing has gotten somewhat easier, and his chest felt weird and buzzy with fresh air, making it harder to feel the aches.

"Now, Peter," Ruth says, causing Peter to drag his gaze over to her. She's smiling playfully, and he notices Charles is hovering by the door. "We have something for you."

Charles grins and opens the door.

Before Peter can register what's going on, a fuzzy blob launches itself at him and lands on his bed.

Peter coughs out a bloody laugh, rubbing the ears of his dog. Finnigan wiggles around excitedly, burrowing in Peter's bedsheets as Ruth laughs. He wraps his arms around the dog's neck and gives him a long hug.

The dog whimpers excitedly, and Peter moves out of the way just in time to keep the dog's long tongue from hitting his oxygen tubes. After another moment of anxious wiggling, Finnigan finally settles, curling up on Peter's lap as if he couldn't get close enough.

Ruth smiles, crossing to Peter and rubbing the puppy's soft ears. "He's just adorable, Peter. I can see how you boys love him so much."

Peter nods, smiling down at the dog. Then, his eyes begin to well with tears. Before he can stop himself, he's crying softly, burying his fingers in Finnigan's blonde fur.

Charles sits on the edge of the bed, placing a hand on the dog's back. "It's okay, Peter."

Peter nods, sobbing uncontrollably now. He wraps Finnigan in his arms, cradling him as if he were an infant. He wants nothing more than to bury his face in his fur, but he knows that wouldn't be safe. How was even cuddling his own dog unsafe now?

Neither adult speaks, they just let him cry. Finally, Ruth takes one of Peter's hands. "I wish you had talked about him sooner. Cameron was more than willing to let him spend the afternoon here."

Peter looks up at her, blinking the blurry tears from his vision. "Cameron?"

Ruth nods. "We've exchanged words here and there, but when I went to get Finnigan, he was there, at the Capitol. So I spoke to him," she straightens the blanket on the bed as she speaks, picking lint from the fabric. "He misses you."

She doesn't need to say more as Peter nods, wiping his nose clumsily. He swallows hard, looking up at the ceiling then back down at Finnigan. The space around him feels empty, feels like something is missing. Then, he speaks, and for the first time in weeks, his words feel truer than they were before. "I miss him too."

Charles and Ruth nod, looking at one another as if they had been waiting – waiting this whole time for Peter to admit it. Admit it in a way where he understood it was true, at least. Ruth squeezes his hand. "And he loves you. Do you want to know something beautiful?"

Peter just nods, worried that if he said too much, he wouldn't ever stop rambling.

"When he told me to tell you that, he smiled," she grins, and Peter wonders if she's ever not boundlessly happy. "I asked if there was anything he wanted to tell you, and he grinned and said to tell you he loves you. Have you ever noticed–?"

Peter cuts her off, eyes fixated on the bedspread, mumbling almost robotically. "The dimple?"

Ruth nods. "Yes. One dimple. And even though it's cold outside, even though the sun is behind clouds most of the day, that boy still has one of the most freckled faces I've ever seen."

Charles chuckles. "His arms, too. I remember when those four were right about to go into lockdown, and he was wearing a short-sleeve shirt, and his arms were freckled, too, just like his face," he glances at Peter. "My apologies if that was a weird thing to notice."

Peter smiles softly, blinking himself back into the present moment. "It's not."

Charles smiles gently, and Peter sometimes forgets how kind his eyes are. "I liked hearing about your adventures from him. It turns these young revolutionaries into more humanlike creatures, surprisingly enough."

Ruth snaps her fingers. "That reminds me." She rises from the bed, crossing to her bag and pulling a magazine from it. "This is an issue from a few days ago, but I saw it in your office. The door was open, and Crown Prince Lucas Rutherland had left it for you, according to the note on the cover." She passes it to Peter, and he studies the front. It's Cameron, leaning out of his office window. Below him is a young boy, and the two are saluting one another. Peter smiles when he sees Cameron's wide grin, and he realizes with a pounding heart that he can't remember the last time he saw that.

He holds it against his chest, almost like he was hugging Cameron again, and as he pets Finnigan, he gets the warm feeling that his family is with him again, no matter how far they really were.

He flips through the magazine, seeing a column about the disease, a chart about rents in the west going up, and a piece about Diana. He reads it over, smile growing wider as he scans the page.

"I miss Secretary Simon quite dearly. I grew up with him. He was, and still is, one of my closest friends. I don't know if I've ever met someone so selfless, so unrelenting in his care for others. He's forever with us in our hearts until he can be with us in person again," said President Monroe regarding the diseased Secretary of Education.

Peter can almost see Diana talking to a reporter, stumbling over her words just a bit but determined to get her message across. The thought makes him smile, and he stares at the cover of the magazine while Ruth clears her throat.

"She's... a good public speaker, yes?"

Peter laughs shakily and shakes his head.

Charles nods too. "I got an earful from Inesh about a similar thing. Apparently, he was the same way Diana is, and when he met Lucas as a little kid, a kid who was such a good public speaker already, he was livid. But he and I agree that it's quite interesting treating a celebrity."

Ruth chuckles, scooping up Finnigan and planting a kiss on his soft head. She eyes Peter, smirking playfully. "He's right sometimes, Peter."

Part Forty-Five: The Taurus

Diana

Cameron and Diana get home at the same time: nine o'clock at night.

"God," Cameron huffs, flopping down on the couch.

Diana takes her shoes off, then her jacket, hanging it on the coat rack just inside the elevator. "You can say that again," she crosses to the couch, grabbing at Cameron's ankle. "Shoes, you slob."

Cameron mumbles a curse word and sits up, untying his shoes and sliding them off. Afterwards, he flops down again, his red hair nestling into the gray throw pillows. Eyes closed, Cameron extends his arms. Diana sits on the edge of the couch, leaning into the awkward embrace. Cameron's forehead presses into Diana's side, and she readjusts as she speaks. "Hungry?"

"No," he replies, voice groggy and more than a little exhausted.

Diana nods, although Cameron doesn't see. She stretches her arms over her head, reaching around herself to grab a cream-colored blanket. She runs her fingers through the fuzz as she drapes it over Cameron. "Where's Finnigan?"

"With Peter. Ruth is gonna bring him back tomorrow morning."

Diana smiles softly. "It's good he has him."

Cameron opens his eyes slowly, and the gray in his irises is almost the same as that of the light pillows his head rests on. "Yeah. It's the next best thing to one of us being with him."

"Exactly," Diana replies. She leans down and plants a friendly kiss on Cameron's forehead. "Night, Cam."

He removes his arms from around her waist and smiles, giving her hand a quick squeeze. "Goodnight, Di."

Diana heads down the hall to her room, pushing the slightly-ajar door open even further. She still isn't used to the sound it makes, or lack thereof. Her door in Sector Seven always squeaked when it opened, a long, shrill noise that reminded Diana of home. But *this* was her home now, no matter how weird it was to get used to.

She closes the door behind her, crossing to the closet door on the far wall, next to the bathroom. She pulls out a gray hoodie and her navy-blue pajama pants, swapping those with the jeans and sweater she had on from work that day. She heads into the bathroom, keeping the lights off.

She'd never been more tired than she was right now. Although, she said that to herself practically every day. She brushes her teeth, shaking out her free hand and letting her muscles relax a bit. She leans down to spit the toothpaste in the sink, and when she rises again, she sees another person's reflection in the mirror behind her own.

She almost screams, but then her eyes adjust to the dim light and she sighs. "Lucas, my God," she mumbles, padding out of the bathroom. The prince is standing next to the bed, a blanket wrapped over his head and shoulders like a long wig, falling over his back and ending around his knees. He's in nothing but boxers, and he lets go of the blanket when Diana passes, letting it rest on his shoulders.

As she walks past, Diana scruffs up his hair a bit, watching as it stays sticking up in a whole bunch of unnatural areas. She climbs into bed, pulling the comforter up to her waist. She looks over at Lucas expectantly. "Staying or going?"

He grins that lopsided grin at her and meanders over. "Staying."

He gets in on the other side of her, pressing flush against her side. He presses a kiss to her cheek and props his chin on her shoulder, dark eyes peering up at her. "How was your day?"

Diana recalls with great difficulty that the last time she spoke to Lucas was this morning in passing, when she and Cameron were in a mad rush to leave and she had barely had time to press a frantic kiss to his cheek. "Hectic," she replies, letting her head drop back against the headboard. "We have so much work."

Lucas sighs, sitting up and mimicking her position. "I can't help but feel like this is partially mine and Kiara's fault. If we hadn't taken the lab work-"

"Lucas, no. We *love* that you're in the lab. In fact, without you guys there, we probably wouldn't have gotten so many healed cases in Sector Five. And we're doing better with finding a cure for Peter, since we have more hands on deck."

Lucas tilts his head and shrugs. "I guess. But I don't like you being so stressed."

Diana glances at him out of the corner of her eye, smirking. "I'm the president. I'm going to be stressed no matter what,"

Lucas chuckles, putting his hand under the covers and threading his fingers through hers. He doesn't speak any more, and Diana leans her head on his shoulder. Lucas kisses her softly on the top of her head. "Get comfortable."

So she does, snuggling down onto her side, facing Lucas. He lies down as well, mirroring her. When they make eye contact, he grins. "Can you-"

Diana cuts him off by wriggling closer, wrapping her legs and arms around him. Lucas laughs, threading his arms around her waist. "I was going to ask you to get closer, but you already got the message, apparently."

Diana nods, burrowing her forehead into Lucas' chest. "No-brainer."

As she closes her eyes, Lucas whispers in the darkness. "Okay, close your eyes," she feels him shift as if looking down at her. "Want me to keep talking?"

Diana just nods.

She can hear Lucas' smile in the dark, even without opening her eyes. "Okay, once upon a time, there was a... dog. Named Finnigan," he pauses, and Diana can feel herself slipping into unconsciousness. "He was discovered by a handsome prince in Alynthia."

Diana snorts. "This is a very narcissistic story."

"Shut up, Monroe. Anyways, the puppy was born in a small bookstore on Main Street. The prince stopped in one day to get a cup of tea, early in the morning. There was a pesky group of Americans visiting, and he needed to get away. One of the American guests mentioned to the prince he had never seen a dog in real life, and so the prince went to that boy's partner and mentioned that the bookshop owner's dog had just had puppies." He pauses and takes a deep breath; Diana feels his chest rise and fall. "They were tiny little golden retrievers, with floppy ears and big paws. And the two Americans adopted one, and named him Finnigan..."

Diana falls asleep with Lucas' gentle voice filling the room, and she finally feels at peace.

Part Forty-Six: The Scorpio

Cameron

"What day is it?!" Lucas asks as Cameron walks into the kitchen the next morning.

Cameron rubs his forehead, blindly accepting a cup of coffee from Diana as Lucas' shouting sends a jackhammer rattling in his skull. "I dunno," he mumbles, sitting down at the counter. "It's like, six in the morning. Why are you yelling?"

"Because it's *lab day!*" Lucas hollers, grabbing a piece of toast directly as it shoots from the toaster.

"Oh, my God," Kiara groans, chomping at an apple from her perch atop the kitchen island, "Lucas, they're spending four hours in the lab. It's practically a Capitol field trip."

Diana snorts with laughter. "I like that. 'Capitol field trip'."

Lucas throws up his hands in exasperation as he takes a seat next to Cameron. "Guys, come on! All of us together, in the lab! You've got the day with us!" He turns to Kiara. "You aren't excited to show them what we've been doing?"

Kiara makes a face, raising her hands in surrender. "Don't look at me! I'm pumped." She sticks her tongue out at Lucas, who mimics the gesture, "I'm just not shouting about it."

Lucas laughs, and of course, everyone laughs with him. Since he moved in, it was almost like Lucas was an unyielding source of happiness. It was like turning on a tap: once it was running, it didn't stop. Cameron could only wonder *how* he did it. Even when his dad started acting up, or things were slowly worsening at the lab, he was continuously smiling, cracking jokes, wrapping people in surprise hugs when they turned the corner.

Cameron's thoughts inevitably turn from one brunette boy to another. Peter is never Lucas. He couldn't be, and nobody wanted him to be. He was the one people pulled aside to confide in, the one people asked for advice. And Cameron loved him for it, and everyone else did, too. But even with Lucas filling the air with his bubbly laugh, a link was still missing.

Diana was the leader: strong, decisive, and smart, she was the head of the pack, they needed her.

Kiara was the warrior: the fighter, the one who stood up for her own morals and advocated for the rest of them when they couldn't do it themselves.

Lucas was the charmer: smile, humor, looks. People's eyes went straight to him, and stayed there, for good reason.

Cameron was the funny one: he was there to lighten the mood, there to talk to strangers, there to give quotes for magazines.

And Peter was the brains: he could solve any problem, respond to any situation. All he had to do was pause and think for a moment, and a solution followed within seconds.

Cameron was no fool. He knew all their roles, and he knew that they played them well. In fact, there was nowhere else he'd rather be than sandwiched between Diana and Kiara, smiling for a camera and falling into his well-known public persona. But they didn't work without Peter there. Lucas' laughter seemed forced, Kiara had less energy, Cameron was just plain out of it, and Diana second-guessed everything.

If only he could come back.

"Cam?" Diana's voice snaps him back to reality.

"Huh?" Cameron asks, jumping nearly a foot in the air.

Diana winces a bit, and Cameron thinks he's the only one who notices. "I *said*, are you awake?"

He shakes his head and forces a smile. "Nope. But ready to see this lab of yours."

The group of four walks through the Plaza, flanked by two bodyguards: Hayley and some other guy whose name Cameron has forgotten.

"Lucas, I swear I'm going to get you a retractable leash," Kiara mumbles. She turns to Diana and motions to the prince, who's at least five paces ahead of everyone else. "Diana, control him."

Diana rolls her eyes and chuckles. "Lucas, stay close."

The prince backtracks a bit, bumping shoulders with Kiara, who scoffs. "Jeez. He's harder to train than Finnigan."

"Speaking of," Diana starts, nudging Cameron with her elbow, "where is he?"

"Peter's room is off the lab. So he's gonna give him back when we leave today. He can hang around for a bit with us, though, if he has to stretch his legs instead of being cooped up in a hospital bed."

Lucas sighs blissfully. "This is *awesome*, you guys. Who knows- today might even be the day we find an antidote for this whole thing."

Cameron ignores him and turns to Kiara. "Is that trial you told me about still healing people down south?"

Kiara nods. "Yup. But we haven't gotten it approved for kids yet, which make up a good bulk of the cases, so we're trying to develop something else for them.

The tricky thing with Peter is he falls right in the middle, not a kid but also not a fully-grown adult, since his weight is plummeting."

Cameron nods, chewing his lip in consideration. Kiara's explanation made sense, but he couldn't help but be worried. If Peter didn't fall under either category, how on Earth would they find a medicine that worked for him?

The group reaches a set of doors – the old schoolhouse. Lucas waves them in as the guards pull them open. "Entrez, s'il vous plaît."

Diana raises an eyebrow as she passes through. "You speak French?"

"Nope," Lucas responds with that trademark grin.

Kiara rolls her eyes. "You're such a loser."

They travel down the hallway quickly, and Diana looks around with a small smile. "Peter really wrapped things up here, didn't he? It looks fantastic."

In truth, it looked far from fantastic. The schoolhouse had been abandoned since Peter had taken over as Secretary of Education. Old schools across the country were reopened, so students were closer to home, and although kids were still split by age, they started at age five, not from birth, and went to school all the way through age sixteen. Then they were churned out into society, to get jobs and settle down or go back to school if they wanted to.

The school building remained to house the lab, but for a while, Peter had wanted it to become a hospital for the people nearer to the Capitol. But then he had gotten sick, and proceedings for that had halted.

They walk down a staircase into a dingy basement, and Lucas waves the two guards off. "We're good from here," he says, pushing open a swinging pair of double doors labeled: 'TO LAB'.

Inside is a huge room, shaped as a big square. The lights are bright and fluorescent, and there's a huge white table shaped like an oval in the middle of the room. That's where Charles and Inesh are sitting, goggles on, hunched over a beaker of something clear. To the right of them was a rectangular table, one that looked a bit like a bar counter, with swivel stools scattered about the edge. There were papers and files on the tabletop, and Cameron recognized a familiar five-letter name across the top of some of the charts.

On the far wall was a big, long countertop, with a weird-looking refrigerator at the end. Cameron assumed, based on the burners and empty beakers, the antidotes were produced there.

Directly across the room from this main entrance was another door, this time with a turn handle and not the swinging ones they just entered through. A sign (clearly made by Lucas) read "TO PETER."

Lucas sees him looking. "That's where Peter's room is."

Cameron nods slowly, eyes stuck on the door. His heart is pounding and he doesn't know why. This was the first time in weeks he had been close to Peter; he was just on the other side of the wall. Cameron should be elated to be in the same general space as him, so why did he feel so nervous?

Cameron nudges Kiara. "Does Peter know all of us are here today?"

She glances at him, expression unreadable. Then she looks to the door. "I don't know. We should ask Charles."

As the words leave her mouth, the older doctor rises from his seat, clapping his hands together. "Ah, Mr. O'Connor and Miss Monroe," he puts his hand out, and Diana shakes it, then Cameron. "Welcome to the lab. If you wouldn't mind washing your hands and putting on a mask, please."

"Just Diana is fine, Charles," she says, waving off the formality as she follows Lucas and Kiara to the sinks. "We're more friends than coworkers now, I'd say."

Cameron smiles and nods as he straps a mask around his ears. "Please, call me Cameron. We're not totally strangers."

Charles smiles wide, and Cameron can understand why Peter likes him so much. "Well, Cameron and Diana it is, then." Just then, the tall, dark-haired doctor comes up behind him. Charles continues to speak as Cameron and Diana shake hands with him. "And you know Doctor Inesh Mahra. He's from Alynthia, and he traveled here... oh, about a few weeks ago."

"Feels like forever," Inesh says, smiling broadly. Cameron realizes the similarities between his showstopping grin and Lucas', and their matching accents, and he wonders if every public figure in Alynthia was trained to smile and speak the same way.

"Charles," Kiara begins, pointing to Peter's door as she shrugs on a white lab coat and gloves, "does Peter know Cameron and Diana are here today?"

Charles thinks for a moment. "I'm not entirely sure. *I* haven't said anything, but I don't know if Ruth may have mentioned it. She's in there with him now."

The others all nod, and Inesh claps Lucas on the shoulder. "Shall we take them around?" he asks. Cameron wonders just how much Inesh knew about them, and why he agreed to come here in the first place. He assumes he knows about Kiara, based on the way the two share a smile and Kiara seems to relax just by looking at him.

So, they wander about the lab, Cameron and Diana loitering in the back of the group as Lucas and Kiara (now dressed in the same white coats as the older men) explain the various charts, instruments, and beakers. They explain that the four of them (five, counting Ruth) were all suited up and scrubbed in every day, and they kept careful track of their symptoms. Visitors, however, had to wear masks as added protection. After about thirty minutes, they all sit around the center table, a pile of charts sitting in the middle of the tabletop. Before anyone speaks, Peter's door opens.

Cameron's heart leaps into his throat, and for a split second, he imagines it will be Peter entering the room, healthy and smiling.

But instead, a big, dark-skinned woman enters, with a familiar golden puppy nipping at her heels.

"This dog is going to be the death of me, Charles, I swear." She sees the teenagers and grins widely. "Oh, hello, you four! I see we have new faces today," Diana and Cameron rise from their seats, crossing over to greet her. Instead of shaking their hands, though, Ruth stretches on her tiptoes to give Cameron a friendly kiss on the cheek. She then repeats the gesture for Diana. She bends down and scoops up Finnigan, passing the wiggling puppy to Cameron. "Good to see you again, dear. I believe this little rascal belongs to you."

Cameron can't fight the grin on his face as he kisses Finnigan's head. "He does. Thanks for bringing him over."

Ruth waves her hand dismissively as she sits at the table next to Charles. Cameron sets Finnigan on the ground and follows suit, and Diana goes back to her seat as well. "It was the least I could do. Peter was elated."

Cameron just nods as the smile slips off his lips. But he doesn't have time to wallow before Charles pipes up. "Ruth, can we have this morning's symptom check, and then we'll get to brainstorming our next steps?"

Ruth nods, pulling out a clipboard. Cameron blinks, eyes getting wide – he hadn't even known she was carrying it. She clears her throat and flips to a page with a chart, although Cameron can't make out what's written. "Headache is worse than yesterday. He isn't as thirsty anymore, but he's still been steadily drinking water. He didn't eat today, but he managed a few crackers last night. He still claims he isn't hungry at all."

"Strange," Inesh mumbles. "That's what, day four he hasn't been hungry?"

"Day five," Ruth counters. "We redid the spirometry test, and his O_2 stats are the same, which isn't an improvement, but it's also not getting immediately worse. The oxygen is definitely helping his airways stay in the same state. His body aches are more sporadic now, also. Still mostly isolated around his operation spot."

"Could that just be a symptom of the operation? After all, it was only a few days ago." Lucas asks, all goofiness from earlier gone. Cameron notices Kiara is also looking serious, and he wonders if they heard these debriefs every day. "Do we think that will go away?"

Charles shakes his head. "On the contrary, I think it will spread. When I spoke to him last night, he said the biggest areas of pain were his head and his torso area. But then, he was holding a water glass, and he said his hand was starting to cramp up." He shakes his head again, expression turning businesslike but also slightly sad, as if a speck of emotion were threatening his seriosity. "I believe his joints are next, or his other muscles. His body is on autopilot, and it isn't used to such strain on two specific areas. So chances are, it will equilibrate that pain across the rest of his body." He pauses and thinks for a moment. "Like... when you fall very hard, you feel the reverberation of the impact everywhere, not only in the spot where you hit."

"A physical therapist, then," Kiara replies. "We need to get him rehabbed as soon as he can."

Cameron swallows hard. Diana looks just as confused as he feels, but Lucas and Kiara seem to be following along, if not actively participating. Ruth rubs her hands over her face and sighs. "It doesn't make any sense. We slowed it down with the operation, and we slowed it down by putting him on oxygen. But in all the other patients we've seen, they just... die. But that isn't happening here, thankfully, but it still makes me wonder why his body is acting differently."

Diana clears her throat, and all eyes turn to her. "Could it just be his age? You guys have trials for adults, but he had a reaction to that. And kids in the south are still infected because they don't have an antidote yet. Could he just slot into the children's age group?"

Charles shakes his head. "I don't think so. The physical aspects set them apart. Although he's lost weight, his physical features still keep him from that group, and his brain and organs are far more developed."

"So is there going to be something developed for teens?" Cameron asks.

"Well, that's the thing. There are essentially no more teen cases in Sector Five, because they all fit under the adults' group. Peter lost an incredible amount of weight, very fast, which left him stuck in this in-between."

Inesh sighs. "Was it just the amoxicillin? Could we develop that trial without it, or with something in its place?"

Charles nods slowly. "It's not a bad place to start. Inesh and Kiara, try to develop that drug with clarithromycin instead of the amoxicillin. Lucas, Diana, you and I will get in touch with Miss Oswald and get updated numbers on Sector Five. Cameron, Ruth, you guys are on Peter duty."

Cameron perks up, glancing across the table at Ruth while everyone else disperses. "Does that mean we get to see him?"

Ruth's brown eyes are full of pity when they meet Cameron's. "No, dear. Today's task is going back to your apartment and getting a few things for him. I requested you join me, as I figured you probably know him best."

Cameron feels a bit foolish, but he nods, rising from his seat and snapping his fingers. Finnigan perks up from his place under Cameron's stool, and he scuttles to his feet as Cameron and Ruth head for the door.

The two walk in awkward silence down the hall. Cameron has only interacted with Ruth a few times, and even then, he barely knew what to say. He felt very much on the outside of things.

"You went to school here, right?" Ruth asks finally.

Cameron clears his throat and nods. "Yup," he points to a passing dorm, number forty-one. "That was my room."

Ruth smiles. "I went here too, shockingly enough. Although the girls' dorms are on the other side of the building."

Cameron smiles softly. "That's cool. What's your sign?"

Ruth laughs out loud, and Cameron chuckles in response. "Sagittarius."

Cameron makes a dramatic disgusted face, and the nurse laughs again. "Joking, joking," Cameron says with a chuckle. "I don't think I've ever really been friends with a Sagittarius, besides Victoria."

She shakes her head in amazement. "It's still crazy to me that you kids are our leaders. Of course, I admire you greatly, and you're probably some of the smartest people I've met. It's good to work with you all, it makes you more human. I'm very lucky."

Cameron nods, although he doesn't really understand. *Was* she lucky to work with them, even under these circumstances? "We're lucky to know you," he replies as they reach the front doors.

Ruth smiles at him as they exit, the two bodyguards showing up out of nowhere. "I'll never get used to this," she mumbles, gesturing to the guards, "the way they just appear."

Cameron chuckles. "They were around the side of the building. It's an old trick."

They fall quiet again. Hayley pulls a black leash out of her jacket, handing it to Cameron. He attaches it to Finnigan's collar, and Ruth glances down at the dog. "It's a very nice collar, I noticed," she says, motioning to the puppy's slate blue leather collar. "The clasp is a nice touch."

Cameron smiles down at Finnigan, touched by the compliment. "Thank you. It was Peter's idea to get the name engraved." He pauses. "Will he be okay after seeing the dog? I didn't realize that it might do him more harm than good."

Ruth smiles kindly. "We took precautions. Trimmed his nails to keep him from scratching, and we were sure to keep him from licking Peter or breathing right in his face."

Cameron sighs in relief. "That's good. I'm sure he was really glad to see him."

They reach the apartment building a few minutes later, and the bodyguards leave, nodding farewell to the doormen stationed outside. "Welcome back, Secretary O'Connor," one of them says.

"Thank you, Kellan," Cameron replies, stepping back to allow them to pull the door open. He waves Ruth inside, pressing a button on the elevator keypad.

The group journeys up the elevator, and Ruth looks around in awe. "I knew it was fancy in here, but not this fancy."

Cameron studies her, one eyebrow raised. "Where have you been staying?"

She waves her hand. "Around. Charles and I have rooms in the schoolhouse, old dorms that were renovated for us to be extra close. And when Peter was at the Capitol, we had offices there too."

They reach the teenager's apartment, and Finnigan dodges between Cameron's legs, racing into the living room. Cameron laughs as he leaps onto the sofa. "Get down, Finn, or Diana is gonna be mad."

Ruth is hovering in the kitchen, and Cameron motions around with his hands. "Um, welcome to the house. I wish you were here under better circumstances, but we've already got a plan to have you and the doctors over for dinner sometime soon."

Ruth smiles. "That's very kind." She claps her hands together. "Now, where's Peter's room?"

Cameron extends a hand, motioning down the hall. "This way." They get to the door, and Cameron pushes it open. Finnigan, who had been trailing them the whole way, whines and sits, right in the doorway. "That's normal," Cameron explains at Ruth's concerned look. "Anyways, what do we need to get? Clothes, toiletries?"

"He has all of that already," Ruth says, stepping into the room and looking around, "and he wears the hospital gowns we provide, so he's all set for clothes."

"Right," Cameron mumbles, watching her walk around the room.

Peter's room was very big: there was a giant desk on one wall, next to the white sliding door that led to his walk-in closet. His bed was to the right of the bathroom door, and he had a huge, almost floor-to-ceiling window on the far wall. The walls next to the main door were covered in big white bookshelves, stark and bright against the navy paint on the other walls. Cameron had made sure nobody cleaned it up when Peter left, so it still felt lived in. A bed for Finnigan was nestled in the corner, a pair of sneakers were next to the nightstand, an empty glass sat on the desk. But the lights were off, the curtains were drawn, and the towels in the bathroom were neatly folded by housekeeping. Even Cameron couldn't keep it all together.

"He wanted something to read," Ruth says, running her hand across the white desk chair. She turns around to face Cameron, who's still hovering in the doorway. "Any suggestions?"

Cameron nods rapidly, entering the room and turning towards the tall bookshelves. "Did he say any specific genre?"

"Um, no."

Cameron chews his lip. "Hm. He likes this one, if he wants a fiction book," he says, standing on his tiptoes to pull a thick hardcover from the shelf. "Or, if he wants something educational, this is one of his favorites." He reaches across a bit, grabbing a book he's seen Peter read nearly every weekend. "It's about a history of American deforestation."

"That sounds amazingly boring."

"It is, trust me. He was reading this one before he left, though." He grabs a smaller paperback. "About the benefits of an agrarian economy."

"You would think this shelf belongs to a fifty-year-old man."

"And not an eighteen-year-old? Yeah, tell me about it. I only ever buy him fiction books. I'm trying to train the elderly out of him."

Cameron steps away from the bookshelf, turning to face Ruth. After a beat of silence, she smiles fondly at him. "You're good for him."

Cameron blushes despite himself. "Thank you."

"No, really. It's clear you two fit well together," she points towards the bathroom. "He wanted face wash, as well. He said you'd know where it was."

Cameron scrunches his nose as he heads for the bathroom. "He hasn't been able to wash his face at *all*?"

"Well, we gave him something, but he complained about it," she chuckles to herself. "He said it wasn't working, although that boy has the clearest skin I've ever seen."

Cameron laughs as he pulls open one of the vanity drawers. "Right? It's insane. When he's here, he washes his face twice a day. Even the girls aren't as on top of a skincare routine as he is."

Ruth accepts the toiletries from Cameron and sets everything on the bed. "Well, that's all he wanted. Anything else we should bring back?"

Cameron thinks for a moment, then nods. "It's in my room, though. I'll be back."

Cameron crosses the hall, pushing his own door open. He goes straight to his nightstand, grabbing a framed photo from next to his lamp and studying it with a small smile. Without a second thought, he returns to Ruth, who has left Peter's room and is packing the things in a bag at the counter. Cameron holds out the picture to her, and he watches her eyes well with tears as they travel over the photo.

"Oh, Cameron," she whispers. "Are you sure?"

"Positive," he replies. "It was on my desk at work, but I brought it here a few days ago. I want him to have it, though."

It was the picture of himself and Peter washing dishes, the one Ms. Miller had seen in his office a while ago. Cameron looks again, and wonders if Peter's smile will look the same as that when Cameron sees him again.

Ruth smiles at Cameron, and he can't help but smile back. She had the same effect on them that Lucas had. "He'll love it."

"I hope so. He's one of the people in the picture."

The woman laughs, and Cameron revels in the sound, a loud, booming laugh that seems to weave its way through the whole kitchen.

Ruth puts the picture in the bag and smiles at him. "Ready?"

"Ready," Cameron replies.

Part Forty-Seven: The Aries

Kiara

Kiara slams her head against the tabletop a little too hard. "Ow, shit."

Inesh laughs. "Language."

"Sorry," Kiara blushes despite herself.

They were at the side table in the lab, three beakers with different trials in front of them. The first was their control antidote, the trial that had given Peter the reaction. The second was the one with the clarithromycin, and the third was completely new, something Inesh had come up with on the spot. Kiara's job while Inesh was revamping the trials was to plug them into a simulation Charles had made, one that made mock symptom charts to show if the medicine would work. The simulation had been set up for Peter's statistics, and so far, it was taking *forever*. And, according to the computer screen in front of her, Kiara noticed that the clarithromycin trial wasn't working.

She waves Inesh to her side of the table, and he leans in, studying the screen. "Interesting," he mumbles, "so not only did the amoxicillin give him a reaction, there was something *else* in the medicine that wasn't working."

"So even if he didn't have the reaction, it wouldn't have worked?"

"Exactly." He crosses back to the beakers, bending down so his dark eyes were level with the middle one. "I think this new one might work. Plug it in."

So Kiara does, and the two watch the red line climb higher and higher. "This is good, right? Incline is good."

"Incline is great," Inesh whispers.

The line continues to climb. If it hits the end of the screen, that means the trial will work. Kiara gasps: they're an inch away. But then the line halts, centimeters from the end of the screen.

"No," Kiara whispers, "what happened?"

"Look," Inesh says, pointing at the line. A blue dot appears at the end of the line, and the red incline blinks blue once, twice, and then disappears. "I can't believe it."

"What was that?" Kiara asks, turning to the man. "The blue dot?"

"I... I don't know," Inesh admits, shaking his head. His eyes are still fixated on the now-blank screen. "I've never seen that before."

"Charles?" Kiara asks, waving the doctor over. "We found something."

Charles listens while Kiara and Inesh explain, and when they're done, the Gemini man is seated, head in his hands. He looks up to speak. "That makes no sense. We've not seen this at all until now?"

"Never," Inesh affirms. "This software is relatively new, but even still, the other trials we've tested on it have looked normal."

"And what happens when those don't work?"

"They just disappear. They stop before the end of the screen and disappear. But never have we seen this blue thing."

"What did the blue look like?"

Kiara juts in then. "Like a dot. Right at the end of the line. Then, the whole line turned blue, blinked a few times, then the screen went blank."

Charles sighs. "What could it mean?"

The other four come over then. "What's happening here?" Diana asks.

Kiara explains the whole situation, and Lucas runs a hand through his dark hair, motioning to the center table. "Group meeting?"

Forty-five minutes later, Ruth has left to be with Peter and the other six haven't come to any sort of conclusion. "Could it be another disease?" Lucas asks.

Both doctors shake their heads. "No," Inesh replies, "we would've seen any other illnesses come up on his weekly scans. If he were sick with something else on top of this, he'd have shown symptoms by now."

"And it isn't just a computer glitch?" Diana counters.

"This software has been used this whole time. Not once has there been a glitch like this," Charles says.

They all fall silent, and Kiara sighs. "Cam, any ideas?"

All eyes turn to Cameron, who is sitting at the head of the table, thumbnail between his teeth. He looks up, shrugging one shoulder. "I think we ask Peter."

Charles' head snaps up at the other end of the table, and he shakes his head. "No. He's going to get someone else sick."

"No, he won't. Not if we prop that door open and he yells to us."

"He can't, not with the state his throat is in. He's had a voice like nails on a chalkboard for weeks, on the rare occasion he speaks to us at all."

Cameron sighs. "I don't want him to get hurt. That's the last thing I want. But nobody thus far has asked him if he has any ideas, right? It's his own body, so what harm could it do?"

Diana nods. "I agree. I know we're the two new kids here, but I don't know why it would hurt to talk to him."

Inesh nudges Charles. "It could work. Maybe he'll know something we don't."

"I'm his doctor."

Cameron shrugs. "I'm his boyfriend. We could go around like this all day."

Charles looks taken aback, but Lucas interjects before anything more can be said. "Charles, I don't think it'll hurt. Masks and hazmat suits, like the ones the guards used, right?"

Charles pauses, propping his elbow on the table and pressing a fist against his mouth. After a moment, he looks up at Cameron and smirks. "You'd make a great doctor, kid. Okay, I'm in. Everybody suit up."

Everyone rises from their seats, heading to an armoire against the wall Charles rifles through, pushing masks and suits into everyone's arms. He, Inesh, and Ruth find theirs on hooks, which they put on with a practiced normalcy. They don them over their clothes, and when they're dressed and ready, they turn to Charles, who has a grim expression on his face.

Without another word, Charles heads to Peter's door, pushing it open as far as it will go.

Part Forty-Eight: The Cancer

Peter

Peter barely has time to wonder what's going on when his door is flung open.

Ruth looks over to the open door, eyebrows raised.

"Good afternoon, son," Charles says. Peter can't see past him; he's blocking the doorway. He's smiling like a child, and he speaks as he props the door open. "Propping this here."

The doctor steps out of the way and all the air is knocked from Peter's lungs.

His doctors, Kiara, Lucas, Diana, and Cameron. They're *all there*.

Peter blinks rapidly to keep himself from crying. They're all there, standing in a group, smiling at him.

The first thought he has is that he died and this is what heaven is.

Then he thinks that if this is heaven, it *definitely* wouldn't look like the lab.

Peter looks at Cameron. He's the only one not smiling, instead, he looks almost sad. Peter wonders why.

Part Forty-Nine: The Scorpio

Cameron

Cameron took one look at him and couldn't smile.

There he was, in a hospital gown, with an IV stuck in his arm, and oxygen tubes in both nostrils.

His heart is pounding. But Peter's face breaks into a smile.

Quietly he coughs, waving his IV-free hand.

Diana, who's standing next to Cameron, gasps quietly. Cameron was just as taken aback by how horrible he looked.

"Hey, Peter," Inesh says, when he looks around and realizes all four teens are stunned into silence.

Before anyone can continue, Diana blurts out: "Does your throat hurt?"

Peter doesn't grimace, doesn't get upset. Instead, he smiles gently and nods.

Kiara leans over and whispers to Charles. "Will it stay like that forever?"

Charles shrugs. "Probably not. It's just the lingering virus, so once it's gone, the symptoms will go away too."

"Peter, we had a few questions," Inesh says, breaking Cameron from his stupor, "so let's get to work."

Part Fifty: The Cancer

Peter

After the doctors explain, Peter thinks for a minute. "*My help?*" he rasps.

Inesh and Charles nod simultaneously. "Do you have any ideas about what it could be?" Inesh asks.

Charles looks down at his notes. "The dot *and* the line, and why they disappeared."

Peter can't help but feel a little excited. It felt *good* to think critically again. It was a distraction from his illness, and it made him feel like he was actually doing something.

Charles crosses to the door, beginning to close it. "Wait!" someone hollers.

Everyone looks at Cameron, even Peter, who folds his hands nervously in his sheets.

God, Peter thinks as he stares at the ginger-haired boy. He grew, somehow. His jaw is more defined, his freckles are so prominent Peter can see them from thirty feet away, and his eyes are bright and alert, despite the dark circles that rest beneath them. He looks silly in a baggy hazmat suit.

"What is it?" Charles asks.

Cameron's eyes are still stuck on Peter's and the two look at each other for a long time. Finally, Cameron speaks without breaking eye contact. "Can we not... talk to him?"

Charles tilts his head. "I don't know-"

Ruth interjects from her seat at the table in Peter's room. "Come on, Charles. They'll keep their distance."

Charles looks at the teens, who all nod rapidly. "Fine. Ruth, out of there, you guys will go one-by-one. Ten minutes each, okay?"

They all nod again.

"Okay. Kiara first."

Everyone clears out, except Kiara, who pulls out a stool from the table. She grins at Peter. "Long time no see, my friend."

"Hi," Peter manages, leaning back against his pillows.

"I miss you! How have you been?"

Peter just shrugs.

Kiara rolls her eyes. "Thank you, genius."

Peter chuckles, then his expression turns serious as he gazes at one of his closest friends. "Thank you for the work."

Kiara smiles softly, shrugging. "I wouldn't do it for anybody else." She pauses, then takes a deep breath. "Peter, I wanted to tell you that... I'm Henderson's daughter. Lucas and I are cousins."

Peter quirks an eyebrow. "Seriously?"

Kiara laughs despite herself, leaning forward in her chair. "Why wouldn't I be serious?"

He shakes his head. "Are you okay?"

"I will be, eventually."

He shrugs, frowning. "I'm sorry." He's interrupted by a fit of coughing, which he buries in his handkerchief.

They fall quiet, and Kiara shakes her head with a sigh. "*I'm* sorry, Peter. I'm so sorry."

Just then, Charles ducks his head in. "Alright, Miss Kiara. Lucas is coming in."

Kiara nods, then turns to Peter, throwing him a little salute. "See you soon, Peter. Stay safe."

Peter smiles, forcing out a few more words. "I'm proud of you, Kiara."

"Me too, Peter."

"I don't really know what to say, Peter," Diana mumbles. She's looking up at him from under those long lashes, and Peter fidgets uncomfortably. "I miss you."

Peter nods. "You too."

Diana smiles, and Peter doesn't know whether to be happy or upset with how relieved she looks. "Okay."

The two sit in silence, and they let one minute pass, then two.

Peter shakes his head, realizing with a start that he *has* to speak. "Diana?" he continues as best he can when she looks at him. "I... I might not get better."

She raises an eyebrow. "Okay?"

"I think that... I think that I couldn't have asked for a better best friend. And really, I'm indebted to you more than anyone, because you were the one who found me. You had to grow up too fast because of me, and I'm sorry for that."

"Peter-"

He isn't finished, fighting against a wave of either coughing or vomit. "And don't ever think I love you any less because of Cameron, because every day I wake up and I think to myself 'thank God I exist at the same time she does and thank God I'm the one who gets to be her best friend.'" His voice cracks and he struggles to battle an onslaught of tears. He lets the coughing take over, and he spits some bloody bile into his handkerchief.

Diana raises an eyebrow, even though her green eyes are teary. "Are you done?"

He nods, wiping at his chin. His IV rattles with the movement, and Diana sighs. "Peter, let me be quite honest with you. I've never missed anyone more than I miss you, even right now. But I know that if I let myself stop hoping, I'll lose sight of what really matters: *you*. Because when we get all sucked into this spiral of grief, we're only focused on how we feel, and how awful it is to feel that way. So I think of you, and helping you, and the day when I can hug you again, because that's what's going to allow us to go on the way we should be."

Peter pauses, looking deep into her green eyes. He can't imagine what she must see: cracked, bloody lips and pale skin? Dark circles under dim eyes?

It doesn't matter, because Diana smiles at him anyway.

It's the moment Peter has been dreading and or waiting for.

Cameron enters the lab with Charles, letting the door swing shut behind him. He first looks at the stool in the center of the room, and then his gaze travels upwards, locking eyes with Peter.

"Hi," Cameron mumbles. Before Peter can reply- before Charles has even left the room- Peter begins to retch, and his doctor rushes into the room.

"What's happening-?" Cameron starts.

Charles gives Cameron an apologetic look and he speaks over Peter's choking coughs. "Sorry, son. But Ruth will escort you out."

As if summoned by Charles, Ruth comes in, gently taking Cameron's arm. "Wait," Cameron starts frantically, "I didn't get to talk to him! Charles, I need to talk to-"

Ruth's interruption is a gentle whisper. "Honey, Peter needs medical attention."

Cameron bites his lip, a small wrinkle appearing in between his brows as he watches Peter's body shake with every breathy cough. "I love you, Peter," he says finally.

Peter swallows a gasp, and he doesn't know why he's so surprised. A million emotions rush through him at once, and he can only decipher a few amongst all his raging, angry sickness. But the thought that makes his heart pound the fastest is that for some reason, it didn't feel normal anymore to hear Cameron say those words.

As Ruth guides Cameron away, Peter wonders if it's the lights that make Cameron look like he's crying.

Part Fifty-One: The Taurus

Diana

The next day, Cameron and Diana were back in the Capitol.

"Lunch in my office today?" Diana asks as Cameron walks past her open door. He shoots her a nod and continues on as she frowns. Since he was practically dragged from the lab yesterday, Cameron had been an almost impenetrable wall of sadness.

"Knock knock," Barbara says as she pokes her head in the door, "can I sit for a second?"

"Yes, ma'am," Diana says, motioning to one of the big chairs beside the door. Oswald sits, fingers tapping the side of the chair nervously, and doesn't speak. Diana clears her throat. "What's up?"

Barbara's eyes widen considerably, and she quirks an eyebrow, jutting her chin towards the door.

"What is it?" Diana asks.

She clears her throat dramatically, eyes widening again. Her lips press into a tight line, and Diana realizes she's hinting at something. She sits completely still and listens.

Cameron's voice is drifting down the hall, and Diana assumes he's talking to Ms. Miller on the phone. Diana glances back at Barbara. "Cameron?" she whispers. Barbara nods. "What about him?"

She finally speaks, her voice a demanding whisper. "We need to leave. Just you and me. And Cameron cannot know."

Diana swallows, blood pounding in her ears. "Why?" she whispers dryly.

Barbara glances back at her, and Diana knows instantly before she even says it. "Peter."

"Oh, my God."

Barbara jerks her head towards the door. "Go tell him you have a meeting with me and can't do lunch. And you'll see him back at the apartment tonight."

Diana swallows, throat and mouth drier than sand. She rises from her seat, and as she reaches the doorway, Barbara grabs her wrist. Diana looks down at her, and her heart leaps into her throat as she takes in the old woman's terrified expression. "Hurry, Diana."

Diana reaches Cameron's door, takes a deep breath, and plasters on a smile. She steps into view and Cameron looks up.

He's sitting at his desk, phone receiver to his ear. He sees Diana and holds up a finger. "Hey, Hayley, I'm gonna have to call you back. Thanks." He hangs up and looks at Diana. "What's up?"

A cold rush of fear rises through Diana, but she forces herself to swallow. "Oh, nothing. But Barbara just came in, and she needs me for a meeting. So I can't do lunch."

Cameron raises an eyebrow. "What's the meeting? Does she need me, too?"

"No – um, no. It's, um..." her eyes lock on something on Cameron's desk. "It's about America's agrarian economy."

He doesn't look any less skeptical. As he studies Diana, she can practically feel the clock ticking. "...Okay. But rain date for tomorrow?"

Diana nods rapidly. "Yes, yes. Of course."

As she leaves and heads back to her office, she sees Barbara at the top of the stairs. They begin the descent together, walking in hurried, agitated silence. Finally,

Diana looks at Barbara, green eyes filled with concern and brows knit together. "Barbara?"

"Yes," the woman answers flatly, eyes frozen straight ahead.

Diana swallows, wringing her hands together. "What's going on?"

Part Fifty-Two: The Libra

Lucas

Lucas and Kiara are disrupted from their work when a million things happen all at once.

The lights go out in the lab.

"What-?" Kiara starts.

The door to Peter's room slams open, and Charles rushes out, eyes wide and breathing heavily.

"Charles-" Lucas begins.

Then, a blaring alarm goes off as hot white floodlights *clank* on.

Lucas and Kiara let out twin shouts and cover their ears as Charles begins barking orders. "Lucas, find Inesh. Kiara, find our surgical supplies."

"Charles, what's going on?"

The man finally looks at the prince, and his eyes are swimming with fear, sadness, and agitation. He takes a deep breath before answering. "It's Peter. He passed out, and before Ruth and I could do anything, he started to flatline. We've got a weak heartbeat now, but it's all or nothing. He's officially in stage three."

Kiara gasps. "Is he going to be okay?"

Charles raises an eyebrow and shakes his head. "Not if we don't operate now. Move."

The two teens break away from each other. Kiara begins rifling through the supplies on the tabletop, and Lucas disappears up the stairs, sprinting down the abandoned schoolhouse hallway, shouting for Inesh.

"Inesh! Inesh, help!"

The doctor emerges from a dorm room, in sweatpants and a gray shirt. He's wearing thick-framed glasses and his hair is tousled from sleep. "Lucas? What's going on?"

"It's Peter, he flatlined, and- and I don't know, but we need you. Now."

Inesh's eyes widen, and both of them tear down the hall back the way Lucas came.

They reach the lab once more and see that Charles has moved Peter to the Operating Room, and he and Ruth were now prepping for the operation in the lab. Kiara is passing Charles his tools, and Ruth is scrubbing in at the sink against the wall.

"Kiara, those gloves and goggles, please," Inesh says, putting out a hand.

Kiara passes him the items from the neat array on the tabletop, and Inesh pulls them on, stepping in between Ruth and Charles. "I've got it from here, Kiara. Thank you." He turns to Charles. "What's going on?"

The two begin to converse as two more people enter the lab: Diana and Barbara.

Lucas races over. Diana's eyes are frantic and full of tears, and he takes her hand, forcing her to look at him. She looks frightened, too. "What's happening?"

"We're not sure. He just passed out, and then his heart stopped. They got his heartbeat going again but now they're getting ready to operate. I don't know anything else."

Diana swallows and squeezes Lucas' hand, eyes stuck on the doctors. "What can I do?"

Barbara has moved to talk to Kiara, and Lucas glances down at Diana. "Cameron doesn't know?"

She shakes her head. "No."

Lucas nods as Kiara and Babara come over. Ruth looks at them with guilt in her eyes and speaks from the foot of the table. "I'm so sorry, you three. But right now, we need to get to work, so the best thing for you all to do is go home."

"What do we tell Cam?" Kiara asks.

Ruth chews her lip. "The truth. But you can't let him come here."

"And what exactly is the truth?" Diana asks, tone more accusatory than she probably intended.

Ruth sighs. "I don't know what they're operating on right now. Peter mumbled something before he fell under, but only Charles heard. Then he asked me to pull the alarm." She sighs sadly. "The most probable outcome is death."

"No," Diana whispers, voice breaking. Her hands clench Lucas' shirt, like she's clinging to a life raft.

"There has to be something else we can do," Lucas says, grabbing Diana's arms to brace himself as much as her.

"There isn't. In this field, you do your best, but you lose people sometimes anyways." She shakes her head, tears beginning to spill down her round cheeks. "And Peter may be one of them."

They're all quiet, until Barbara waves them to the door. "Let's go. We aren't helping anybody by standing here. You all need to go home."

"No, I have to stay with him," Diana mumbles, but she doesn't protest when Lucas begins to pull her towards the door.

They reach the apartment after a slow walk in silence. Barbara leaves them a floor below theirs, hugging them all in turn. When they get to their floor, Cameron is waiting at the counter.

"Hey! How was your...?" he trails off when he sees Kiara and Lucas, still in their lab coats, behind Diana. "What's wrong, guys?"

Diana opens her mouth, but nothing comes out except a sob. Lucas grabs her arms, guiding her to a seat and standing next to her, rubbing her back. Kiara walks around the counter, across from Cameron, taking his hands in hers. "Cam, something bad happened."

"What?" he whispers, expression almost crazed. His eyes flick from one person to the next, and his chest hitches. "Is it Peter?"

Kiara just grimaces. Cameron rises from his seat, heading for the door. "I have to go, I have to see him-"

"No, Cam, you can't, he's in surgery," Kiara says.

Lucas strides quickly to the elevator, grabbing Cameron by the arms. The two push against one another for a moment, matched in strength, until Cameron finally relents. "Kiara, tell me what's going on. Why is Diana crying?"

"Because he passed out, and now he's in surgery."

Cameron stands there, eyes frozen on his friend. His gaze is filled with a flash of anger here, a glimmer of tears there, and then he pulls himself from Lucas' grip and sinks to the floor, a broken cry escaping his throat.

The others rush to comfort him, and in a moment, all four friends are on the ground, arms around one another and yet missing a vital piece.

Part Fifty-Three: The Cancer

Peter

Peter is sitting in bed, with Ruth and Charles at the table in his room, keeping him company. Ruth is laughing at something Charles said, and Peter just likes to watch them.

He's glad they're sort of together. It gave him some odd sense of achievement, knowing his ailment played a part in their matchmaking.

Suddenly, he swallows. His breath stutters, and he grips the bedsheets. Ruth looks over when he begins to gasp. "Peter, what's happening?"

He can't answer; his vision is cloudy. He can't breathe, he can't breathe. *His eyes lock onto Charles, who is standing over him, gaze frantic.*

Only one sentence comes to mind, one he had been turning over in his head all day, and Peter pushes it from his lips with the last breath of air he has.

"My power."

His world goes dark.

Peter wakes with a gasp, sitting up with a hand over his throat. He's breathing so hard he gags, retching onto the ground, but nothing comes up. His hands press against the warm cement beneath him.

He's sitting on cement.

He rises to his feet, feeling suddenly energized, a feeling that had been foreign for so long. Looking around his surroundings, he realizes he's in the Plaza; there's the schoolhouse, the Capitol, their apartment building.

It's deserted, even though the sky is clear and the sun is directly over his head. A cool gust of wind blows through his hair, and he turns around as a wisping shout drifts through the air.

He gasps when he sees the scene in front of him. It's almost a hologram: him and Kiara, in the woods. He recognizes Sector Five's huge, reaching magnolia trees behind them, shimmering in the illusion.

"I think you should shoot at me," Kiara says.

Peter – or his hologram – looks perplexed. But he doesn't answer, and after a moment, he fires a blue ball from the palm of his hand towards her. It swallows her up, and before the real Peter can blink, the whole picture disappears.

He doesn't have time to process before he hears more talking. Well, this time, it's more like shouting: the hologram appears, and Peter cringes.

It's the Battle of Zodiacs. Peter sees himself, Kiara, and Maya fighting; he knows what's coming, he can tell by the immediate tightness in his chest.

A guard turns towards Maya, and the image seems to zero in on Peter. His dark curls are falling over his forehead, sweat is beading on his brow, and a ball of blue border material is sitting in his palm. He grits his teeth, aims, and the ball flies towards Maya, swallowing her up in a protective shield. Real Peter barely has time to register the relief on Picture-Peter's face before the whole image fades again.

His body feels warm and tingly and somehow, he knows the next image that's coming before it appears to his left. He turns to see himself and a holographic Cameron, kneeling by a border source in the woods.

Peter is standing away from him, and Cameron is crouched by the base of a tree. They don't speak, but the two boys in the image share an intimate look before Cameron presses a hand against the border wall. It flies from the ground into a compact ball in Peter's hand, and Peter's holographic twin smiles a big, broad smile at Cameron before the image fades away.

Peter is left alone now, standing in the center of the vast Plaza. He feels like he should call out, but he knows somehow that nobody would answer. Then, he hears a whisper, a familiar voice in his ear.

Cameron.

"Peter, look," Peter's hands rise up, at a ninety-degree angle to his waist, and he looks down at his palms. He has two clumps of the border material, round and glowing, sitting in his hands. Cameron's voice returns. "You know what to do, right?"

"What?" Peter whispers. His voice is normal again.

Then he sees it.

Standing on the outskirts of the Plaza, by all the buildings, in a big half-circle, are people. But they aren't *really* people, they're shaped like them and instead gray, half-formed shells of humans.

They have no faces, but Peter decides that's the second scariest thing. The first is that they're all marching towards him, mechanically, militarily.

"You know what to do," Cameron says again, his voice fading into the distance.

Peter realizes he *does* know what to do. He raises his hands, and as the figures get close, he releases the projectiles with a scream of exertion, pushing all his strength into hitting one after the other. As soon as the border walls leave his hands, more appear in their place. But more people keep coming, too, and he can't hold them all off. There are too many people, only one Peter, and he has no one to help.

He continues to throw projectiles as they converge on him, reaching towards his throat and legs and arms.

"No!" Peter screams as he's shoved to the pavement by somebody, by something. He has a fleeting thought that he might die, and his whole body is paralyzed with fear. "Please!"

Just as a fist closes around his throat and Peter's vision begins to go black, a girl's voice ricochets through his head.

"It's okay, Peter," Diana whispers. "You can go now."

So he does.

Part Fifty-Four: The Scorpio

Cameron

Cameron, Lucas, Diana, and Kiara are sitting on the couch.

Nobody speaks, and they're all apart from one another, even Diana and Lucas. Lucas's leg is bouncing up and down, Diana's thumbnail is between her teeth, Kiara's head is in her hands, and Cameron is staring straight ahead, at the empty fireplace.

For some reason, before this disaster of a day, Cameron had been good at processing his thoughts about Peter. He thought rationally, or rationally *enough*, and most of the questions he asked himself he was able to answer. But now, only one question was boomeranging back and forth in his brain, and as soon as he finished asking it, it started over again, leaving him unable to answer.

What do you do now?

They were all in separate stages of grief at this point. Diana was in denial: she kept shaking her head, mumbling contradictions to herself as if that would bring him back. Kiara was angry: Cameron could read it in her creased eyebrows, the flashes of madness in her dark eyes. Lucas was unreadable to Cameron, but he could see the prince's eyes occasionally well with tears. And Cameron was just a mess.

Often, Cameron asked himself what Peter was to him. Was he just his boyfriend? No, Peter was more than that. He was his second half, a person so much better than him who, by some twist of fate, was sent to be with Cameron, to keep him upright, keep him whole.

So what would he *do?*

They had been sitting for an hour. In the same spots, in the same positions. No call had come through, and Cameron didn't know if he wanted it to or not.

Diana clears her throat. When she speaks, her voice is watery. "Should we call Ruth and ask?"

Lucas shakes his head. "She's probably busy. I'd assume he's still in the operating room."

Cameron feels bile rise in his throat, but he swallows it down, tears pricking at the corner of his eyes. Kiara glances at him, frowning. "Cam, why don't you go rest? We'll wake you with any news."

Cameron nods numbly, standing and walking down the hall without another word to anybody. He gets to his room, slips under the covers, and is asleep before his head hits the pillow.

He's woken up however later by Diana. His eyes open slowly, and they adjust to the others standing over his bed. "Hey, Cam," Diana whispers. "Ruth called."

Cameron's heart leaps into his throat. "What did she say?" he whispers.

One agonizing moment passes as Kiara and Diana share a look. Then, Diana looks back at Cameron and her face splits into a grin. "He's gonna be okay. He's alive, and in recovery."

Cameron sighs, then smiles as relief floods through him. He flops back against his pillows, grabbing the one to his right and pressing it over his face. He screams into it, letting all his loose emotions out into the fabric.

Diana laughs and sits on the edge of the bed, putting her hand on Cameron's leg. "But there's something else." The smile slips off her face, and

Cameron's heart begins to pound again. "Ruth said they were about to lose him. She says... she says even Inesh was about to give up, but then Charles remembered something Peter said to him before he passed out."

"'My power'," Lucas mumbles, interrupting the story.

Diana nods. "Charles wondered why Peter warned him about his power, and then it hit him. The power was what was blocking the trials. That's why the line turned *blue* and disappeared."

Cameron's mouth falls open slowly, and he huffs out a disbelieving breath. "His own power was killing him."

Diana nods. "They extracted it. He flatlined again, but they revived him. About twenty minutes later, he woke up."

"And is he okay?"

Kiara barks out a laugh. "It's Peter. He's the strongest person you know, Cam. He's going to be okay eventually."

"He needs lots of physical therapy and a few more weeks of antidote testing," Diana smiles softly. "But now that the power is gone, they're hopeful something will work."

Cameron smiles as the image of a healing Peter pops into his brain. "Thank God," he pauses. "Does this mean he can come home?"

Lucas shakes his head. "In a few weeks, if he's feeling better. He'll be continuously monitored and tested."

"Like they did with us," Kiara adds.

"Wow," Cameron says. He's happier than he's been in a while, he realizes. "I... I can't believe it."

Diana leans in, and Cameron accepts her hug. "We'll leave you to rest more." She lowers her voice to a whisper. "He's still with us, Cameron."

The three leave, and Cameron leans against the headboard, unable to fight the hope blooming in his chest.

Part Fifty-Five: The Cancer

Peter

Peter has been sitting in bed day after day after day, staring at nothing.

He felt empty.

What was he without his power? What was he even worth?

He knew he sounded dramatic, or ungrateful. But he couldn't help it. He had been relieved for a little while, but then Charles had told Peter what they had done to save him when he eventually came to.

He could only think about the Battle of Zodiacs. He knew for a fact he wouldn't have survived without his power, and the crazy thing was that so many other people wouldn't have survived either. One of his fondest memories was when he saved a civilian, in the midst of the battle. He hadn't been close enough to help, and he had thrown a shield to the guard the girl had been fighting, blocking her from harm.

It hadn't been a revelation. It was only a few seconds. But the look of relief, then happiness, that had bloomed on her face was enough for Peter.

And he'd never be able to do that again.

He remembered how good it had felt to train with Cameron. And the moment they had shared when they realized they could work together. But now he couldn't.

He couldn't, he couldn't, he couldn't. He had lost a part of himself against his will, and he could never get it back.

He had thought maybe they could re-inject the power. That's how they gave it to the next heirs, right?

But Inesh had studied the vial with the blue liquid for less than five minutes and declared it contaminated. And Charles told Peter a little while later it was destroyed.

Peter felt bad now for not responding when Charles had said that, but before he hadn't. In fact, he hadn't spoken to anyone for a while. He could go home tomorrow, after three weeks of physical therapy and monitoring and daily conversations with Inesh, and he hadn't yet thought about what he would say to the others.

He sighs and pulls the blanket up a little further. He should probably sleep; he was leaving early the next morning.

His mind wanders to Ruth and Charles. Would they stay in the Capitol? Or in America, at least? He knew for a fact Inesh was probably leaving. Peter would miss him too, but he really couldn't stand the thought of not seeing Ruth and Charles.

Peter sniffles as his eyes fill with tears. He doesn't know why he's *sad*. He should be elated, all packed and ready to get out of here, not dragging his feet and crying about leaving a hospital room.

But the people who had practically become his parents were leaving him. The only gift that made him important was gone.

He's crying harder now, into his pillow like some heartbroken princess. His nose is running and his eyes sting, but the floodgates are open: he hasn't cried like this since Maya died.

Someone knocks on the door and then pokes their head in. "Hi, Peter," Inesh mumbles in that posh accent of his.

"Hi," Peter replies. His voice did feel better.

He'd been meeting with Inesh every afternoon for therapy, and Inesh often found him in a state like this one.

"Why are we crying?" Inesh asks as he sits at the now-cleaned table in the room.

"I'm going to miss Ruth and Charles."

Inesh nods. "Are you excited to go home? You've spent a very long time in this lab."

Peter shrugs a little. "I am. I don't understand why I feel so..."

"Horrible?"

"Yeah."

The doctor readjusts and discards his notepad on the tabletop. He'd stopped taking notes after their first few sessions. "It might be to do with the unfamiliarity of the thing, Peter. You've been here while life has continued outside, and you know now that you won't be the same Peter you were when you were diagnosed."

Peter nods, wiping again at his eyes. "What if I'm never the same Peter again?"

"You might not be. But that isn't a bad thing. You've lost things, like your power, but you've kept all the important stuff that makes you *you*."

Peter sniffles. "I feel like I'm nothing without my power."

Inesh thinks for a moment. "When you closed this school to build a hospital, did you use your power?"

"No?"

"When you traveled to Sector Five to bring hope and help to those patients, did you use your power for that?"

Peter understands the game they're playing. "No, I didn't."

"Peter Simon, Secretary of Education, doesn't need his power to make him important or special. For a while it was just an added bonus," Inesh says with a wink.

Peter can't help but give him a sad smile in return. "I guess you're right."

"It'll take a while to heal from this, mentally and physically," Inesh says as he rises, "but heal you will, my friend. You've already made a splendid start."

Peter nods. "Thank you, Inesh."

The man smiles, and Peter can't help but feel a pang as he thinks of him leaving, too. "Don't thank me. I'm going to sign my paperwork and get you out of here, back to the life that wants and needs you. Don't forget about your physical therapy and try to remember how strong you are, please." He leaves with a wave and a sparkling grin.

After a long few minutes of running through his hand exercises, he yawns. His cheeks are numb and puffy; his vision is blurry. But he's also tired.

Peter's hazel eyes flutter closed, as aching sorrow makes way for sleep.

Part Fifty-Six: The Scorpio

Cameron

Cameron hasn't felt this way in forever.

Peter was coming home today, after four weeks of physical therapy and staying all cooped up in that hospital room.

And Cameron wanted to be ready for him. So he had been cleaning the house all day, flitting around nervously.

"Cameron, relax," Kiara says as she walks into the kitchen, seeing the ginger-haired boy aggressively washing the countertops. "He isn't the King of Alynthia."

"And thank God for that," Lucas mumbles, entering behind her. Diana is hot on his heels, and she just smiles softly. Cameron knew she was worried too, but she certainly wasn't showing it as outwardly as Cameron was.

"I just don't know what he wants when he gets back," Cameron says, tossing the dishrag onto the countertop in mild frustration. "Like, what am I even supposed to do?"

The three sit at the counter almost simultaneously, as if they were waiting for him to ask. "Well, he'll probably want to rest," Kiara says. "Maybe a bath, a nap?"

Lucas nods. "That's what I'd want if I were him."

"And we've all got the day off, so we'll be here if he needs anything," Diana says. She takes Cameron's hands as he leans against the counter. "But remember, they took his power away. He's probably going to be upset about that, and he'll probably take a while to readjust."

Cameron's heart pangs. He had been trying for weeks to put that little detail out of his mind. "Right."

Diana taps Lucas on the shoulder. "But I think it's a good idea if he sees you first. So, Lucas and I will go get lunch."

Kiara pushes away from the counter. "And I have a meeting with Inesh, a little final therapy session. So I'm out too."

Cameron nods, heart hammering. Was he... nervous to be left alone with Peter? "Okay. But you'll be back soon, right?"

Lucas shrugs. "Couple hours."

Cameron just nods as they rise and put their shoes on, chatting to one another. The three exit with gentle goodbyes, but Cameron barely hears them.

He decides that he'll tidy up his room, since it's the only part of the house he hasn't tackled yet. He makes the bed, ignoring the way his hands shake. Then he cleans off his desk, pushing papers and empty pens to the trash and notebooks or stuffed files to the side.

The elevator dings and he almost has a heart attack.

Taking a few deep breaths to steel himself, Cameron heads down the hall.

And there he is.

He's standing with the help of a cane, which is shockingly the first thing Cameron notices. Peter is looking around as if he's never seen the place before, although his mouth is pressed in a tight line. His hair had gotten longer and remained untrimmed, but Cameron thinks it suits him.

"Hi," Cameron says gently.

Peter's hazel eyes find Cameron's, and his lip quivers. "Hi."

Then he bursts into tears.

Cameron crosses slowly to him, as if trying not to spook an animal. Gently, softly, he wraps his arms around Peter's shoulders. "Hey, shh. It's okay."

Peter doesn't reply, just curls further into Cameron, putting his weight onto Cameron's body. Weakly, his free arm comes up around Cameron's waist and he buries his face in Cameron's chest.

Cameron recalls something Kiara said, and he leans down to whisper in Peter's ear. "Hey, do you want me to run you a bath? Just to relax a bit?"

Peter sniffles and nods.

"Okay. Come on," Cameron leads them down the hall, into his room. They enter the bathroom, and Cameron turns on the bath, kneeling down and running his fingers under the water. When it's warm enough, he rises, turning to Peter, who's watching him intently. Cameron wonders how that works: his eyes are alert, but the rest of his body is almost slow motion, like he was rusting at the joints.

He turns and grabs a towel off the shelf as Peter begins to remove his clothing, starting with his shirt. Cameron turns around and gasps before he can stop himself.

Peter's chest and stomach are covered in scars: a big one by his kidneys, slightly more faded than the others. There are two long ones, symmetrical to each other, in between two of his ribs. Then there are some by his armpits, and smaller ones down towards his pelvis: surgical cuts that were rushed and desperate. Cameron clears his throat, but says nothing.

Peter doesn't speak, just reaches out and takes Cameron's wrist, guiding his fingertips to the scars. When Cameron's fingers come into contact with Peter's skin, the curly-haired boy sucks in a sharp breath, and energy courses through Cameron's veins. "Peter, I-" Cameron whispers, out of breath for some reason, "I'm so sorry." He doesn't know what he's apologizing for.

"It's okay," Peter whispers back, letting go of Cameron's wrist and beginning to undo his belt. Unlike the other times he's undressed in front of Cameron, Peter doesn't turn away, and Cameron is torn between simply averting his eyes or leaving the room completely.

He decides on the second option, turning towards the door. But then Peter's still-gravelly voice makes him halt in his tracks. "Stay." Cameron turns around, heart thumping, and he sees that Peter's eyes are swimming with tears again. "Please stay."

He's standing in just his boxers, and Cameron swallows, nodding as he tries to keep his eyes from wandering. Peter undresses completely and steps into the warm water, sitting with his knees pulled awkwardly close to his chest. He's just staring at the wall, and Cameron kneels down next to him. Without a word to one another, Peter carefully tilts his head back, and Cameron grabs a cup from the side of the bath, filling it with water and pouring it slowly over his dark curls. He repeats the process cup after cup, and when Peter's hair is wet enough, he pours some shampoo into his palm and runs his fingers through Peter's hair. He sighs contentedly, and Cameron smiles instinctively.

He rinses the shampoo from Peter's hair, and then grabs a brush, combing out the knots in his long curls. They don't talk, they don't have to. It's the small smile on Peter's face that makes Cameron's heart soar, the way his eyes drift closed, the way his shoulders relax.

When Peter doesn't open his eyes, Cameron lets his own wander down the length of Peter's body. He swallows, feeling indescribable things alight in his stomach. In a moment of weakness and probable stupidity, he bends down and plants a soft kiss on Peter's bare collarbone.

Peter's eyes open, and he glances up at Cameron, mouth hanging slightly open. Cameron sits back on his heels, clearing his throat. "I'm sorry, I didn't think-"

Peter shakes his head, reaches out one damp arm, grabs the front of Cameron's shirt, and pulls him in slowly for a searing kiss. Cameron is the one to pull away, and he puts both hands on either side of Peter's face, leaning their foreheads together. A few loose water droplets drip from Peter's curls down both boy's faces, and Peter pushes into Cameron, their lips and noses brushing one another's.

Peter pulls away and hits the bathtub drain, rising to his feet with Cameron's assistance and reaching for his towel, which he wraps around his waist, tucking it in securely. Cameron stands and backs up, watching his every movement. Peter catches him staring.

"What is it?"

Cameron grins, he can't help it. "I just really missed you."

Peter smiles, a big, genuine smile that lights up the whole room as he dramatically shakes his head, flinging water droplets everywhere. "I guarantee I missed you more."

Cameron laughs as the tension diffuses, and Peter steps towards him, backing him into the counter. Cameron wraps his arms around Peter's waist, fingers playing in the fabric of the towel. Peter's hands rest at the base of Cameron's neck, and he runs his thumbs across Cameron's cheeks, gazing up at him. Their waists and chests are flush against one another. "Cam, I... I don't really want to talk yet about everything that happened. But I just want to make sure you know that I'm grateful for everything you did for me."

Cameron smiles and his dimpled cheeks smush under Peter's hands. "This sounds like you're dumping me."

Peter shakes his head with a chuckle. "The opposite."

Cameron raises an eyebrow playfully. "You're proposing? I didn't think you'd be in a bath towel."

Peter shuts him up with a kiss, and Cameron parts his lips as Peter pushes further into him. Cameron grips the towel at Peter's waist. "Do you want to go to bed?"

"Are you joining me?" Peter asks with a raised brow.

Cameron laughs instinctively. "You bet."

Peter kisses him again.

Cameron smiles against his lips and guides him backwards, out of the bathroom. They continue walking until Peter's legs hit the bed frame. Cameron grabs him by the waist and grins. "Do you want my sweatpants?"

Peter nods, and Cameron's heart soars. "And a t-shirt, please."

Part Fifty-Seven: The Taurus

Diana

"I can't believe you're home," Diana says, adjusting her position by propping herself up on her elbows.

Peter follows suit, and he glances at her out of the corner of his eye. In the moonlight, his hair looks almost streaked with gray, and one curl falls across his brow as he turns his head back towards the stars. "Me neither."

Diana sits all the way up, running a hand through her hair. "You probably have heard that a lot today."

Peter smiles, shrugging one shoulder and nearly knocking himself off balance. "Yeah. But don't worry, I'm enjoying the attention."

Diana laughs and the two lapse into silence. They had been up on the roof for almost an hour, since neither of them could sleep. They had met by accident in the kitchen, where Diana had gone in to make a cup of tea and seen Peter at the counter, reading a book. The pair had noticed the stars were out, and so they had gathered their blankets and a few pillows and headed to the roof. They had briefly made small talk but quickly fallen into an unfortunate silence. It was difficult to go back to talking about everything, Diana had realized.

Their first meeting had gone smoothly. Peter was seemingly elated to see them again, and the others were too, with him and Lucas hugging for a record four minutes.

But Diana had soon realized there was something off. Apart from the fact Cameron and Peter had been glancing knowingly at one another, for something Diana most certainly did not want to know about, Peter had been quiet through dinner and their nightly routines, shutting himself gently in his room around nine o'clock.

It is a little past one now, and Diana looks over to see Peter looking up at the dark sky, bright hazel eyes scanning the constellations. "What are you looking at?"

Peter smiles softly but doesn't tear his eyes away from the stars. "Scorpius."

Diana nods and grins, looking up as well. "Since when are you an astrologer?"

"Since Cam told me about the constellations, when I was in the hospital."

Diana lays back, sticking her hands under her head. "And what did you learn?"

Peter glances her way with a playful smirk. "That it's really attractive when a guy talks stars to you."

Diana snorts with laughter. "I can't say I've ever noticed."

Peter chuckles as well. "That's okay. Now you know what to look for."

They fall silent again. After a long few minutes, Peter points up at a cluster of stars. "That constellation is Andromeda. It's *huge*. The book I read says there's one trillion stars in it."

Diana follows his point and squints, finally locating the constellation. "It's pretty." She turns to Peter. "But why is it so important to you?"

Peter sighs, letting his hand drop. "Well, I was bedridden since I got diagnosed. But if I turned my head just so, and if it was the right time of night, I could see Andromeda through the window. And I told myself as long as Andromeda was there, I wasn't really alone." He shakes his head with a slight frown. "That probably sounds really dumb."

"No, it doesn't," Diana says, reaching across the blanket and taking his hand. "It sounds really *nice*."

Peter nods. "It helped me remember that I could get out of there. And then I did." A wisp of a smile appears on his face, and Diana notices a flash of white teeth before his expression turns neutral again. "And now I'm back with you guys."

Diana squeezes his hand. "I hope you're happy, Peter." She clears her throat against a lump of emotion. "I... I know it was hard. And even that's putting it lightly. And I know you won't be the same. But I hope, even if you aren't the same Peter, you're at least a happy one."

Peter nods, turning his head to look at her. Diana looks back, and the two share a melancholy smile. "I dunno if that's where I'm at yet. It'll take a while to heal, quite literally." He runs his free hand through his hair and then looks back at Diana. "But I couldn't ask for better people to do that alongside."

Diana nods, letting herself turn over his words. "I'm glad you and I were thrown together by the universe, all those years ago."

Peter grins now. "Twelve years."

"Twelve?"

"Well, yeah, pretty much. When I was six, I remember we bumped into each other in the hallway at school. I apologized; you just kept walking. But then at lunch the next day, you came up to me and introduced yourself. Do you remember what you said?"

Diana smiles. "No."

"You said, 'I'm Diana. I figured we may as well make each other's acquaintance, since I ran into you yesterday.'" They both laugh, and Peter shakes his head. "I remember thinking, 'what is she talking about?' But I was six, so I guess the word 'acquaintance' flew right over my head."

Diana is laughing considerably harder now, knees curling up to her chest as Peter begins laughing due to her less-than-graceful movements. After a moment, Diana sighs, wiping her eyes. "God, that's crazy. I can't believe you remember that."

Peter chuckles. "It was the start of my whole life. I guess little Peter knew that, and so he decided to engrave it in his brain." He turns pensive then, pulling his lip between his teeth. "Di, do you... know anything about visions?"

"Visions?" Diana asks, unable to keep the curiosity out of her tone. "Like, prophecies?"

"No, well, I dunno," he mumbles, "but when I blacked out, and the doctors... took my power, I kinda had a bunch of visions, of all the important times I used the power. And the whole time, I felt like I was awake as ever, in the Plaza."

"Weird," Diana whispers. "What happened after that?"

"Well, a bunch of... people, I guess, but not really people, they didn't have faces, all started coming towards me. And I had to fight them, using my power. But they overpowered me and pushed me to the ground. One started choking me, and then-" his voice breaks. He turns towards Diana, eyes swimming with tears. "And then I heard you."

Diana swallows. "What do you mean?"

"I heard your voice. You whispered to me. You said, 'it's okay, you can go now,'" his breath catches in his throat. "And then everything went dark."

"When you flatlined again," Diana whispers.

Peter nods, mouth set in a grim line. "Exactly." He swallows. "I just... I don't know why it was you who told me to... you know."

"Die?"

"Yeah." Peter swallows. "I think it might've been because I trust you the most. I mean, I trust Cam, and Ki, and Lucas, but it's always been you, Di. It's always been you who won't ever judge me, who won't ever let me down." He looks at her, his gaze unreadable. "So I think when my body was shutting itself down, it knew that if there was anybody who was going to make me feel the calmest about dying, it would be you."

Diana sniffles, tears threatening to spill from her eyes. "I'm sorry, Peter. I'm so sorry."

"Don't apologize. It's beautiful, in a way. You're my person. But I think you know that," he smiles softly. "I've never felt as safe with a group of people as I do with you."

Diana smiles, sitting up and pulling Peter with her to wrap him in a hug. "Because we love you, Peter. You'll always be home with us."

Peter smiles, burying his forehead into her shoulder and hugging her harder. "I know."

Part Fifty-Eight: The Aries

Kiara

"Good morning, Miss Kiara," Ms. Brewer says as she pokes her head into Kiara's office. "How are you?"

Kiara smiles at the woman, who looks very put-together, probably in preparation for their public meeting today. Her dark hair is pulled into a bun at the base of her neck, her navy dress goes down to her knees, and her long, beige coat rests just below the dress's hemline. Kiara, on the other hand, hadn't yet changed: she was just in jeans and a sweater. "I'm good, thanks. Just wrapping up a statement for Peter."

Ms. Brewer nods, letting herself into the room. Her hands, which had previously been behind her back, appear now, full of mail. "Barbara wanted you to do mail today. Cameron is swamped with all the non-disclosures."

"I bet. You can leave it here." She motions to the mail bin on her desk, and Brewer deposits the letters there. "What time should I change?"

The woman pulls her bottom lip between her teeth as she thinks. "Oh, well, I'm not really sure. Barbara told me the reporters are coming at noon, and the public comments will start the meeting off. Then, Peter has his speech, then Diana will close. So I would assume we need to be on the floor by eleven, for prep. I would be dressed by ten forty-five."

Kiara grins, jutting her head towards her bookshelf, where a garment bag hangs. "And when should this be steamed?"

Ms. Brewer throws a hand dramatically over her heart, shaking her head. "Oh, Kiara. You wound me. One day, you'll be excited to wear a dress to a press conference."

"Not anytime soon."

With a smile and a wave of her fingers, Ms. Brewer exits. Kiara reaches for the mail and shuffles through bills, citizen's letters, and the occasional magazine.

But at the back of the pile is an unmarked envelope with a red seal.

Kiara swallows and opens it, squeezing her hand into a fist to stop her fingers from shaking. Inside the envelope isn't a letter, or a photograph, it's a piece of fabric.

The edges are frayed, as if someone took scissors to whatever garment the patch came from. The fabric is white, but a little dirty, as if it had been worn over and over, rubbed against skin for months or even years. Attached to the piece of fabric with small white stitches is a nylon tag. And written in blocky, permanent marker letters, reads:

KIARA, ARIES 333

Kiara swallows the bile rising in her throat and takes a deep breath, trying to think calmly.

The patch was obviously from her school dress. That would explain the dirtied fabric, not to mention the tag. But her coherent thoughts ended there.

Who could've gotten the patch? And how would they have managed to cut it out of her original dress? Kiara knew that when kids turned in their old clothes, in exchange for their sector colors, the outfits were washed, and the tags were removed. But Kiara's dress had most certainly not gone through a washing machine, and the tag was sewn in quite securely. Someone had saved her dress, but who?

And *why*?

Kiara glances at the clock, which reads ten-twenty. She had twenty minutes to be dressed, which means she needed to forget this and move on.

But when she reaches to put the patch, which has been returned to the envelope, into the trash, she pauses.

Without a second thought, Kiara meticulously re-seals the envelope and gently places it in the back of her desk drawer.

She'd think about it later. But she just didn't have time right now.

Part Fifty-Nine: The Libra

Lucas

Lucas was *nervous.*

It was his first press conference as a primary player in the American government, although he had done his American tour broadcast what felt like forever ago. But for some reason, this felt different.

Seated in a line were the nine government officials. At the far left was Ms. Brewer, then Cameron, then Barbara, then Kiara, then Diana in the middle. To her left was Peter, Ms. Miller, Lucas, and Mr. Boone on the far right.

Lucas didn't know Ms. Miller or Mr. Boone very well personally, so it was more than nerve-racking when Barbara had explained the importance of who was on either side of him.

"If there's a question you can't answer, whether because it's too uncomfortable or because you simply don't know, the people sitting on either side of you are your biggest allies. So remember to help each other," she had said, with a steady glance towards Lucas. He suspected she was still sort of upset about the whole "your dad isn't really the Aquarius heir and you're actually Kiara's cousin" situation. And he couldn't *really* blame her.

Lucas clears his throat and adjusts his pressed collar as members of the public begin to fill into the Congress floor, through the big wooden doors. They take their seats, and Lucas watches as some families and groups whisper and point at certain members of the group seated like gods on the raised stage at the front of the room.

A little girl, walking in with her father, points to Ms. Miller. "Look, dad! It's Miss Miller!"

The father shushes her, but to no avail, and Ms. Miller looks up at the little girl. To Lucas' shock, she smiles and waves, although she doesn't get up. She beckons the child closer to the stage, and the little girl meanders right to the edge. "Hello, darling," Ms. Miller says, voice soft, "what's your name?"

"Penelope," the girl says, batting her lashes and sticking her thumb into her mouth. Lucas cringes, only semi-disappointed in the fact that he was still reverting to the old Alynthian story that sucking your thumb meant bad luck for the child.

"Well, Penelope, why did you come today?" Ms. Miller asks, leaning forward. Lucas glances to his left, but Mr. Boone is busy talking to some bodyguards. So, with nothing better to do, the prince turns back to the exchange to his right.

"My dad has some questions for you all," the girl responds, "but I remember you."

Ms. Miller's smile falters for the briefest moment. "From where?"

"I'm a Libra!"

Ms. Miller grins, nodding her head. "Ah, I see. Well, between you and me, I think your sign is the best."

The girl nods rapidly, and Lucas can't help but smile, feeling his own personal alignment alight a feeling of pride in his chest. Ms. Miller looks over at Lucas, grabbing his wrist. "Penelope, do you know who this is?"

The girl's mouth drops open, and her blue eyes go wide. "*Prince Lucas*," she whispers.

Lucas smiles and waves. "Hi, Penelope."

Ms. Miller chuckles. "Penelope, do you want to know something cool?"

The girl is too stunned to speak; her eyes are still stuck on Lucas, so she nods.

"Prince Lucas is a Libra, too."

The girl gasps. "No way."

Lucas smirks and nods. "Yes, ma'am," he leans forward. "So is the *king* of Alynthia."

"Wow," she whispers. Her eyes light up, and she stands up and down rapidly on her tiptoes, practically bouncing with excitement. "Is it very pretty there? In Alynthia?"

"The prettiest," Lucas responds. "But it's very, very pretty here, too."

"And have you ever been to Sector Nine? Or where it used to be, I guess?"

Lucas thinks for a minute, then shakes his head. "No, I haven't. But I'd definitely like to."

"Well, maybe if you do, you can visit me and my dad!" Penelope says, voice rising to an even higher tone, which Lucas didn't think could be possible.

Just then, Diana rises, and Lucas motions with his hands as if shooing her back to her seat. Before she turns away though, he shoots her a smile. "I'd love that," he whispers, even though he isn't certain she heard.

Part Sixty: The Cancer

Peter

Diana's welcome speech goes smoothly, and Peter readjusts in his seat as the room is filled with applause. Moments before they had begun, Barbara had told Peter he would speak after Diana, rather than after public comments.

Diana continues, introducing the members of the government sitting behind her, and Peter glances towards Cameron. He's one in on the end, and Peter recalls with a small smile his incessant complaining about being so far from everyone. Cameron catches Peter's eye and smiles, tilting his head as if talking out loud.

Peter smiles back right as Diana's voice breaks him from his stupor. "And now, I'd like to welcome our Secretary of Education, Mr. Peter Simon."

As the applause starts back up again, Peter rises from his seat, putting weight on his cane and straightening his suit jacket. Diana turns away from the mic and reaches her arms out to Peter, and the two embrace briefly before she sits back down. Peter steps up to the microphone and waves, trying to locate the cameras in the crowd based off of the places the various clicking noises come from.

"Hello everybody. Wow, is it good to be back!" Applause once more, and Peter motions for the crowd to quiet with his hands. "I wanted to take the time today to speak a bit about what my time was like with the Sector Five disease. Firstly, I want to speak to my fellow Cancers, who are still isolated in Sector Five." He looks directly at the large camera in the back of the room, which he knows is broadcasting the speech to the still-blockaded sector down south. "For those of you who are sitting in your homes, unable to leave due to this invisible danger, I thank you. For those of you who have lost loved ones to this disease, I thank you. I thank you for being relentless in your courage, and showing me, an eighteen-year-old boy from the same place as you, that I could make it too.

"When I was first diagnosed, for the first little while when I was stuck in isolation, I still had hope. I had faith in my team, and, for reasons I still find semi-immoral, I had the best medical team in the country, so who was I to assume they *couldn't* get me better? But then, things got worse. Even in the Battle of Zodiacs, I had never felt worse pain than I did in the hospital. But the most awful thing about it was that I was suffering by myself. When I'm sick at home, I have President Monroe to make me cold compresses and soup, I have Prince Lucas to sit and chat with, I have Secretary O'Connor to flit around like a nervous wreck." Some chuckles ripple across the crowd, and Peter smiles. "But I didn't have that when I was sick with this disease. And before I flatlined for the first time, before I had allergic reactions to my trials, before my lungs failed, part of me died.

"I don't say this to scare anyone. I say this because it's true. People assume what's happening in Sector Five is people are ill, and then their bodies fail, and most of the time, those who are infected inevitably die. But while that does happen, there is a mental aspect to it as well. So for those of you who plan on supporting Sector Five from afar, please remember that it isn't just about healing your body. This is a setback that will need years to heal, maybe even years after we're through running this government and the next group of politicians have taken over. I ask, no, I *urge* everyone to continue supporting the Cancers in

251

any way that you can." He sighs and swallows. "And now, I need to wrap it up with a... difficult piece of news." He looks behind him and sees Cameron nod slowly. Peter turns back towards the crowd.

"Days ago, I flatlined in my hospital room. In order to save me, my two incredible doctors, Doctor Charles and Doctor Inesh, had to remove my power. While I recognize that this is incredibly difficult to heal from, especially mentally, I take this time to thank my team and say that I am *incredibly* lucky to have had the opportunity to be healed so quickly from this disease. Millions of Cancers suffer until they get the antidote, and my solution was quick and relatively painless compared to what happens to some others. But this means that the Cancer power has since been destroyed." Peter blinks back tears, trying to put on a strong facade. "Finally, I want to thank a few people in particular. To Diana, Kiara, Lucas, and Cameron: thank you for sticking with me. Thank you for never giving up hope, even when I had none. To Inesh: thank you for traveling all this way to help me. Without you, who knows if I'd be standing here. And finally, to Ruth and Charles: thank you for being... well, for being there for me, really. I know it sounds silly, but you were, and hopefully will remain, the family I never had as a kid. Thank you for being so devoted and kind, and loving. I won't ever, ever forget you two."

Peter is crying just a bit now, and he wipes away a tear that begins to roll down his cheek. He manages to squeak out a "thank you" before he turns and stumbles back to his seat, and he blinks away his tears as Ms. Miller takes his hand, squeezing gently. Diana rises, and with a concerned-yet-kind glance towards Peter, she steps back up to the mic. "And now, I'd like to open the floor to public comments."

Almost an hour later, the nine had fielded dozens of questions, whether aimed at Diana and Barbara and their plan for Sector Five, for Cameron about the borders around the sector, or for Peter about his sickness.

Peter is exhausted, but he forces himself to sit up and fold his hands in his lap as Diana points to a group of people in the back. "Yes, you three?"

The three people stand, and Peter blinks rapidly, trying to confirm if he was seeing them correctly.

It was three men, in dark sunglasses, dressed entirely in red. As they rise from their seats, a few people scattered about the audience stand as well, in the same glasses and the same harsh outfits. The biggest, burliest man crosses his arms. "This is a question for the Citizens' Liaison."

Kiara rises from her seat, approaching the mic. Her steps are confident, but her face is a picture of caution. "Yes?"

Peter doesn't fail to note their guards' slow, autonomous movements, their hands slowly reaching to cover their holsters.

"We want to know if you know," the man says slowly.

Kiara swallows. "Know what?" Her tone is astoundingly even. Peter scoots closer to the edge of his seat, gaze flicking between Kiara and the people in red.

The man grins a slow, sickening smile. "Nevermind that. Did you receive our postage?"

Kiara takes a long, deep breath. Then, she turns around, facing the left, near where Mr. Boone and Lucas are seated. She waves to a guard standing on the wall behind Mr. Boone. "Hayley, could you please get your team to escort these people out of the building?"

The woman nods and hurries to the other guards, and the man laughs, waving his hand dismissively. "Not to worry, we're leaving. Thank you, Kiara."

As they turn to leave, a skinnier, older man waves to Kiara as he passes by the stage. When he speaks, his words are just to the nine people onstage. "Goodbye, Kiara Henderson."

Kiara stumbles back as if she's been pushed, moving backwards until she lands in her chair. Barbara takes one glance at her and stands, clapping her hands together. She doesn't even bother crossing to the mic before she speaks. "Alright, everyone. Thank you for attending this conference. If you would all exit the way you came, please have a wonderful rest of your day."

Peter glances at Kiara out of the corner of his eye, heart thumping in his chest when he takes in her vacant expression. As people file out of the room, whispering and pointing at the terrified girl, Cameron walks over to Peter, standing in front of his chair.

"What was that?" Cameron whispers, looking down at Peter.

Peter shakes his head, wringing his hands together nervously. "I'm not one hundred percent sure. But whatever it is, we're not safe."

Part Sixty-One: The Taurus

Diana

"Do you want some water, Ki?" Diana asks as she enters the living room.

It's around six, and after putting in a quick two hours at the Capitol – damage control, really – the five teenagers had gone back to their apartment. Now, Peter and Cameron were snuggled on the couch, flipping through a magazine, Lucas was off picking up food, and Kiara was seated in the big chair next to the fireplace, wrapped in a plush blanket.

Kiara shakes her head as she robotically drags her fingers through the shag blanket. Her dark eyes are clouded, and her expression is vacant. Diana plunks a mug of water in her hands anyway, seating herself on the floor in front of the fire. Finnigan trots over and curls up next to her. "Kiara, what did that guy mean? About receiving something in the mail?"

Kiara blinks, clearing her throat. Diana notices Cameron and Peter look up as well, suddenly tuned into the conversation. "I... I got a letter this morning."

Cameron raises an eyebrow, waiting for her to continue, and he leans back against the couch cushions. "From?"

Kiara shrugs, turning the mug in her hands but not drinking. "I dunno. Those weird people, I guess. There was nothing written on the envelope."

"And what did the letter inside say?" Diana asks, rubbing circles on Finnigan's back.

"There was no letter. It was a piece of fabric, the tag cut out of my old dress."

"Old dress, as in, school dress?" Peter asks. "From six years ago?"

Kiara nods, and Cameron grimaces. "That's disgustingly creepy."

Diana's eyebrows knit together, and she scoots forward, putting her hands on Kiara's legs. "Ki, are you okay? We can fix this easily, we'll have Hayley and her team track them down again if you want. But I want to know that you're fine first."

Kiara swallows and nods slowly, finally meeting Diana's gaze. "I'm... I'm fine. And don't make Hayley do that. I'm sure they've learned their lesson by now."

Diana feels like she's lying, but she pushes the worry out of her gut. Kiara knew what was best for her, and Diana knew *that* as well as anybody. "Okay. But make sure you tell us if anything happens again."

"I will," Kiara says with a small smile.

Just then, the elevator door dings open, and Lucas enters, holding a large paper bag. He sees everyone in the living room and grins as he uses his toes to push his shoes off. "Picnic in the living room, I see. I can get behind that."

Diana rolls her eyes as he starts passing out food. "If anyone spills anything, I'm going to be very upset."

"We know," Peter says with a chuckle.

Diana glances at Peter, and her heart warms. All of a sudden, there he was, as if nothing had changed, snuggled up with Cameron and reading in the living room as if he'd never left.

But Diana knew that wasn't right. She knew from the wrinkles in the corners of his eyes, she knew from the scars that stretched like vines across his stomach, she knew from the way he winced every time someone brought up the disease or the Powerful Ones. Every time someone mentioned Ruth and Charles were moving away, further west. She knew he'd never really be healed.

"Lucas, I saw you talking to that little girl today," Cameron says between mouthfuls. "What was that about?"

Lucas shrugs. He had seated himself on the other end of the couch, takeout box resting on the edge of the coffee table. "Her name was Penelope. She was visiting 'cause her dad wanted to see the press conference. She remembered Miriam from when she reigned over Sector Nine."

"Ew, don't call it a 'reign'," Diana mumbles.

"That's what it is. Anyways, Miriam introduced us. She was *appalled* that I was a Libra."

"Aren't we all," Cameron mumbles with a smirk.

Lucas wads up a napkin and throws it at him, but it falls short by about a foot. "What *other* sign would I be?" he asks, mouth full.

Kiara shrugs. "Sagittarius?"

Diana and Peter laugh out loud at this, pointing at one another and repeating: "Forgetful, unthinking, rash!"

"Ouch, you guys!" Lucas yells. He grins and straightens his posture, rattling off his next words on his fingers. "Libra positives: artistic, idealistic, reasonable."

Diana rolls her eyes. "We *do* work in the Capitol, Lucas, we know what a Libra is like."

"And don't forget your negatives, Your Highness," Cameron says. "Hesitant, lazy, careless? You've got one of the worst lists in the zodiac."

"*You* have the worst list in the zodiac, Cam," Peter says.

"Rude," Cameron responds, turning his back to Peter in a standoffish manner and leaning against his shoulder. Peter laughs and leans his head against Cameron's shoulder, and the group falls quiet again.

Diana sighs, grinning at nobody in particular.

Part Sixty-Two: The Cancer

Peter

"I'm *tired*," Cameron mumbles.

Peter tugs on his pant leg, pulling him closer to the edge of the bed. "I don't care. You're not allowed to go to sleep before you wash your face."

Cameron sighs and sits up, and Peter crosses his arms, trying his best to glare at him. "Fine," Cameron says, standing and entering the bathroom. As he begins rubbing a wet towel across his face, Peter looks around.

He hadn't been in Cameron's room much since he got back. Actually, in the three days he'd been home, he had only been sleeping in his own room. Cameron's bedroom was relatively dark, because of his drawn blackout curtains, but it was cleaner than usual: the ginger-haired boy had spent hours the night before putting away laundry that he had let pile up over the weeks.

Cameron emerges from the bathroom, his hairline slightly damp, and Peter rubs the moisture off with his thumbs. Cameron climbs into bed, leaving the blanket folded so Peter could see the gray sheets underneath. Cameron was wearing a black short-sleeved shirt and dark green pajama pants, ones that were so fuzzy Peter would often catch Cameron rubbing his hands down his legs. Cameron glances up at Peter, who is still standing in his sock feet near the bedside table. "You okay?"

Peter opens his mouth to reassure him, but no sound comes out; instead, he just nods. Cameron pushes himself into a seated position, patting the bed next to him. Peter ambles over and sits, tucking his legs beneath him.

"Talk to me," Cameron says, grabbing Peter's hands and beginning to play with his fingers.

Peter shrugs, looking down at their intertwined hands. "I dunno. I just feel off today."

"Like, sick?"

Peter shakes his head. "No. Just weird."

Cameron bites his lip, nodding slowly. Peter wanted to applaud Cameron's reaction to his return: Cameron was always there to listen, to talk to, or just sit in silence, on the odd occasion Peter couldn't bring himself to speak his thoughts aloud. "What can I do?"

Peter laughs softly, for a lack of a better reaction. Letting go of Cameron's hands, he places his own on either side of Cameron's face, tilting his head down to plant a kiss on his forehead. Peter leaves his hands there, running his thumbs along Cameron's cheeks and forcing him to meet his eyes. "Don't worry about it, Cam. There isn't anything either of us can do. I just need a little while to get better."

Cameron's gray eyes are sad, and his lips quirk downward briefly. "Peter, I *am* worried. I don't want you to be upset."

"I'll be upset forever, Cameron. But that doesn't mean I won't eventually be happy. I'll just always have a little bit of an ache, that's all."

Cameron swallows, leaning into Peter's touch and placing one of his hands over Peter's. "I guess so."

Peter puts on a semi-forced smile and kisses the top of Cameron's head. "Are *you* okay?"

Cameron blinks, his expression one of shock. "I... I dunno. I haven't thought about it."

Peter doesn't know whether to laugh or be sad about that revelation. "Well, think about it for a second, and then let me know."

He releases Cameron and sits back against the headboard, and Cameron does the same. Neither boy talks, and the two keep about a foot of space between them as they stare straight ahead. After a couple minutes, Peter glances back over at Cameron.

He's crying.

Peter almost gasps. Cameron was sitting there, crying absolutely silently. He sees Peter looking at him and reaches out his arms, and without a word, Peter wraps him in a strong hug. Cameron, always the taller one in the embrace, tucks his head into Peter's neck, wrapping his arms around his waist.

"Hey, shh," Peter whispers as Cameron's gentle tears turn more violent, "it's okay. It's okay."

Cameron turns his head a bit, enough to whisper: "I missed you so much. I was so scared."

Peter's heart practically breaks in two. "I know. I'm sorry."

"It isn't your fault. I just..." he trails off as another sob escapes him, and Peter just squeezes him tighter.

"No, I'm sorry I never asked you sooner," Peter says, chuckling a little. "This would've probably been a healthier breakdown to have on the day I got back."

Cameron laughs, but it sounds broken. "Probably, yeah." He pulls away, wiping his puffy cheeks. Peter smiles sadly at the sight of his wet eyelashes and red face. Cameron looks at Peter, gaze unwavering. "I love you."

Peter leans in and kisses him softly, savoring the feeling. He leans his forehead against Cameron's, closing his eyes. "I love you too."

Part Sixty-Three: The Scorpio

Cameron

Cameron's heart was pounding.

He was pacing the car of a monorail, all alone.

He was dressed to the nines: a pressed black suit with a white undershirt under it. His tie was gray, an ode to Sector Five, which is where he was headed.

That morning, he had gotten the call from Barbara: Sector Five was cleared for release.

In the five days since Peter had been healed, the almost hundred-thousand cases had dwindled lower and lower, until finally, at midnight the night before, the last person had been declared healed of the disease.

It was finally over.

Cameron had asked Barbara if Diana could come, or Peter. But she had refused: both were needed for a radio conference after Cameron dropped the borders.

So, aside from two bodyguards, Cameron was on his way down south alone, awaiting a mass of citizens, a live television broadcast, and the walls.

Cameron hadn't seen that material since he and Peter had returned from Sector Five, days before Peter's diagnosis. For some odd reason, he was strangely nervous. He wondered if it was because he was doing this all alone, and the solidarity of the thing was scaring him. Or if he was just scared to go to the place that had nearly killed Peter.

He had no speech prepared, he wasn't there to talk. He would exit the monorail, then get driven to the very point of the triangle that was Sector Five, along with a group of cameramen and his guards. When he was there, he'd crouch by the wall and press both hands on either wall, so the whole sector could be released in one fell swoop.

"Fifteen minutes, Secretary O'Connor," Hayley says, poking her head into the car.

"Thanks," Cameron says, voice wavering.

She smiles and exits, and Cameron crosses to the window. They were passing over a large swampish area, and he chuckles to himself when he recalls their bathing misadventure after they had found Peter.

Cameron turns, crossing to a phone hanging on the wall of the train car. He knew it was an emergency phone, but he figured his pounding heart qualified as an emergency. He dials a number from memory and waits as it rings once, then twice.

"Hello?"

"Peter, I'm freaking out."

"Do you just... *know* my office number?"

"Yeah, shut up. Anyways, I'm panicking, and I dunno why."

"What can I do to help you?"

Cameron huffs. "Nothing. I just wanted to hear your voice."

Peter chuckles. "Well, I wish I was with you. I miss Sector Five."

"You won't be able to call it that much longer."

"Ugh, I know. I miss 'the south'."

"Better."

Both boys are quiet for a long moment, until Cameron sighs. He leans against the wall, staring up at the ceiling as he speaks. "I miss you." He isn't telling the full truth: that he was also terrified.

"I miss you too," Peter's voice is soft and reassuring, and Cameron hears a rustling noise. Peter must be reading something. "But what's really the matter?"

Cameron bites his lip. He should've known Peter of all people would see right through him. "I'm scared."

"I gathered that. Why?"

"I dunno. I just... I haven't done this in a while, not since Alynthia, when we were training, right? So what if I mess it up? What if all the Cancers are mad at me for butchering the very last release? What happens if my power hurts me the same way yours hurt you?!"

He hadn't meant to say that last part. Cameron was breathing heavily, having yanked himself back from falling off that mental cliff at the very last second. Peter is quiet on the other line, and Cameron wonders if he made him upset.

After a few agonizing moments of silence, Peter speaks again. "Cameron, my power hurt me not because I was using it, but because my body was sick. So you don't need to worry about yours hurting you. I remember when we first trained, way back when, I thought you were one of the most insanely powerful people I had ever met, and you had confidence to go with that power. But then, after the Battle of Zodiacs, I realized that you were *talented*, too. You were the one with no fear of what you could do. You didn't hold back, and you were obviously the one person there who would always, always be able to rein in this crazy power."

"But-"

"Wait, listen. Remember the meeting we had that night, with Diana and Barbara?"

Cameron blinks rapidly; his eyes are welling with tears and he has no idea why. "Yeah."

"Me too. We decided that you and I would keep our powers, same as Diana. But what they didn't tell you was that it was for separate reasons."

"Diana said it was because the two of us were the most in control."

"Well, I know, but that isn't the real reason. They kept me because out of me, you, Olivia, Jesse, and Claire, mine was the most useful in battle. Barbara and Diana wanted a weapon, just in case, and they chose me."

Cameron feels his blood boil. The whole reason they had started the revolt was so that nobody would be used as a weapon again, and now the very Capitol he worked for was doing that to the person he loved. "Peter, I-"

"Don't get mad," Peter says with a chuckle. "I agreed. I knew I wouldn't ever have to *be* that weapon, and I was right. But anyways, they kept you because-"

"They needed me to drop the walls?"

"Partially. But mostly because they saw what we could do, and they said 'Cameron can do it best. He's the one with control, he's the one with talent.' And they were right. So don't go thinking you can't do what you're about to do, because you're wrong."

Cameron swallows. He should say something poetic, something that would make Peter feel like all his pep-talking was working, because it was. But all that comes out is a squeaky "I love you."

Peter chuckles. "I love you too, Cam. You're amazing."

"Thank you, superhero."

"Make my sector proud."

"I'll do my best."

"And that's enough."

With that, Peter hangs up the phone. Cameron blows out a long breath through puffed cheeks as the monorail halts, and moments later, his guards come through. "Secretary O'Connor, it's time," the male guard says as he enters the room.

Cameron can't help but feel a little braver than before. "Great."

Part Sixty-Four: The Cancer

Peter

About forty minutes after Peter gets off the phone with Cameron, he's gathered on the Congress floor with the others. Lucas and Diana are sitting around the table, hands intertwined, Kiara is standing by the entrance talking to Ms. Miller and Mr. Boone, Ms. Brewer and Barbara were seated across from Lucas and Diana, and Peter was standing at the edge of the stage, pacing.

A television screen had been set up on the far left of the stage. The plan was originally to make this border-dropping a public event, where people could come in similarly to the press conference and watch onscreen. But for Kiara's safety (a phrase that worried Peter to a great extent) it was canceled, and now the eight were alone, watching the livestream.

Peter halts about four feet from the screen and watches.

"Peter," Diana says, voice soft but assertive, "there's nothing on screen yet."

Peter was, in fact, staring at a blank screen. "I know. But I don't want to miss anything when it does come on."

As if he was summoning Cameron himself, the screen blinks on, showing the corner of Sector Five. In the background, a little way away from the camera, was the point where the two main walls intersected. The terrain was familiar and made Peter's heart ache: tall trees arched over the camera, so huge Peter couldn't see the tops.

The chattering from the other Congress members stops, and as if waiting for complete and utter silence, Cameron steps in front of the camera.

Peter's heart leaps into his throat as he studies the ginger-haired boy. The vibrant colors on the screen made him seem almost supernatural: his black suit was stark against the dirt, his tie was a bright gray that matched his eyes. His freckles stood out, even through the translation to the screen.

Cameron doesn't say anything, just turns his back to the camera and studies the wall. Peter watches his fingers twitch at his sides, as if they were eager to touch the blue material. Cameron takes one step forward, two. Then he stops, shoes making a small scuff in the dirt where he digs in his heels.

"Come on, Cam," Diana whispers. Peter was certain no one was supposed to have heard her.

Peter's heart was pounding. He knew he had cheered Cameron up over the phone, but would it be enough? Peter knew as well as Cameron did that the job at hand was not easy. Peter could only hope Cameron would push through.

Cameron straightens his shoulders and goes right up to the wall. Peter realizes the video they were watching was muted; he would've heard Cameron's shoes crunching in the dry dirt. Cameron usually crouched down when he dropped the walls, he had everywhere else. But this time, he stays standing straight up, and slowly, mechanically, his arms come out, palms pressing flat against both walls.

"Yes," Barbara whispers from behind Peter.

Cameron stays that way for a long moment. The wall fades in vibrancy, flickers.

But it doesn't disappear.

Cameron scrambles away from the wall, pulling his hands towards him in one fluid movement as if he'd been burnt. A collective gasp ripples through the room, and Cameron turns around, looking towards someone behind the camera.

A moment passes. Cameron shakes his head and runs a hand through his hair. He mouths something along the lines of *I'm trying* and hold up his hands.

They're covered in spots. Burns.

"No," Ms. Miller says, "it's hurting him."

"What's going on?" Lucas asks, rising from his seat.

Peter shakes his head, eyes frozen on the screen. "His power. It's not working."

"It's going away," Kiara whispers.

Cameron turns back to the wall. His eyes are sparkling with tears, and Peter shakes his head as Cameron begins pressing on the walls again. "No, no. It's hurting him, he has to stop."

But no one responds, instead they watch as Cameron steps back again, pulling off his suit jacket and discarding it on the ground. He goes back to work, neck and arms straining with effort as he shoves his palms against the wall. He turns his head ever so slightly, and Peter notices his mouth is open in a painful, clenched shout.

The walls disappear and Cameron falls to the ground.

A guard rushes towards him, holding a roll of bandages, and he bends down next to Cameron and begins wrapping his hands. Peter catches a glimpse of the burns and grimaces. His skin is red and peeling already, and his palms and fingertips are covered in welts.

"It could've been much, much worse," Barbara says as she steps up behind Peter, placing a hand on his shoulder, "he could be dead."

"What happened to his power?" Peter whispers, watching Cameron rise to his feet and begin walking out of frame. "Why wasn't it working?"

They all move to sit at the table. "We'll have to ask Cam when he gets home," Diana mumbles, hands fidgeting nervously on the tabletop.

"He still has to drop the back wall," Ms. Brewer says, drumming her fingertips on the table, "I hope he does fine."

"That one is smaller, easier," Peter says quickly, reassuring himself more than anyone else, "it'll be okay. It has to be."

Kiara shrugs. "I hate to say this, but at least his power is failing on the last sector. At least we aren't left with others to release."

"Exactly," Peter mumbles, "I'm sure he's okay."

Part Sixty-Five: The Scorpio

Cameron

Cameron had never felt worse in his life.

He was sitting in the monorail car he had ridden earlier, head in his hands, elbows propped on his knees.

He had dropped the last wall with far too much effort, and, per his request, with a lack of livestreaming. When he rode back through the main part of Sector Five, people weren't screaming and cheering as they had been when he had arrived. They were absolutely silent, staring at him with mouths agape.

When he had gotten on the train, his hands had been rubbed with a burn cream and re-wrapped, and he had been left alone with water and a blanket.

He had thought about calling Peter but decided against it. He would see him in a few hours, and he needed a second alone with his thoughts anyways.

He wasn't necessarily upset about losing his power. In fact, he was surprisingly okay with it. He had dropped the last border, so it wasn't like he needed it for anything. And besides, being one of last Powerful Ones wasn't exactly something to brag about, considering the losses all the others had gone through.

He just felt like a *failure*. He was the Secretary of Security. And there he'd stood, shouting in pain as he idiotically pressed his hands harder and harder against the walls. He couldn't have done a worse job at reassuring the Cancers, much less the rest of the country, who had watched him struggle over a live broadcast.

How could he protect everyone now?

He almost laughs as he realizes he and Peter had been so distant, and now they had practically gone through the same things in the span of weeks.

He groans as a fresh wave of nausea washes over him. It wasn't the burns themselves, it was the sudden jab of pain that made him remember pressing his hands against the border, and fighting against the white-hot pain that flared from it was making him sick to his stomach.

"Secretary O'Connor?" a woman says as she pokes her head into the car. It's Hayley. Cameron waves her in with one bandaged hand and she sits across from him, on another one of the leather-lined benches. "How are you feeling?"

Cameron leans back against the back of the couch. "I'm okay. My hands hurt."

"Do you need more antibiotics?"

"No. I'll be okay, and I can bring some of that cream home with me."

She rises and brushes herself off, straightening her black blazer. "Well, I'll leave you to it. I wanted to tell you it'll be a half hour until we're back."

Cameron nods. "Thanks, Hayley. By the way, were you at the dropping? I didn't see you there."

Hayley smiles, the corner of her mouth twitching. "Strange. I was there, yes."

Cameron nods as she exits, pulling his bandage tighter around his fingers with his teeth.

Forty-five minutes later, Cameron is on his way up the elevator to his apartment. He blows out a big breath as the door opens, and before he can process anything, he's tackled into a group hug.

"Cam, are you okay?!" Diana asks, flinging her arms around his neck.

"We were so worried!" Lucas says.

"I missed you," Kiara mumbles into his chest.

Cameron reaches his arms away from them, to avoid hitting the burns, and chuckles a little. "I'm fine. A little banged up, but fine." He looks around the room. "Where's Peter?"

"Here," a familiar voice says from the hall. Peter is by the door to his room, Finnigan standing at his feet. Cameron sighs and begins walking as fast as he can to him, and Peter's strong arms wrap around his waist, pulling Cameron into a tight embrace.

Cameron tucks his face into Peter's curls. "Hey, superhero," he whispers, voice thick with emotion.

"Hi. Are you okay?" Peter whispers back.

Finnigan whines and bumps Cameron's leg with his nose, and Cameron pulls away from the embrace, sniffling as he nods. "Yeah."

Diana clears her throat. "Cameron, is your power... gone?"

Cameron shrugs. "I dunno, really. I think maybe it's completely faded by now. The last wall was hard."

Kiara raises an eyebrow as everyone settles around the kitchen counter. "And are you... *emotionally* fine?"

Cameron just nods.

Lucas nods slowly. "Okay. What does everyone want for dinner? I'll cook."

A few mumbled replies come from Diana, Peter, and Kiara, but Cameron shakes his head. "Nothing."

The conversation halts as all four turn to look at Cameron. "Are you sure you're okay?" Diana asks.

Cameron's cheeks get hot. "Yeah, I'm fine. Trust me. I'm just not hungry," he pushes away from the table and waves a bandaged hand at everyone. "I'm just gonna go to bed."

He disappears down the hall before anyone can respond.

Part Sixty-Six: The Cancer

Peter

An hour after Cameron had left, the other four had fed Finnigan, discussed their next steps for the newly released Sector Five, and, in Lucas' case, begun cooking for the rest of them.

Peter sighs as Finnigan jumps onto the couch, curling up with his nose tucked under his tail. "I'm gonna go check on Cam."

The others nod, and Diana reaches over from her stool closest to the fridge and squeezes his hand. "Tell him we love him."

Peter smiles softly at her and nods. "I will."

He enters Cameron's room without knocking. However, the ginger boy is nowhere to be seen, and before Peter can think anything of it, a clatter comes from the bathroom along with a string of expletives.

Peter pulls open the bathroom door to see Cameron sitting on the sink counter, fumbling with his half-unwrapped bandages. The noise in question had been made by a bottle of face wash he had knocked off the counter.

Cameron looks up as Peter enters, and Peter notices his cheeks are puffy and his eyes are red. Peter smiles at him. "Need help?"

Cameron huffs out a laugh that sounds more bitter than he probably intended. "Yup."

Peter crosses to him, taking the burn cream and bandage clips from his hands and setting them on the counter. Carefully, slowly, he takes Cameron's elbow, guiding Cameron's left hand towards his chest. He begins unraveling the bandage, eyes trained on Cameron's hand. As he methodically unwraps, he begins speaking in a low voice. "Why'd you storm off?" He feels Cameron shrug.

"I dunno. I just wanted to be alone."

"Well, I'm here."

"You're the exception."

Peter pulls the last of the first bandage off, revealing Cameron's blistered, red hands. Cameron sucks in a sharp breath, and Peter looks up at him, noticing Cameron's face is pinched in an expression of pain. "What do I do next?"

Cameron flushes red and clears his throat. "Um, burn cream."

Peter smirks as he reaches for the tube. "Are you embarrassed?"

"A little."

Peter begins massaging the burn cream gently into Cameron's shaky hands. "Why?"

"I dunno. I hate that you have to take care of me like this."

Peter chuckles, moving his thumbs in slow circles. "I don't mind. Really."

They fall into silence again, and Cameron moves his other hand towards Peter, who begins unwrapping it. There's something warm, comfortable about the energy in the room: Cameron moves so his legs are open, and Peter steps between them, bringing the two even closer as Peter pokes his tongue out of his mouth in focus.

He frees the bandage and reaches for the burn cream, beginning the process again. The burns are somehow worse on this hand, and Peter doesn't fail to notice the way Cameron occasionally gasps in pain. Peter glances up at him. "Are you okay?"

Cameron swallows, nodding after a long moment. "Uh-huh," he sniffles. "Keep going."

Peter takes Cameron's first hand and begins wrapping it again with a clean, new bandage. Slowly, he weaves it around his fingers and thumb, then down his wrist a bit. He secures it with the clips from before, then repeats the process with the other hand. When he's done, he places Cameron's hands gently on his thighs and smiles up at him. "See? So much better."

Cameron chuckles and shakes his head, holding up his hands. Only his fingertips poke out from the gleaming white bandages. "As better as I can be."

Peter places his hands on Cameron's cheeks, pulling him down for a kiss. When they part, Peter leans their foreheads together. "I am *so* proud of you."

Cameron laughs again. "Thanks."

"No, I'm serious. Anyone else would've given up today. But you went back."

Cameron shakes his head, rustling Peter's curls. "I had to."

"No, you didn't. You were getting hurt. But you went back anyways. Jeez, Cam, I know you're a Scorpio, but you can take this one compliment."

Cameron laughs, pulling away and placing both hands on Peter's head and shaking him lightly. Using just the fingertips of his bandaged hands, he tilts Peter's chin up to face him. "Thank you. Really."

Peter smiles, then his expression turns pensive again as he rests his hands on Cameron's legs. "Why'd you do it? Go back, I mean."

Cameron shrugs, as if it were obvious. "I owed it to the Cancers. It's my sworn duty to protect them, and they weren't safe there anymore. They've waited too long to be free."

Peter grins, heart warming. "What were you thinking, then? When you realized the walls were hurting you."

"I remember it was fine, for a few seconds. Then it felt like my whole body was being ripped apart. I dunno if you saw, but I looked down at one point."

"Yeah, I did see that," Peter raises an eyebrow, "I thought you just were closing your eyes, or something."

Cameron laughs out loud. "No. I was looking to see if my stomach was being torn open, because that's what it felt like." He bites his lip, pensive. "Anyway, I pulled my hands away after a sec. You definitely saw that. The guard I was with, he said, 'drop it.' That's it. 'Drop it'."

"And you said, 'I'm trying'," Peter whispers, eyes stuck on Cameron's face.

"Yes. And all I thought about then was the disease. The revolt. Everything Sector Five has gone through in the past little while, it all came to me. And I swore I would drop that border, even if it killed me."

Peter frowns, but Cameron doesn't look down. He's too engrossed in his own recounting of the tale. "What about Congress? And all of us?"

Cameron shakes his head. "I dunno. I think I should've thought of you. I definitely did, when it was all over. But right then, it was the Cancers."

Peter swallows. Suddenly, he feels overwhelmingly impressed by Cameron. The seriousness of what he had done hits Peter all at once. "I'm amazed by you sometimes."

"All the time, hopefully."

"All the time," Peter laughs. Cameron leans down and kisses Peter slowly. Peter tucks himself further into Cameron's waist and grins when a low sound comes from Cameron's throat.

Cameron jokingly pushes Peter away by his shoulders, giving him a stern look. "You're gonna have to wait until my hands work again to do that."

Peter laughs, stepping closer again and brushing his fingers up Cameron's legs until he pauses at his hips, index finger sliding under his waistband. Cameron shivers and wiggles away, and Peter laughs, finally relenting. "Okay, okay," he quirks an eyebrow. "Can't wait."

Cameron's gaze travels across Peter's frame, making the brunette boy's heart speed up and his stomach begins to burn with wanting. "Me either."

Part Sixty-Seven: The Aries

Kiara

"Are we almost done yet?" Kiara mumbles.

Diana laughs, setting her napkin down. "Almost. Just waiting on Peter."

The five teenagers were seated around a table at a restaurant that evening at seven. They had been through meetings all day about various things regarding Sector Five: what to do with the land, how to split up school districts, and how to create new housing plans that were better integrated with the architecture surrounding the sector. It was exciting work, work they'd been looking forward to doing and finally could.

It was Peter's idea for them all to go out. Cameron was struggling with using his utensils, but as the night carried on, he got better and better at using his fingertips to hold his forks and knives.

Lucas watches as Cameron uses a spoon to bring a bit of dessert to his mouth. "It's frustrating how good you got at that in literally two hours."

Peter chuckles and nods as he signs a check. He had refused to let them go out that night unless dinner was on him, and he tucks the paper into the leather-bound book that held the receipt. "Try dating him."

"I'm good," Lucas laughs.

Kiara nabs her jacket off the back of her chair and shrugs it on. She runs her hand over her hair as she looks around the table. "Ready to go?"

Diana smiles, and Kiara has to pause for a moment. The girl's blonde hair was curled down her shoulders, her makeup was light and natural and the candlelight on the table made her skin almost glow. Her teeth were a blinding white, and Kiara can't help but grin back from across from her. "Ready."

The five get up to leave, pulling on jackets and pocketing wallets and other items, when a waiter approaches them. He steps towards Kiara almost timidly. "Miss Kiara, Citizens' Liaison?"

Kiara doesn't fail to note the way Cameron, Lucas, and Peter all inch closer, or the nervous look Diana casts around the rest of the dining room. "Yes?" Kiara asks.

The waiter nods, raising an eyebrow and stepping even closer into Kiara's space. Kiara backs up as he begins to speak, voice monotonous and robotic. "You're all being watched. But you most of all, 333. Watch out." He blinks, tilting his head in an almost unhinged manner. "Watch out, Henderson."

"Hey, back off," Lucas says, stepping between Kiara and the man.

Diana grabs Peter's arm, and Kiara catches her whisper: "Where are the guards?"

The man begins to laugh maniacally, placing both hands on Lucas' arms and shoving him to the side. Lucas plows into the table, sending silverware clattering and drawing the attention of the other guests, who stand and begin congregating conspiratorially. The waiter pays them no mind, and begins walking towards Kiara, who backs up further and further. "Watch out, Kiara! Watch out!"

Cameron, now positioned behind the man, grabs one of his arms and yanks him back, grimacing in pain as his bandages rub uncomfortably on his burns. The man grunts but the crazed expression lingers in his gaze. Cameron wrestles him to the ground as Peter heads for the door, returning momentarily with two guards, Hayley and another man.

"Get him out of here, Hayley," Diana commands, voice cold as she gazes down at the man. "Now! Put him in the Capitol jails for questioning first thing in the morning."

Hayley glances at the man and nods. "Yes, ma'am."

The man is cuffed and dragged away, and Diana turns to Kiara, who is pressed against the wall, chest heaving and fingers shaking. "Ki, are you okay?" she asks, taking Kiara's hands.

Peter, always the socially aware one, takes each of the girls by the arm and guides them towards the door as Cameron helps Lucas brush any remaining crumbs from his jacket. "Let's talk, but not here."

Cameron shakes his head as he trails the group, and Kiara catches his mumble. "I have a feeling people are gonna eat this up no matter what."

Part Sixty-Eight: The Libra

Lucas

"Americans are roaches."

Diana rolls her eyes. "Thanks."

Lucas leans back in his chair. The five teenagers were all gathered around a tabloid in Diana's office, and he was seated at her desk. "Well, they are. Revolting, really, the way they're so addicted to their tabloid magazines."

Peter crosses to one of the seats against the wall, two cups of coffee in hand, and passes one of the mugs to Cameron. "That's the most British-Canadian thing you could've possibly said."

"I'm *not* 'British-Canadian'. I'm Alynthian."

Cameron chuckles, swallowing a mouthful of coffee. "Which was Canadian land."

"I'm still not *British*."

Diana rubs her temples and places her hands on the table. She was standing at the end of the desk, staring down at the magazine. "That's unimportant right now," she points to the cover of the magazine. "What the hell do we do about this?"

The cover of the magazine is jarring to say the least: Diana and Peter are huddled out of the way, arms protectively around the other, Cameron has the waiter pinned on the ground, Kiara is up against the wall with teary eyes and her hand over her mouth, and Lucas is sprawled awkwardly against the table, jacket and arms covered in discarded food. The headline reads: "Scandal in Capitol Restaurant Leaves Government in Tatters!"

Kiara sighs from where she's leaning against the bookshelf and covers her face with her hands. "God, I'm so sorry. When Barbara finds out-"

"Diana Florence Monroe!"

Diana grimaces. "I think she *might* already know-"

Just then, the door to Diana's office slams open and in storms Barbara Oswald, followed closely by Ms. Miller, Mr. Boone, and Ms. Brewer. Clutched in Barbara's hand is another, slightly more wrinkled copy of the tabloid, and she holds it out towards the president, her face a picture of rage. "Care to explain this?!"

Diana clears her throat. "Barbara, it's not what it looks like-"

"No? I'll tell you what it looks like. It looks like the Crown Prince of Alynthia is trying to start a food fight, it looks like the Citizens' Liaison is having a mental breakdown, it looks like the Secretary of Security is *attacking* a food service worker, and it looks like the Secretary of Education and the President are having a little rendezvous in the corner there!"

Diana holds out a hand. "I don't want you to shout. Let me explain."

Barbara finally seems to take a deep breath, face turning a lighter shade of red as she begins to calm down. "Fine. Explain."

Diana also takes a deep breath and begins pointing to different places on the magazine cover. "Firstly, this guy-" her finger travels to the waiter on the ground, "-tried to attack Kiara. He told her to watch out, said we were all being watched, and he also knew her last name. That's why she backed up, and that's why Cameron grabbed him. This is after Lucas tried to intervene, and this guy shoved him into the table. I'm with Peter over there because I was telling him to go get the guards. The picture was taken at the wrong moment, and it makes *us* look like the villains here."

Barbara thinks for a long moment, then turns to the other four teens. "Is this true?"

They all nod rapidly.

Barbara sighs, smoothing her skirt. "Well, where is this man now?"

Diana sits on the arm of her desk chair, perching herself next to Lucas. "The jails. I left Hayley in charge of questioning him."

"Good," Barbara says, taking her magazine and passing it off to Ms. Brewer, who looks equally as scandalized and confused as the other adults, "I'll have her call you when she's done."

"Thanks," Diana says. As the adults move to leave, she calls out again. "And Barbara?"

The older woman turns, raising an eyebrow. "Yes?"

Diana smiles, and Lucas notices the way her expression is one of authority. "Don't doubt us when we tell you we want what's best for the country just as much as you do."

Part Sixty-Nine: The Scorpio

Cameron

Cameron is sitting in his office an hour later when his phone rings. He fumbles for the receiver, bandages restricting the movements of his fingers.

"Hello?"

A girl clears her throat on the other end of the line. "Hello, Secretary O'Connor. This is Hayley."

Cameron leans back in his chair, propping his feet on his desk. "Hello, Hayley."

"I wanted to call and let you know the updates on the man we took into custody last night."

"Alright."

"Well, um, we questioned him. He started babbling like a baby, all tears and such. He was obviously under the influence of something."

Cameron raises an eyebrow although Hayley can't see him. "...Okay."

"And he told us he was drunk, and in a bad place financially, and he saw you all and got carried away. We ran a polygraph and determined it was true, so we let him go with a warning."

Cameron nods slowly. "Okay. Is there a record of the polygraph?"

"Yup. In the archive files. I had John bring it there this morning."

"Perfect," Cameron says, moving to sit normally and leaning into the receiver a little more, "thank you. I'll tell the others."

"Great. Have a good day, Secretary O'Connor."

Cameron mutters a quick "you too" and hangs up, leaning back and steepling his fingers together. He waits for one minute, then two, in complete silence.

His eyes land on the pile of unopened mail that had come in that morning, and his gaze travels to a red envelope on the top of the pile. Cameron's heart begins to pound, and his blood runs cold as he slowly reaches for the phone, as if moving too fast would give him an electric shock.

Carefully, methodically, he dials a number.

"Hello?" The voice on the other line answers.

Cameron's wavering voice is barely above a whisper. "Kiara," he says, taking a deep, shuddering breath, "you need to get out of here."

Part Seventy: The Cancer

Peter

Peter is walking through the lobby of their apartment building when someone grabs his arms from behind, shoving him into the open elevator.

"What the f-?"

"Shh," Cameron commands as the doors slide shut. He keeps Peter pressed against the wall, one bandaged hand over his mouth. After a long moment, he steps back. "Peter. I need you to listen to me. It's a matter of life or death."

Peter laughs, shaking his head. "God, Cam, I know you can be dramatic, but this is..." he trails off as he takes in the ginger boy's terrified gaze. Peter's eyes widen and he reaches out, taking Cameron's hands in his. "What is it?"

Cameron shakes his head. "Kiara. Someone's out to get her. And I know who."

Peter swallows. "Hayley said the restaurant thing was-"

"A drunken accident? Yeah, no. Let's review. We find out Ki has a crazy stalker who somehow got ahold of her old dress."

"Right."

"And then she gets assaulted in a restaurant, and apparently she's 'being watched.'"

"I *was* there."

"Listen. I got the call from Hayley, saying that the guy was innocent. And then when I got the mail this morning, there was a red envelope in the pile. No address, nothing. Same as the first one."

Peter pauses, then his eyes get wide. "So you're saying they're all connected somehow."

Cameron nods slowly, taking a step closer and lowering his voice. "Superhero, who was with us when we went to Sector Five the first time?"

Peter considers. "Hayley and her team."

"And who was Lucas' personal guard when he came to America?"

"Hayley."

"And who traveled with me to drop the walls?"

Peter gasps. "Hayley's been there the whole time." He pulls Cameron even closer, looking around frantically as if there were cameras, which in hindsight, Cameron should've checked for before he began conspiring.

"And remember Diana complaining about all those missing things? Hayley has been around everyone, at multiple points. She probably took them!"

"Cam, are you implying Hayley is *stalking* the Citizens' Liaison?"

Cameron shakes his head. "No. She helped, but it isn't only her."

"Then who is it?"

Part Seventy-One: The Taurus

Diana

Diana, Lucas, Kiara, Peter, and Cameron were all seated around their kitchen counter. The lights were off, besides a flashlight held between Cameron's palms. Diana had done her good-old-fashioned camera trick, and although they couldn't find any bugs in the apartment, they still left the lights off for added discretion.

Sitting on the countertop between them was the red letter, and the group had read it minutes before.

Kiara had her hands over her mouth, eyes full of tears.

Diana's expression was completely vacant, and her shaking fingers were folded in her lap.

Cameron's expression was one of anger: although he was in pain, his hands were white and clenched around the flashlight.

Lucas looked confused and terrified, all at once.

Peter's mouth was hanging open, his hazel eyes frozen on the paper.

Slowly, Diana reaches across the countertop and pulls the letter closer to her, rereading it to make sure she had seen what was there correctly.

It's been a long time, hasn't it?
I figure you thought you were rid of me.
Well, my child. You were very, very wrong.
I'm back.
And I will not have mercy this time. I will not run away again.

I won't rest until this country is back in my control.

Right where it belongs.

-George H.

"What do we do?" Diana whispers, eyes welling with tears.

"Could it be fake?" Lucas mumbles.

Just then, a scream erupts from the Plaza, so loud Peter jumps and his shoulder rams into Diana's.

The group barely has time to cast nervous glances at one another before more shouting and screaming drifts through the windows.

They get up so fast their stools scrape the floor, rushing past one another to jam the elevator.

They get to the bottom floor, and sprint from the building into the Plaza.

People are gathered in a huge crowd, screaming and pointing up at the side of one of the buildings, where a hologrammed image is projected there.

The group of five slams to a halt, and Diana gasps as she registers who is sitting there, a malicious grin plastered on his face.

"I'm glad you got my letter, President Monroe," George Henderson says as he makes direct eye contact with Diana. "I can see I've caused quite a fuss," he waves dramatically, causing another round of screams to ripple through the crowd. "Ah, Mr. O'Connor, move over, will you?"

Cameron swallows, face paling, and he takes a step to the side, revealing Kiara. Henderson smiles again, and Diana's skin crawls as her heart begins to pound. "Ah, my Kiara. It's so nice to see you again, daughter."

Before Kiara can respond, another figure steps out of the crowd. It's Barbara Oswald, and she glowers up at the hologram. "George, I'm warning you right now. Tell us what's going on, or we'll send people out to hunt you down."

Henderson just laughs. "Go ahead. In fact, I'm sure you could figure that much out," he levels his gaze at the five teenagers, still isolated in a clump in the center of the Plaza. "You better be fast about it," he smiles, and Diana's stomach churns at his crooked teeth and the manic gleam in his green eyes. And the next four words Henderson mutters send a chill down her spine.

"Time is running out."

www.ingramcontent.com/pod-product-compliance
Lightning Source LLC
Chambersburg PA
CBHW050925030726
47503CB00007BB/2470